SOUTH BEACH STAR

James Cubby

Liberty Collins Press
Miami Beach

COPYRIGHT © 2021 by James Cubby

All rights reserved.
No part of this book may be reproduced in any form whatsoever without written consent of the publisher, except for brief passages quoted in reviews. This is a work of fiction, and any resemblance to events, localities, or actual persons, is entirely coincidental.

COVER DESIGN: BRIGITTE ANDRADE

Author's Email: cubbysobe@hotmail.com
Author's Website: www.southbeachstarwriter.blogspot.com

Fame is an illusive thing -- here today, gone tomorrow. The fickle, shallow mob raises its heroes to the pinnacle of approval today and hurls them into oblivion tomorrow at the slightest whim; cheers today, hisses tomorrow; utter forgetfulness in a few months.
-Henry Miller

This book is dedicated to Gilbert Stafford and everyone who ever passed through his velvet ropes.

1997

ONE

A New Kidd

White hair a la Jean Paul Gaultier was just the touch I needed to strut among the fabulous shallow South Beach royalty and even pass as one myself. Michael, my good friend and hairdresser, had bleached away my oh-so-boring brown hair color giving me the new "It's All About Me" look I needed to be noticed and visually hip enough to mingle with the crème de la crème of the South Beach nightlife circuit that included celebrities like Madonna, Gloria Estefan, Prince, Gianni Versace, Calvin Klein, David Geffen, Barry Diller, Mickey Rourke, Kate Moss, Donald Trump, Leonardo De Caprio as well as some of the top models and photographers in the world. Of course, let's not forget the pioneers of South Beach who made it all happen, the gays and the international circuit boys who come to South Beach every year for the world famous White Party at Vizcaya, which was the forerunner for the "circuit" and continues to set the party standard. This world-renowned event attracts nearly 15,000 gay party boys from all over the world for a week of events, the highlight being an over-the-top fête that takes ostentatious to the extreme, held on the grounds of an opulent Italianate villa located on Biscayne Bay. Those who think these international circuit parties are just massive orgies with music aren't far from the truth, however this one happens to be a creative and well-produced fundraiser for a very good cause. While thousands of dollars in funds are raised, the focus of the week is primarily sex and drugs.

For at least a month before the event every South Beach store window displays white clothes, white accessories, white jewelry, and anything else white since white is the required dress for the gala. Gay circuit boys spend months working on elaborate and often expensive costumes comprised of beads, bangles, sequins and feathers that act as frames for their gorgeous bodies so when they're not sewing they're at the gym so they'll be pumped up for this non-stop party. The muscle boys come in groups wearing white jockstraps and large wings made of feathers, although you'd be hard pressed to find a real angel in this group. Most of their costumes are designed to reveal as much skin as possible and to be removed quickly.

This being my first White Party Week and my introduction to the circuit scene, I thought I might as well be introduced as a sleek platinum-coiffed journalist hoping that it would give me a little sex appeal. I had spent my life trying to become a serious journalist and even had a book in the works but for now it was on the back-burner since my new job took all my time. When I inaugurated my nightlife column I used Kidd, my last name, as my byline. As a result everyone started calling me Kidd. At first it seemed odd but it was another step to a new life so I went with it. So, with this White Party I christened myself Kidd. I figured that's one way to stay a kid forever, if only on paper, yet at the time I was a young-looking thirty-something. At least that's what I kept telling myself.

I'm not sure if it was luck or fate that had made me the hot new celebrity nightlife reporter for the *South Beach Star* but if anyone asked, I'd say it was the result of hard work and incredibly long hours. In my wildest dreams, I would never have dreamt of myself in the situation where I had landed. I had never even considered covering something as frivolous as nightlife and my goal had been to be a published novelist before I reached thirty-five but here I was covering the South Beach nightlife scene. Being a popular columnist wasn't enough for South Beach and I needed a little help being fabulous even though I was having a ball playing shallow. I had not spent my life hanging with the literary geniuses of the world but the crowd I had infiltrated were more interested in fashion trends, celebrities, and club openings than current events or novels. Luckily my dry wit and blatant honesty were welcomed, which was quite surprising in a town where phony and shallowness were the norm and lies were expected. The Beach was full of one-dimensional people and I had to constantly bite my tongue to silence the wise cracks and put-downs whenever someone made some dim-witted comment. Not that I'm such a critical person but the people were walking stereotypes screaming for attention. In print, nobody was safe but it seemed like all anyone cared about was having their name mentioned in print. I could literally rip someone to shreds but if I ran a photo of them with their name in the caption, I was a hero in their eyes.

Problem is, nobody reads in this town, unless it's a feature about themselves or the captions that accompany the photo pages of every publication in town. Phrases like "Did you see my photo in *South Beat?*" or "I saw your photo in the *Star*," were typically thrown about like greetings. Everyone in South Beach is fabulous, just ask them.

Actually, you don't have to ask, they'll tell you, dropping the names of their famous friends, or acquaintances as part of the conversation. And what really amazed me were the South Beach drag queens, like no where else in the world, were considered celebrities and even photographed and pampered like stars. But the fabulous quotient didn't stop there. Almost every man, woman and busboy in South Beach was a star in the making. The Beach was famous for its rags to riches stories. Madonna had a child with her trainer so he became a star. Yes, one day a busboy or a lifeguard, the next a Bruce Weber discovery modeling all over the world. So everyone was a star, some just hadn't been discovered yet. And there was nothing sexier than fame.

Sitting in Michael's chair, I could hardly believe I was staring at my own reflection in the mirror, a white-haired reincarnation of the once dull, brown-haired writer whose face I was used to seeing. Michael ran his fingers through the new whiteness for my entertainment as I gazed at the two of us in the mirror. Michael was a handsome hipster who dressed the part and was a notorious flirt but I knew not to wander down that path. I didn't want to have to search for another hair dresser.

"Everyone's talking about the big party tonight," Michael whispered in my ear. "And you get to go, you fucker."

"I'm sure it'll be a big bore," I said, trying to seem blasé about the whole thing. "You know it's just work, but I must admit I'm dying to see the inside of Madonna's house." I was actually creaming in my pants. Madonna's party was a private cocktail reception given by Miss Blonde Ambition herself with an invitation list of only 75. God knows how I got invited. I guess I'd become more important than I thought but whatever the reason, I had planned on making a good impression and working it to the max. I heard that the press wasn't invited except for Tasha Simon who was known as "Queen of the Night," the name of her weekly gossip column for the *Miami Herald,* and me, who had not accepted any royal titles yet.

"It's fabulous, I love it," yelled Angie, the owner of the salon. "It makes you look so much younger and it brings out your eyes. Good job, Michael." Angie was a cute brunette-sometimes red-head, who resembled the actress Bonnie Franklin from the sitcom *One Day at a Time* but was not the mother type at all even though she treated all her employees like her children.

Angie first started styling my hair when I wrote a cover story on her for the *South Beach Star*. Now that Michael's my stylist, her compliments were less sincere, but I was still in her salon so she'd still get press. That was the name of the game with her, just mention her shop in print and she's happy. Michael on the other hand was a good friend and could care less about press. He also changed his hair color every week, going from red to blue, yellow then white, and back to red again. With that many color changes he still had his hair, so I knew he'd be the one to take me to white when I was ready. So here I am with white hair and looking fabulous. Well, at least Angie thought so.

"You're going to get so much attention it won't matter what you're wearing," said Michael. I certainly hoped he was right. I wanted some personal attention and not because I put someone's name in my column.

"Wow! Is that really you? Let me get a picture," yelled the photographer Jesse Garcia, as he pulled his camera out of his bag. Jesse was one of the photographers from *Ocean Drive* Magazine, one of the big glossies, and has shot every celebrity that has landed in town. His photos also appeared every Friday in the *Herald* with Tasha Simon's column, so he was in demand and equally pampered. Jesse was a typical photographer type, long stringy hair who underdressed for every occasion.

"And what are you doing here?" I shouted, a little too accusingly.

"I'm here to get my hair trimmed. I know it doesn't look it, but it takes Michael a lot of work to make my hair look like I don't care," Jesse said, in his casual been there, done that kind of way. "So let me be the first to record the transformation. By this time next week, the world will have seen your new look." Was he being serious?

"Only if Michael says I'm camera-ready and we must get Angie in the shot." I hated having my photo taken and I certainly wasn't going to pose for Jesse alone. Even though my face had appeared in the people-pages of so many publications, I was much more comfortable on the other side of the camera.

"Angie, come here for a photo," I yelled. "If everyone hates my hair, I want them to know who to blame." Of course I knew I was only adding points to my merit with her, since undoubtedly the photo would find its way into a future issue of *Ocean Drive* Magazine if not the *Miami Herald*. And I would make sure her salon was mentioned and her name spelled correctly.

"Oh Kidd, you're so sweet. You always remember me," she gushed. Angie quickly ran to the nearest mirror and restyled her hair and added a new coat of lipstick.

"You're my cover girl," I replied. Ever since Angie was on the cover of the *South Beach Star* as one of the fabulous people in my series 'The Fabulous People that make the Fabulous People Look Fabulous' I could do no wrong. Not only did she have the cover framed and displayed in the window of the salon, but she told me I'd never have to pay for services in her salon again. Just another example of what people will do to get their name in print.

"Okay, smile," directed Jesse, while Angie and Michael gave him their biggest smiles, posing on either side of me, who Michael had called a cuter version of Jean Paul Gaultier. Little did I know that very same moniker would be used to describe my new look and on several occasions I would even be mistaken for Mr. Gaultier himself. Well, I could be mistaken for worse. My life had taken an odd turn, my path as a serious journalist hoping to finish my novel had been sidetracked by a life of pretending to be fabulous and going to celebrity-studded parties. I guess I was on the 'live now, write later' path.

It was air kisses for all, except Michael whose friendship I truly cherished, and he got a big hug before I made my way out the door and back to the *Star* office just steps away across Lincoln Road. The transformation of Lincoln Road, a walking mall of ten blocks or so, running from Washington Avenue to Alton Road, was giving progress a bad name. The Lincoln Road reconstruction plan had begun and the whole Road was being redesigned. Already rents were being raised and the local retailers weren't pleased with the whole scheme. Not long ago Lincoln Road was nearly empty until the artists resurrected the area by renting the storefronts for galleries and the loft spaces on the side streets for studios. The gays claimed it as the perfect cruise street for walking their dogs. Kremlin, a hot dance club, filled the space that was once a Saks department store and other gay-themed shops popped up nearby. Lincoln Road became the crossroads where everyone would meet, if you happened to be awake during daylight hours. Now the 'Road' was getting a major face-lift. With prices going higher, everyone feared that some of the locals' favorite places like the Hollywood Juice Bar, Il Libra, or G.W., the Gay Emporium, would be pushed out by rent increases. So far only a few stores had closed but the retailers on the street had banded together, and complained that if the rent hikes didn't finish them off, the loss of business because of the construction certainly would.

The office of the *South Beach Star* was located just off this colorful South Beach thoroughfare which made my life a bit more interesting but more importantly it was very convenient. To keep current on news, drama and up-to-the-minute gossip, I'd just take a quick trip to the Hollywood Juice Bar, a lunch-counter with two sidewalk tables serviced by a waiter on roller blades, who at night became Trixie the drag performer. At the Juice Bar, I'd hear all the dirt I hadn't discovered at the salon. Today Lincoln Road was packed with shirtless circuit boys marching almost like a parade, proudly displaying their buffed bods that they'd worked all year on. Some even pretended that they were window shopping, as they admired their own reflections while cruising.

"Hey Kidd," yelled Bobby, a hot little rave kid who worked at the Juice Bar. I had met him my first night in town at local gay bar called TWIST. Bobby had been my welcome party to South Beach and he welcomed me all night long. I think he thought I was a tourist and would never see me again and he was shocked when I reappeared. Bobby and I had become friends after I had moved into the neighborhood and was proud to be my friend since I was the nightlife columnist at the *Star*.

"Hey yourself," I yelled. I was tempted to reveal my new hair color to Bobby but kept my new hair-color hidden under my black baseball cap. To Bobby, I still looked like the normal Kidd. I was not ready yet to unveil my new look but the new me was waiting in the wings. Every day I was amazed at my new lifestyle, not one a serious novelist might travel, but if nothing else I could call it research and who knows use it in a novel someday. South Beach had opened its arms to me, quite literally in some cases, and I was ready to revel in my new life.

TWO

Mistaken Identity

Usually the *Star* office was quiet at this time of day so I felt safe coming in so late. The *South Beach Star* was run by Anthony Deerpark, who had traveled the world and made a fortune twice and lost it twice. Anthony was one of the pioneers of South Beach and after several failed business ventures, he had given birth to the *Star*. With the help of his two best friends Jack Daniels (on the rocks) and Johnson Donne (the wealthy ex-socialite whose contributions kept the *Star* in print), along with his caustic tongue, even more biting than Truman Capote's, and his comic charm, Anthony had managed to make the *South Beach Star* the longest running weekly on South Beach. Anthony was for the most part a loveable character with an emphasis on character who was a true performer, especially after a couple of cocktails.

The office was just around the corner from the Hollywood Juice Bar, off Lincoln Road in a loft-like space that once was the studio of the famous, but deceased artist Gregory Moone, known to many as Lady Lola (his drag nom de plume). The small front office consisted of a counter with a desk where a receptionist sat (that happened to be Mindy Morgan's battle station), a layout table and a wall of bookshelves. The back office was a series of desks, usually empty until an hour or two before deadline and then the place was filled wall to wall with advertising sales reps, columnists, photographers (a term used loosely at the *Star*), and a few *Star* groupies.

All the way in the back (near a door often used for quick exits) stood an antique credenza with packed shelves, which was Anthony's official throne. No chair for him, he worked standing up. When he tired, he took a very long lunch, or if it was the afternoon he announced that he had a meeting and left for happy hour at LINCOLN, a trendy bar located less than a block away. Of course he never returned until the following morning unless it was Tuesday, press day, and then he returned to approve the layout boards. Sometimes the boards weren't ready for approval until 9 or 10 p.m., but Anthony made the sacrifice and stayed at LINCOLN with his good friend Jack Daniels and an audience that hung on his every word. On Fridays the entire staff followed Anthony to LINCOLN for free cocktails, courtesy of an advertising trade with the bar. Anthony held court at the end of the bar but only the newest staff members or advertising reps hoping for a cash advance listened to his stories, the other staff members were there solely for the free booze.

"Well, if it isn't the star of the *Star*," bellowed Mindy Morgan, in her husky English accent as I entered the office. Sitting guard on the front desk so she didn't miss a thing, she was on me like a dog to a bone. "So Mr. Hotshot, who are you taking to the big party tonight?"

"Mindy, you know I always travel alone." Knowing full well she was hinting for an invite and knowing that I'd never ask her, Mindy still attempted to bully me into taking her to the party. She was the first person at the *Star* who gave me any attention but I later discovered she merely took me under her wing so she could smother me immediately if she sensed any competition. As soon as she decided I was lifeless and just a fact-checker with no dreams of glory she totally erased any concern from her calculating mind. Of course, she'd hated me since the day I first started my 'What's Happening?' column and swore that she had the idea first. Luckily Anthony stood by me and told her since she had actually never voiced her idea she should never ever mention it again. As the popularity of the column grew, so did her animosity.

While most saw Mindy as a ball-breaking broad, she saw herself as a glamorous journalist/vamp. Both titles lacked credibility, however, if you think Roseanne Barr (the "Roseanne" version) is glamorous, you'd love Mindy. If it wasn't bad enough that she thought every hunk was after her, I later learned, and she made no qualms about hiding the fact, she also liked women. The label 'rude and obnoxious' didn't do her justice, but the poor dear was just another vicious beast clawing her way to the top as aggressively as she could. If anyone dared to call her a vindictive bitch she said, "Fuck 'em." Everyone in town knew her and some even attended the events she produced, only so they wouldn't have to endure her vicious attacks in her column if they didn't attend. These events often focused on a ridiculous theme like her birthday and those invited who didn't attend got either a personal screaming session or were blasted in print. Some received both. Mindy Morgan never minced words.

"But tonight you should arrive with someone on your arm," she whined, pretending that she loved me, forgetting that I didn't have a memory problem like some.

"And don't you think everyone else in town has already suggested that?" I replied. "I already called Gina, Madonna's secretary, and told her I'd be attending alone." And then I walked quickly back to my desk to avoid any more confrontation. No wonder Anthony leaves every day for happy hour. After just five minutes with Mindy I needed a cocktail. At my desk, I called my service and checked my messages. Celia (my best friend and nightlife side-kick), Sally (*Star* ad rep and nightlife photographer who managed to take out-of-focus photos with an auto-focus camera, but I still loved her), Lester (my dear friend who was also a very talented artist but played the dumb blonde yet was smart enough to stay by my side since he knew the cocktails were always comped), Holly (an ex-beauty queen who acts like she's still wearing a crown but she's officially a local gossip columnist who decided to be my friend when she needs an escort for an event), Tasha (that's Tasha Simon, "Queen of the Night" who ruled South Beach and always looked fabulous for her brief appearances), and Justin (*Star* ad rep who hated me from the day I first walked into the *Star* office and didn't give me the time of day until my column became one of the selling points of the *Star*). They could all wait until later. Wonder what Justin wants? He never calls me? I took a deep breath and thanked the universe that no one else was around. I'd just grab lots of film from my desk drawer and run out, hopefully without another Mindy attack.

"Hey, what do you think of my hair?" I yelled at Mindy with my hat in my hand as I headed toward the door.

"It's fabulous, love. I hope every hair on your head falls out, you little twit," she screamed, without the phony charm she previously tried to feed me, then she stuck out he tongue just to make a point. God, I hope I don't have nightmares from that image.

"Oh, but do enjoy the party," she brayed. "Tell Madonna and Tasha I said hello."

"Sure love, ciao," I said, as sarcastically as I could before rushing out the door. I needed to pick up my clothes for Sunday's White Party event. Luckily a cab had just dropped someone off and I jumped in. Imagine if I had taken Mindy to Madonna's party? I'd have been blacklisted by Madonna, who has said repeatedly that under no circumstances will she be in the same room with Mindy. Mindy was famous for ruining a party and then blackballing the host the following week in print. Somehow Mindy's column, originally a film review, was transformed into Mindy's world view and opinions with a little film review at the end if space permitted. Anthony only allowed her column to run as written because she acted as the *Star* receptionist at no charge.

The traffic on Washington Avenue (the busiest street in South Beach) was horrendous today. Normally I'd be traveling on my bike, which is not only cost effective, but usually faster than a taxi.

My mind was rushing and I mentally checked off my to-do list as I entered Zoo 14, a boutique on Washington Avenue famous for dressing circuit party gods and male go-go boys, both of course having the same body types. Maria Consuela, the owner of Zoo 14 and star designer, offered to make my White Party ensemble gratis after her cover story in the *Star* (she's also one of the Fabulous People who make the Fabulous People Look Fabulous) doubled her business for nearly a month plus prompted *Ocean Drive* Magazine to profile her as well. Maria really does make people look fabulous and I hoped she could at least make me look presentable. Versace, who lived a couple of blocks from her shop, fell in love with her and Maria made swimsuits for him and his boyfriend. The circuit gods have had her custom design their duds from day one when she had a shop in Cherry Grove (that's on Fire Island for those not in the know). Maria designed for those beefy guys who wear their pants so tight they have to lie down to put them on, even if they're made of stretchy fabric, and the shirts are just as tight. The drag queens swarmed around her like she was a goddess and she even taught the diva of all drag queens, Paulina DeSoto, to sew. Maria was considered family to the nightlife crowd and treated everyone like a star client. Although Maria hid from the limelight, the stars found her and demanded her services, including the likes of Aretha Franklin, Melba Moore, Rod Stewart, Mickey Rourke, and Patti Labelle. She even dressed the boys of the NEW Menudo for one of their videos. Maria rarely went out, but her clothes made the rounds and she was known by every go-go boy on the circuit. Since I didn't have the typical muscular body that she was used to dressing, Maria asked me to come and try on the clothes she had made for me so she could be sure of the fit.

"Kidd's here," Renaldo yelled, as I walked in. Renaldo Perez Gonzalez was the hot Latin stud who managed her store and possessed the body of death, but had the heart of a Sunday school teacher, sweet and attentive. I thought if I could only afford him I'd make him mine but Renaldo was loyal to his boyfriend of five years. Actually I had no desire or time for a boyfriend and my heart was still in disrepair from my last emotional devastation.

"Kidd baby, how are you? It's so good to see you," Renaldo gushed, as he gave me a hug and a kiss on each cheek. "What have you done to your hair? Let me see."

"It's a surprise, just a little change," I said meekly as I took off my cap.

"Little change, it's fabulous! So Jean Paul Gaultier," he shrieked. "I love it! Wait till Maria sees it. Come," he said, as he pulled me through the crowded store into the backroom where Maria and two seamstresses were frantically sewing all the orders for White Party. The backroom was wall to wall fabric, clothes and photos of designs worn by muscle boys or drag queens. The two seamstresses were stationed at sewing machines in front while Paulina DeSoto, out of drag, was hand sewing white sequins on jockstraps. Just to see Paulina DeSota in the daylight out of drag, working on any project that wasn't for her, merited headlines.

"Hey Kidd," said Paulina. "Ready for the big night? Baby, I love your hair." As one of the reigning drag divas on the Beach, Paulina would be at the party. In fact Madonna probably asked Paulina to do a little surprise performance and I bet these costumes were for her back-up dancers. So she was sewing for herself after all.

Maria sat in the back at a sewing machine away from the crowd. Her desk was opposite the sewing machine so she could roll back and forth from sewing machine to desk as she often did.

"Maria, look at Kidd," Renaldo shouted.

Maria looked up from her sewing machine and saw me. Her face lit up like I'd never seen before. "It's incredible," said Maria, as she walked over to me. "Turn around, let me look at you," she commanded.

I turned and realized there was an audience of about a dozen watching. I stood proudly practicing my new persona as the new Kidd. I needed as much practice as I could get since I wasn't comfortable being the center of attention.

"You're a new person," she screamed. "Give me a hug." She hugged and kissed me and then gave me a long look. "You look so much younger and handsomer. It's a look that fits. You look like a star," she said finally.

"Thanks, I like it but I'm not quite used to it yet," I said, blushing. "Every time I see myself in a mirror I can't believe it's me."

"Renaldo, do you have Kidd's clothes?" shouted Maria. "I made special things for you because you're so good to me and I love you. Now my fashions won't even be noticed because of your beautiful new hair. Oh well, you deserve to look beautiful. Renaldo, get his things. I've got to get back to work. I can't believe how many designs I've yet to construct. I'm so busy, but I can't complain. Thank god for White Party and Winter Party, otherwise most of my work is for Halloween and the drag queens."

"Kidd, follow me," instructed Renaldo.

Maria gave me one more kiss and went back to her sewing machine. "Stop by next week when it's all over and bring pictures," said Maria, as she sat down. "I know you'll be at every party so I won't miss a thing. Be careful and don't push yourself and try to have some fun." Maria was one of the people who seemed to really care.

I followed Renaldo back into the front of the store where a crowd of muscular boys were looking for outfits. "I've put your things in the middle dressing room," said Renaldo. "If you need any help just yell. Here, let me take your backpack."

I closed the flimsy fabric of the dressing room curtain and changed into the new clothes. White has never been my color; in fact I was known for wearing only black, but I was adhering to the all-white dress code for this party of all parties. I couldn't believe that Maria made me white alligator pants. They were beautiful and with a matching vest. Oh, but this sheer white t-shirt, I wasn't so sure, it would reveal every pore on my white un-tanned body. Well, we'll see. When I looked into the mirror I couldn't believe the image I saw reflected. The pants fit like a glove and actually pushed up my rear, giving me a better looking butt. The white, sheer see-thru t-shirt would be a definite no for me with all the circuit bodies around (my body is so un-circuit) but the vest covered my little bulges and somehow magically lifted and separated giving the illusion that I have a chest. Hopefully no one would try to touch or the charade would be over. God, was Maria amazing or what?

"Come out, let me see," yelled Renaldo.

"It's okay, it fits. I don't need to come out," I shouted.

"But I want to see," Renaldo demanded.

"Then you come in," I said, shyly peeking through the curtain. "I'm not going out there with all those gorgeous bodies walking around. They don't need to wear clothes, I do." Most of the guys in the shop were parading around half naked. Of course if I had a body like theirs I'd never wear clothes and I'd try on g-strings and skimpy swimsuits in the dressing booths without closing the curtains just like they did.

"Let me see," ordered Renaldo, as he pushed the curtain aside so he could check the fit. "Turn around, let me see," he said, as he pulled the vest down and smoothed the pants. "Seems to fit perfectly. Oh la la. Looking good. How does it feel?" I never thought I'd get such a look of approval from Renaldo and it sent chills throughout my body. I'd better not be getting an erection because I was going to have to take these pants off.

"Like a padded bra," I said, blushing again. "I'm definitely going to have Maria make me more pants, my butt never looked better." Butts were more important than nightlife columns in some circles.

"It does look nice," said Renaldo, patting my butt and smiling. I was definitely getting an erection.

"Stop it," I said. "You know what it really looks like; you measured me for these pants."

"Oh, but it still looks good," he said smirking.

"Renaldo, how you flatter me," I replied, trying to hide the growing bulge in my pants. "Now get out there and flatter that parade of bubble butts while I change. I've got to get out of here. I have so much to do before the party," I said, even though I knew this was my last errand before I went home. If truth be known, I'd love to have kept him in that changing room with me and undressed him. I glanced at my watch and realized that I had less than two hours before the party started. Shit. I undressed quickly and headed to the counter with my bag of clothes. Renaldo glanced down towards my crotch and smiled. Shit, he had noticed my erection. I was so embarrassed. I had to get out of there.

"Gotta run, Renaldo. Thanks, and tell Maria I love her," I said, as I turned for the door.

"Wait, I've something else for you behind the counter," said Renaldo. "It's something special from Maria. Don't look until you get home."

He pulled another bag from below the counter. Something completely wrapped in black tissue paper was inside with a card on top. I smiled and waved goodbye.

"Hey Kidd, your hair looks fabulous," said Juan Carlos, one of the muscle-bound dancers from Kremlin, a hot gay dance club on Lincoln Road. Oh, the body on that one. He was probably there shopping for a dozen g-strings. As one of the hottest dancers at the club, he probably wore out those g-strings quickly, the way the crowd grabbed for him and stuffed dollar bills down his pouch, as if he needed any help filling it. What a show he'd put on in the dressing booth. He'd take everything off, very slowly, and wouldn't close the curtains. A show I'm sorry I had to miss.

I needed to get my mind back on Madonna's party, so out the door I ran. I was already beat and I had a full night ahead of me. Thank God my dear friend Celia would have a little treat to pick me up. Yes, my new lifestyle had added some bad habits but weren't writers known for their excesses? How did I ever make it through a night of going out without a bump of coke?

THREE

A Party I'll Never Forget

The cab Renaldo had called was waiting for me at the curb. What a sweetheart. I jumped in with my bags and was glad to be sitting at last. Years ago when I had spent a year in New York and worked as a waiter, the back of a cab became my only safe space between interviews and jobs. Now I cherished the calm before the storm as we traveled to my little second floor studio over El Rancho Grande, a hot little Mexican restaurant on Pennsylvania Avenue.

My apartment was "drag-queen elegant"--not my description--decorated in leopard print, flea market buys and tossed clothes. My place was merely a closet for outfits given to me by designers or stores that wanted free press and a place to sleep after an exhausting night of hitting as many parties and clubs as possible. I may have led what seemed like a fabulous life, but this South Beach writer could barely pay his bills. My luxury deficient studio featured cracked walls and barely running water, but the price and location couldn't be beat. One block from the *Star* office and a half block from Lincoln Road, my apartment couldn't have been more conveniently located.

The first thing I noticed after entering my apartment was that the light from my answering machine was blinking. Everyone always called me and wanted to talk when I barely had time to spit. It was already seven and Madonna's secretary said they would send a limo to pick me up at eight. I'd arrive around eight-fifteen. Shit. I had just enough time for a shower and a wardrobe check.

I really should call Celia or she'll kill me. We're meeting somewhere after the party. That's if she gets it together. Punctuality is a concept that most South Beach residents don't comprehend and Celia doesn't even understand the word. At least I'm not meeting her at her place. Usually when I meet her at the appointed time, after she has sworn that she's dressed and ready to go, I walk into her apartment to find her naked or nearly naked, and have to watch her change clothes at least a half a dozen times. When she's ready, she's a flawless beauty that turns heads wherever we go, but the process drives me crazy if I have to watch. I love her like a sister but enough about her or I'll never get to the party. Now I have to decide what to wear tonight. Let's see what Maria's surprise could be.

"Oh, my Lord in heaven!" I screamed, as I held up the most beautiful leopard shirt I've ever seen made from some silk-like fabric. Why it is silk, how stupid of me. Maria knows me so well. She knows my whole apartment is decorated in leopard including the bedspread, my curtains, and the chairs. There's even leopard fabric artfully placed on tables. I say artfully, someone else might say carefully arranged to hide the scratches and stains. All designed with leopard fabric that came from Maria's studio. Now, I know what I'll be wearing to Madonna's party.

Just as I stepped into the shower the phone rang. Of course, it was Celia. "Kidd, pick up, I know you're there. It's me," yelled Celia. "You better not be avoiding me, I know you're there," she snapped.

Dripping wet from the shower, I ran for the phone nearly tripping over the shoes I had just taken off. "Shit. Hello, hello, Celia." She had hung up. If she knew I was here she should have stayed on the line a bit longer. I'll call her when I'm dressed, otherwise I won't get dressed at all. I jumped back in the shower and the phone rang again. Yes, it was Celia.

"Kidd pick up, I know you're there," she whined. "I talked to Renaldo and he said you had just left the shop. Where else could you be? You've got to be there. You shithead, you better call me. Love you. Oh, if I don't talk to you before the party, but you better call me, asshole, I'll meet you at the Delano for drinks and then we'll go to Liquid. I'm bringing a new friend along named Tina. You'll love her. You better not stand me up. Love you. Heard about your hair, can't believe you didn't tell me about it. Asshole. Renaldo says it"....beep.

Thank god for answering machines with a time limit. Celia usually called back and back until she had said everything on her mind, which amazingly was a lot. Once she called back eleven times just so she could tell me the whole story of her incredibly awful day, the result of not being able to find the perfect dress for an event. Of course, she had to spit out the entire story again when we met for drinks later because she knew that I hadn't listened to the story on my machine. That was my Celia.

I'll never forget the night I met Celia at SWIRL, one of the coolest bar/hangouts on Washington Avenue that featured a bar full of toys and stools filled with more drug dealers than regular customers. SWIRL was so outrageously illegal, and I say that in the nicest way, I usually made it my last stop of the night. One night I turned around and Celia was just standing there staring at me. I thought she was a pre-op transsexual with flawlessly perfect makeup that looked like it was airbrushed on with a pair of incredible tits on display. How she loved to show them off. Once she even tried to convince me they were real, forgetting that she had told me the whole story of her operation and even told me the name of her plastic surgeon. Celia was just like Marilyn Monroe's character in "All About Eve" except that Celia was a brunette. She was a walking sex machine who wore her heart on her sleeve. Her heart happened to be gold, but hollow. Her only talent, besides looking fabulous and not accepting a "no" from anyone, was makeup. She could make anyone look beautiful. She was a complete mess and sometimes I thought her only purpose in life was to screw up mine. Somehow I fell head over heels for her. Celia also fell for me and wanted me to physically prove it. Unfortunately, for her, I gave up having sex with women years before we met. Celia loved sex, drugs and gay men who couldn't give her the physical love she needed, so they gave her clothes, jewelry and drugs. Like a character out of a novel, Celia was my Sally Bowles with a little Holly Golightly thrown in.

Sometimes I fantasized that if I had been straight, Celia and I would be incredible together. Then Thank God, that thought quickly passed. We had fantastic adventures together and she was the perfect accessory and photographer magnet. Not that I wanted my photo taken but she seemed to crave the light from a camera's flash. If her beautiful designer ensembles didn't have the photographers all over us, she walked up to them and with her sexy Marilyn Monroe voice asked them to take a photo of her and her friend. They never said no. She was one of those people who never really worked, knew everyone and never wore the same outfit twice. Celia even looked fabulous when she was too drugged or drunk to walk.

There goes the phone again. I'd better get my butt in gear or I won't be ready when the limo arrives.

"Kidd, hello, it's Tasha. If you haven't left for the party yet, please give me a call. I'm just finishing my column and I just got a tip of a sighting of Jean Paul Gaultier, but I need to verify it. Call me. Thanks." That said a lot for my placement in town, when Tasha Simon called me for confirmation of a celebrity sighting.

Clean, all toweled off and smelling of, can you believe it, Jean Paul Gaultier's cologne Le Male which was a birthday gift from my friend Lester, I put on my black velvet pants and new leopard shirt with a Versace belt. All gifts, thank you. I could never have afforded even the pants on my *Star* salary and the belt, don't even ask. One look in the mirror and I still didn't believe it was me. Yes, very Jean Paul Gaultier, but better looking. I think I just had a vain South Beach moment.

When I first arrived in town nearly a year ago, I was a big nobody without a job and I knew no one. Now, not only do I get invited to every party, but I'm friends, okay casual acquaintances, with most of the celebrities that I write about. Why me? I guess I know what to write and don't take the scene too seriously and only show them in a favorable light. Go figure. I always ask before I take a photo, unlike the strolling paparazzi photographers that have begun stalking South Beach. I'd never publish a photo of someone looking bad and often I'll call and ask if they're still speaking to the person who's in the photo with them. If they don't want the photo printed I pull it and if they don't remember the person or the night then I definitely pull the photo. Deeds like that get me invited as a guest to parties while the paparazzi have to wait outside. Of course none of the tabloids would ever hire me, which is a fact that I'll always be proud of. I still feel that I've sold myself out, writing fluff and shooting party photos. Someday I'll get back to writing that novel.

Often the paparazzi took my photo with some of the celebrities and if it was a slow week they'd take my photo with whomever I'm with. In the last couple of months my photo had appeared in almost every local glossy, Tasha's column in the *Herald* and even in a couple of national publications like *People* and *US Weekly*. My friends and the staff of the *South Beach Star* kid me that I've become a local celebrity, whatever that means. I shudder at the thought because I know a few so-called "local celebrities" and I certainly hope I don't act like they do. One of them, one who will remain nameless, has "local celebrity" printed on his business card and this character tries to work his "celebrity" for all it's worth. He may be a local celebrity but he wasn't invited to the party tonight. For Madonna's party, the paparazzi would be waiting with baited breath all over town because they know that Madonna, Mickey Rourke, Antonio Sabato Jr., Patti LaBelle, Calvin Klein, Barry Diller, David Geffen, Versace and his sister Donatella, as well as a long list of other celebrities would be in town. Every club on the Beach swore that the stars would be in attendance but the best parties would be held in private homes of celebrities like Madonna, Gloria Estefan, Ricky Martin and Sylvester Stallone. And I was invited to the hottest party of the year. Shit, the limo would be here in ten minutes.

"Celia, Kidd here. Don't talk, just listen. I'm being picked up in two minutes. I'll meet you at the Delano at midnight. Love you. How dare you call me an asshole. You shithead. Love you. Bye."

She hates it when I do that, but knows when I say don't talk, just listen, I really mean business, but it only works on the phone. When we're together I can barely finish a sentence before she butts in. Hopefully I have time to return Tasha's call.

"Tasha, Kidd here."

"Kidd, thanks for calling me back. I'm just finishing my column and just got a tip and I knew that you'd know if it was true. Someone called me and told me Jean Paul Gaultier is in town and was just seen at Zoo 14. My celebrity service never mentioned he would be in town and I was shocked to hear he was at Zoo 14. Why would Gaultier be there?" She was smart not to believe everything she heard.

"I can't believe it," I said, between laughs. "It's happening already."

"What do you mean?" asked Tasha.

"When did you get the call?" I asked, still laughing.

"Just about an hour ago, they said they saw Gaultier leave the shop carrying two Zoo 14 bags. I find it totally implausible that he would be shopping at Zoo 14," she added. Tasha had a biting tongue that she hid from her public.

"It wasn't him," I said, trying to compose myself. I couldn't believe this was happening. "Tasha, it was me. I dyed my hair white today for White Party. Everyone says I remind them of Jean Paul Gaultier, but I look fabulous, or at least I've been told I do. Wait till you see me tonight, I look like an entirely different person. That was me walking out of Zoo 14 with two bags." I paused and waited for Tasha to speak. She was speechless which was so rare. "Didn't Jesse tell you about my hair?" I added, waiting for a response. "He was at the salon and took my photo just after I went blond. I didn't tell anyone so it would be a big surprise."

"I can't believe Jesse kept that from me," Tasha screeched. "I just got off the phone with him and even mentioned the Jean Paul Gaultier sighting and he didn't say a thing. He's crazed with celebrity madness and was rambling on in Spanish about not being invited to Madonna's party. Security will be very heavy and photographers won't be able to get anywhere near the house."

"That's great. That'll make them even more frenetic on the Beach trying to get shots of the stars. We're going to have an incredible time. If you need any photos I'll have my little Minolta with me," I said, smugly. I couldn't believe how excited I felt.

"I guess I'd better carry my little camera with me too," Tasha replied. "I can't wait to see your hair. You're going to get so much attention and you're already making everyone crazy looking for Jean Paul Gaultier. And what are you wearing tonight?" she teasingly asked.

"Just a little something that Maria made me," I said, proudly. "You'll see. Madonna won't be the only blonde at her party tonight. Gotta go, the limo is here. See you at the party. I know you'll be dressed to the nines. Look for a Jean Paul Gaultier type with a camera. We'll gossip. Bye."

I hung up and took one last quick look in the mirror. I couldn't believe that was really me. I locked the door to Kidd Manor and rushed downstairs hoping that the limo would still be waiting. Out front on the steps was the regular gang of hot Cuban guys that lived in the building. They threw me a look and didn't even recognize me until they saw my camera.

"It's Kidd. Hey papi, you look good tonight," one of them yelled. "You come back home to me early tonight."

Yeah, right. Someday I'll get the nerve and turn around and confront them and say, "Why wait till later, why not now?" That would have to be the day that I moved out of the building since I didn't have the balls to be so bold.

Thank God, the limo was waiting. The driver opened the door for me and the Cuban guys all whistled. I jumped inside and the door shut the whistles and the rest of the world out. Madonna's voice sang softly on the limo's stereo system, thanks to a very details-oriented secretary. The seats were plush, the temperature controlled and an ice bucket with an open bottle of champagne sat waiting on the console.

"The champagne's for you Kidd," said the driver on his intercom. It's like he was reading my mind. I'd better be careful what I think. Madonna would be the one to hire drivers that could read minds, not so much for the service but so she could find out exactly what her guests really thought about her. What a luxury. I could live in this limo. "There's a note for you next to the ice bucket," announced the driver, just as I spotted the envelope. How scary. Gina, Madonna's secretary, knew how to make everyone feel special. Inside was a note that read, "A toast to you. Tonight will be a grand celebration. I can't wait to see your new hair." Signed "M." Wow, that's so sweet but also very scary. How did she find out about my hair?

I looked down and saw that there's a little baggie of what looked like coke on the floor. I don't know who left it there but I certainly could use a little pick-up. I had done bumps of coke with Celia, but this was the first time I'd had a whole little baggie to myself. Celia usually just stuffed it up my nose with her fingernail. I guess I could do a little bump or two before I get to the party. My God, I was drinking champagne and doing coke in the back of a limo headed to a private party at Madonna's house. Someone pinch me. I really felt great and suddenly wasn't feeling tired at all. No wonder coke was illegal?

what's HAPPENING?
ramblings on South Beach nightlife
by KIDD

ROMANCE AT KREMLIN: It was a night to fall in love...and I did, several times. **KREMLIN**, the fabulous Lincoln Road gay club known for its hot-hot male dancers, was decked out with a romantic celluloid theme and filled with lots of men ready to be romantic. **DJ David Knapp** kept the music pumping for the shirtless dancing men who were already pumped. The "if I was any closer I'd be on the other side of you crowd" included legendary South Beach icon **Louis Canales**, actor **Rupert Everett**, designer **George Tamsitt**, the fabulous drag divas **Adora** (no one has bigger hair), **Taffy Lynn, & Damien Devine** (no one has bigger lips), **Peter Estrada** (Kremlin's owner), photographer **Jose Antonio**, designer **Calvin Klein** (with an entourage of pretty boys), makeup legend **Kevyn Aucoin**, socialite **Curtis DeWitz, Nikki Haskell** (diet queen to the stars), artist **Aaron Von Powell**, photographer **Dimitri**, and **Rubio & Kidd Madonny** (doing an obscene dance under a white veil in the upstairs performance area).

WHITE PARTY UPDATE: Everyone's talking about the Saturday night event for **White Party Week** at **First Union Plaza** in downtown Miami which features the incredible sounds of **DJ Mark Tarbox** in an ultramodern 15-story open atrium. Shopping for White Party Week fashions has been like an Olympic Event in South Beach. With so many added events and a multitude of private parties a whole new wardrobe is necessary. **ETE** (the popular Lincoln Road boutique for the fashionably dressed male) has just reopened in a new location across from the **Lincoln Theatre** (just in time for White Party). **Zoo 14** seems to be able to fulfill the most unusual custom order, be it a white g-string for one or white sailor suits for twenty. **Maria** at **Zoo 14** has her hands full with all the orders and who knows how many assistants are helping her sew for those circuit boys.

WHO'S THAT GIRL: Everyone is talking about **Madonna's** party. The material girl is upstaging the **White Party** buzz (even though it doesn't conflict) by throwing an A-List invitation only party at her house. Guess who is invited? Yes, I'm one of maybe two journalists on the list, so you can read about it here next week. Photos next week.

SEEN SHOPPING FOR WHITE PARTY: Egon Von Furstenburg (at ETE), **Rupert Everett, Kevin Crawford,** and **Joe Bon** (at Zoo 14).

EVENT OF THE WEEK: Back Door Bamby opens at **KBG** this Thursday night with hot promoter **Mykel Stevens** (now sporting a shaved head) at the helm. His new feisty sidekick is the fabulous artist **Attila Lakatoush** (which team does he really play for?) who has promised us a series of exciting Thursdays. Can you say **Debbie Harry** with a whip? Have you ever experienced public bondage with an open-bar? Do you enjoy watching drag queens mud-wrestling while lip-syncing to **Madonna**? It'll be another night of beautiful people (they pose and smile while the rest of us talk about them) with assorted hipsters and maybe a few drug dealers.. Entrance to Back Door Bamby is not in the back.

TREND OF THE MOMENT: Sex instead of a resume.

BARTENDER OF THE WEEK: Dotty (formerly of **West End**) is now at **LINCOLN**. There may not be any hot go-go boys at LINCOLN but there you don't have to watch your wallet. Need to relax? Dotty is also an incredible masseuse if her cocktails don't do the trick.

QUOTE OF THE WEEK: I wouldn't mind meeting a Cuban Drug Lord.

NEXT WEEK: If you see someone dressed in all black with short bleached hair and a camera, it's probably me. As always, buy me a cocktail (or three) and share some juicy dirt. Until next week, see you out.

A YEAR EARLIER
1996

FOUR

Becoming A Star

I wanted to die! Never in my life had I felt like ending my life, but suddenly I was quickly weighing the options in my mind as I lay in bed hoping that God would do the dirty work for me. Always the eternal optimist, I had never encountered a situation that had pushed me to the edge that my life was standing on at that very moment. I wanted to jump off the cliff of life but found myself flat on my back barely able to move from my bed.

Last night I had arrived in South Beach, a total new world compared to my home in Virginia, searching for a new life. After lying awake in my bed, I came to the conclusion that there were only two solutions to get rid of my misery, start a new life or kill myself so I quickly got up and packed my car. I'm not the suicide type so I decided to drive as far away from my troubles as possible. It wasn't just that I needed to start a new life, I had to discover a reason for living.

On the surface it seemed that success and happiness had come my way. The arts magazine that I had started a couple of years ago had flourished and I was happily involved in a relationship with my business partner. There was one drawback to that relationship. It was totally secret. No one knew of our involvement since he publicly pretended to be straight. The normal person might have seen the trouble in such a relationship but I wasn't that person. I'm basically a private person and thought I had struck pay dirt when I found someone who wanted to keep our relationship private *and* wished to live in his own apartment. I didn't even get jealous when he dated girls as I stupidly thought it was just a cover. How could I have been so blind?

One morning I went into the office and discovered a note taped on the computer screen that simply said that he had left. The fucker didn't just leave with my heart, but he had emptied out the business account, stolen my spare camera (the old Nikon that I used when I first fell in love with photography) and left town with my favorite jacket (a black cashmere Ralph Lauren suit jacket). This man, I still couldn't bring myself to say his name, had ruined me financially but had also wrecked me emotionally. The saddest part was that I could turn to no one for solace. There was not one single person, absolutely no one, who knew of this relationship. Certainly anyone that I mentioned it to would think me crazy since there had not been a clue of our secret relationship. We were that clever and I was that stupid. I didn't want to talk about it anyway, I just wanted to die.

For days I prayed to God, hoping He'd strike me dead as I didn't have the courage to kill myself. Suicide had never been an option for me, even when faced with such misery and pain that the only solution was death. The checks written on the business account were already bouncing, and payroll, rent and thousands of dollars worth of other bills needed attention. I was broke but wasn't able to deal with the financial disaster because I was wallowing in the misery of losing a lover. Every day the avalanche of problems worsened and I just couldn't cope. I escaped to the comfort of my bed and didn't answer the phone or the door. The idea that my only two choices were suicide or escape scared the hell out of me. While I felt like all the life had been drained from my body, I wasn't a quitter and really didn't want to die. I had too much living to do yet and still had a novel to write. There had to be some place that I could start over without looking back, a place where people didn't ask questions. Miami Beach was the first place that came to mind.

It took three days of trips to the ATM to empty my bank account. Luckily, I had kept my personal account separate and secure. I packed my car with provisions for a new life, my camera, my favorite art pieces, clothes for every occasion and my photo negatives. Every picture that I took from the wall I replaced with another and rearranged my apartment to look like nothing was missing. If I was to vanish it had to look as if I had disappeared in thin air and I would tell no one. My empty bank account would be a major clue to anyone investigating that my disappearance had been planned but my destination was to be a mystery. My plan was to disappear without a trace.

Anyone wondering about my whereabouts would never have guessed that I was sitting in a South Beach bar called LINCOLN, a bar named after its location on a walking mall called Lincoln Road. I could barely believe I was sitting in South Beach myself, waiting for Anthony Deerpark, the editor and publisher of *South Beach Star*, the man who was going to be my ticket to a new life. The desertion of my former life had not solved my emotional state as I still wallowed in depression and lacked all motivation to write or pick up my camera until I picked up a publication called the *South Beach Star*, a publication that reminded me of the one that had been my life in Virginia. *South Beach Star* was a tabloid with irreverent style that followed no rules, including punctuation or spelling, publishing the news, dish and dirt of South Beach weekly. As if sent by a messenger from heaven, this tabloid was left by the person sitting next to me at the counter of the Art Deco diner where I was having breakfast. I grabbed it and started thumbing through the pages. It reminded me so much of my paper in the early stages. While I had hoped I might work on my novel that I had started a couple years ago, I had a strange feeling about this paper.

The *South Beach Star* seemed to need assistance and being needed had always been an inspiration and driving force in my choices. The feeling that I wasn't needed or even wanted seemed to be my downfall and at the moment I certainly didn't feel either. I could not shake the sensation of being totally alone and unwanted in a town that was swarming with strangers. I had never experienced such a feeling of doom and numbness where for a moment I actually thought death was my only solution. Luckily, I had thrown out that choice but now I needed to find my spark again, a reason to live, and I wasn't going to find it by sitting around doing nothing.

Two years previously, I had visited South Beach with a DJ friend who had been hired to spin at a new club. We walked the streets of South Beach after his gig and looked in the windows of the art galleries and boutiques that populated a run-down street named Lincoln Road. South Beach seemed like a place where anyone could be who they wanted to be and I always wanted to see if that was true. I had heard that Miami had a rapidly growing nightlife scene and had become a popular location for fashion shoots. I was hoping that Miami might have a place for me.

Sitting alone at a table in this trendy South Beach bar, I waited for Anthony Deerpark to bring us back cocktails. I could barely believe that I was sitting in a strange bar with Mr. Deerpark and surprise of all surprises, I was having a cocktail. In the afternoon, no less. After three failed attempts to meet this man in the *South Beach Star* office, where I had left my resume three different times, I decided I needed to be a little more aggressive. The chubby English girl at the front desk seemed friendly enough when I left my resume with her. The blond guy, who said he was the art director, was more than polite and even seemed to be flirting with me when I left a resume with him. The handsome fellow, who looked like a model but told me he was head of advertising, said, "I'll make sure that Mr. Deerpark gets your resume," when I left my third resume with him.

Little did I know that none of those documents would ever reach the intended destination.

So, after not hearing a word, yes or no, no or yes, I decided to try to get to the boss myself. I gathered up my courage and marched right into the *South Beach Star* office, and luckily enough, no one was there. Well, not in the front office anyway.

"Who's there?" screamed a voice from the back office. It just happened to be the voice of Anthony Deerpark, who for some reason took an immediate liking to me after I showed him my resume, a copy of my magazine, and volunteered my services. At the time, I didn't need money. I needed a reason to live. He quickly grabbed me by the arm and led to this bar located just around the corner from the *Star* office, where he said he conducted all his meetings.

Although it was just after 4 p.m., the bar seemed quite active. A time only drunks or losers were found in bars in Virginia, or so I thought. Here, gorgeous men rushed back and forth setting the bar up for the busy evening that they apparently anticipated. LINCOLN was designed to the max, all modern lines and high tech accessories mixed with savvy and flair. Miniature lights hung on suspended wires and appeared to be spaced haphazardly but were not, since each fixture lit either a piece of art on the wall or one of the many art pieces exhibited on the shelves behind the bar. A giant light fixture that resembled a paper canoe with water wings hung over the bar. The bar stools were black metal each with a bight red vinyl seat. Sheer black fabric covered the front windows that looked out on the busy activity of Lincoln Road, enabling customers to see out, while the outside world could not see in. Four tall black steel tables lined the wall opposite the bar, each with matching stools like those at the bar.

"Here we go," said Mr. Deerpark, as he set our drinks down on the table. Mine a vodka and cranberry. "Now, that's so much better than bottled water," he said, commenting on my first choice of beverage which he

37

would not allow. "I don't like to drink alone, even though I always drink with my best friend, Jack Daniels," he said, with a mischievous grin. "Now tell me, what was your name again?"

"My name is Jamie Kidd. I left three resumes with your staff hoping that you might call," I said, quite timidly, but gained more courage with each sip of my cocktail.

"Apparently my trusted staff chose to keep you and your resume from me, since they think they're the only staff I need," said Deerpark, with another of his grins. This time there was a bit more mischief and what seemed like a look of pleasure on his face. "So tell me, my dear boy. What is it that you do?"

I took a deep breath and told him the story of my life, of course listing my credentials, my writing background, my credits as a photographer, how I happened to get into the publishing business in California, and how I finally landed in Virginia writing for an arts publication that I had started. For the next hour, with the help of cocktails which never stopped coming, I shared my love of the business and told him how I couldn't get a writing job in Virginia so I had started my own publication, where I basically did everything from selling advertising, to paste-up and promotion, including most of the writing and all of the photography. I shared the details of how I transformed a small town publication into a statewide monthly in less than three years. While arts publications never turn much of a profit we were paying the bills and landing more advertising accounts every month. Unfortunately I had a partner who had emptied the company bank account before he left town. I didn't mention that he had also stolen my heart as well.

The cocktails slowly transformed the timid Jamie into the eager journalist who saw a place for himself at the *South Beach Star*. Anthony Deerpark listened to each word as if he had been waiting for their delivery while he sipped his drink. I would soon learn that this was a rare and historical moment as Anthony Deerpark never listened, without butting in, or made offers where money was involved. Anthony saw this as an opportunity for both of us, one for me to start over and one for him to get back at his staff.

"And why have you landed here, my dear boy?" inquired Anthony, which he demanded I call him as he couldn't stand being called Mr. Deerpark.

"Well, that's a very long story," I said slowly. I took a deep breath and looked in Anthony's eyes before letting the words escape from my mouth. "I had to flee while I could, otherwise I would be stuck there the rest of my life. If I had stayed, I know I probably would have killed myself or but I left because I really felt dead already. I'm not suicidal so I had to escape." I was trying to make light of the fact that a publication that I had started and given me life to for years had been crumbled so quickly by one man. Being a private person, I chose to keep my heartbreak and emotional distress a secret. I just wanted a job as a writer or photographer and didn't need to share my emotional baggage. I had hopes of saving enough money so I could take time off to write that novel I had been formulating in my mind for the past couple of years, but I was having trouble putting words to paper.

"Well, let's have another cocktail," said Anthony, as he quickly grabbed our glasses and went over to the bar. I had been totally wrapped up in telling my story and had not noticed that the bar had begun to fill with people. The mood had completely changed as the sun had set and now the bar was covered with tiny votive candles that complimented the light hanging from the ceiling making the place appear a bit magical. The voice of Peggy Lee sang 'Is That All There Is' and I thought "how apropos." I realized that my life wasn't over and I wasn't about to accept defeat. I was ready for a new life and thought I had found it. That wasn't all there was, I wanted more.

"Here we go," announced Anthony, as he brought us fresh cocktails. The actual number of cocktails that I had consumed while sitting with Anthony was a mystery and for some odd reason I didn't feel inebriated but energized. "My dear boy, my staff tried to keep you from me but they have a little surprise in store for them. What a gem you are and with all that experience, well let's just say, you could be an asset to my publication. Why, I think you're just the person that I've been searching for to be my assistant. Consider yourself hired and you started working for me an hour ago. LINCOLN is my other office. All late afternoon and early evening business is usually discussed at the end of the bar. This bar is the meeting place for all great minds. There's the owner, let me introduce you. Paul, come here a minute," shouted Anthony.

"Anthony darling, how are you?" said a little balding man with a big cherubic smile that looked almost like it was pasted on. "I noticed you earlier but I never interrupt meetings of the mind." This man was Paul Reed, one of the owners of LINCOLN, who had also designed the bar. Paul had bought the place on a whim because he said he needed his own bar where he could feel comfortable. Paul and his partner happened to be among the most sought after designers in Miami, to say nothing of being two of the most successful. LINCOLN had become Paul's little toy and the watering hole of the local hip and trendy of South Beach.

"Paul, you must meet Jamie Kidd, my new assistant," barked Anthony, who then motioned to me as if I were some prize in a game show.

"Congratulations. I'm Paul, one of the owners of this humble little establishment," said Paul, as he clinked his cocktail to mine. "I hereby welcome you to the family. I'll have to take you to lunch so I can find out all about you without Anthony cutting in, besides I've heard all his stories and he's heard all of mine. I have to rush off now to change into something a bit more fabulous but I'll be back later. We're having a special party for all the volunteers from Winter Party, but you're both welcome." Later I was to discover that Winter Party was an annual fundraising event primarily attended by gay men who traveled from all parts of the world to attend. It was a circuit party and I had yet to discover what a wonderful thing a circuit party could be. I thought it funny that it was called Winter Party. It was indeed winter and cold in New York, where the majority of the men came from, but in Miami it was warm and beautiful.

"Oh no," said Anthony immediately. "Tonight I'm going to show Jamie the town, we'll be back tomorrow. Toodles." And with that said, Anthony grabbed me and led me out the door. We rushed down Lincoln Road with Anthony waving and greeting almost everyone that we passed. He either knew everyone or acted like he did. Rushing towards a waiting taxi on a street that crossed Lincoln Road, Anthony opened the door and jumped in pulling me in behind him.

"Driver, next stop TWIST," shouted Anthony, with the flourish of a practiced train conductor who was indeed announcing the next stop. As the cab sped along, Anthony looked at me and smiled. "Remember," he said, seriously as if making a point. "Your job is to remember because sometimes I forget. My good boy, I have an incredible memory but sometimes the alcohol wipes away portions of the night and sometimes even warps my recollections. I do hope you have a good memory because an important part of your job is to remember. Welcome to South Beach, hold on, the taxi ride can be a bit bumpy."

Little did I know I was about to take the ride of my life and yes, it would get more than a bit bumpy.

FIVE

Easy Come, Easy Go

My life had purpose once again and soon I'd be writing about the glamorous and famous people who live and visit South Beach. Or would I? This was to be my first day on the job as the assistant of Anthony Deerpark, editor and publisher of the *South Beach Star*, who himself was one of the pioneers of South Beach. The *Star*, as it was called by locals and those in the know, chronicled the South Beach nightlife scene and interviewed local celebrities while Anthony's coverage was the political waterfront. In fact, sometime during the previous night's excursion someone had mentioned that Anthony had even run for mayor, but as a joke. Could he really have done that?

When Mr. Deerpark had hired me yesterday he had not exactly told me what my duties would be as his assistant. I guess I'd find out soon enough. He had just said that my job was to remember. Anthony had stated that he always came into the office at 9 a.m. but I didn't have to come in until 11 a.m. He told me that I would need my rest after a night of celebrating and I believe he had said that he wanted to make sure his entire staff was there when I walked in the door. That frightened me a bit, but promptly at 11 a.m., I stood in the open door of the *South Beach Star* office ready to begin my first day of work.

"It's by invitation only and you are all invited but you each must bring a friend," announced a loud female voice with a strange English accent as I walked in the door. It sounded like that chubby English girl, who had first taken my resume but I couldn't see her since the desk by the door was surrounded by handsome young men. If I wasn't positive that this was the office of the *South Beach Star* I would have thought I was walking into a model casting. For a moment, I was afraid to enter since I wasn't nearly as attractive as any of these guys and imagined that I might be turned away.

"Excuse me," I said, timidly, but loud enough to get someone's attention.

"Hello and who are you?" yelled the chubby English girl and the men scattered.

"My name is Jamie Kidd," I said politely while gazing at two fierce eyes staring at me like I was bad news. This rather buxom woman was the source of that harsh-accented voice that I'd first heard. I immediately assumed that it had to be her position at the *Star* that attracted these men to her, since looks, charm and personality eluded her, judging from her greeting. Usually I wasn't so quick to judge a person; however this woman seemed to play all her bad cards up front.

"Here, take an invitation to my Oscar party," she demanded, without adding any charm to her voice. "I'm Mindy Morgan and I'm hosting the party. You can bring a guest but the dress is formal," she snorted. She looked me up and down as if I was being inspected for final approval. "Do you have a tux?" she asked, spitting the words in disdain, ready for my negative reply.

"Yes, I have a tux and tails," I proudly replied. "How dressy is this affair?" Runaway that I was, I arrived in town with a wardrobe suitable for any occasion, or so I had thought.

"Tux and tails," she sneered. "My, I like that in a man," she said, adding a bit of friendliness to her tone, however I felt as if she were talking about ingredients in a tasty dish and if it suited her she'd have me for lunch. "And what do you do?" she finally asked.

"I'm a writer and I'm supposed to start working here today," I announced. "Mr. Deerpark hired me as his assistant. Is he here?"

"He hired you as his what?" came the reply in shriek form. The words that I had spoken were certainly not the ones that she wanted to hear. Ever. Now the evil stare was back and anger had been added to her voice and face. "Anthony," she yelled, as loud as she could, giving a start to me and all the guys in the office. I imagined that everyone within a block could probably hear her shrieking voice. The handsome guys that had been gathered around her desk were now looking at me like I was the enemy. "Anthony," she yelled again with a voice that could, if possible, actually wake the dead and send them running. I sure felt like running. "There's someone here to see you." This Mindy Morgan glared at me while I tried to look as pleasant as possible without falling through the floor. I could only think of how Dorothy must have felt when first accosted by the Wicked Witch of the West.

"Morning boys, what's all the commotion out here," said Anthony, as he came out of the backroom. "Mindy, what's gotten into you," said Anthony, and then he saw me. "Oh, my word, it's, oh yes...hello there," he said, as if he could barely believe I was standing there. "Why it's Jason Kidd, good morning. Glad to see you made it." I could tell that he was uncomfortable but he did remember me, which was a good sign.

"Morning, Mr. Deerpark," I said, afraid to call him Anthony in the light of day. "It's Jamie Kidd, sir."

"Oh yes, so sorry. Mindy, this is Jamie Kidd, he's a very talented writer and photographer and he is to be my new assistant. Hold all my calls. Jamie, come with me." Anthony turned and swiftly walked into the backroom and I followed. I dared not look back as I was sure that Mindy and the boys were all staring daggers at me.

Anthony had walked into the backroom, which was filled with desks and a shelf of books covered the entire right wall while the left wall was filled with bizarre but very colorful art work. I followed behind Anthony like an obedient child walking behind a parent. He stopped in front of an antique cabinet in the back that seemed to be a work area for someone; however you'd have to stand to utilize the space. Anthony walked straight to the cabinet as if it were home. He touched some papers, and then spoke without looking at me. "Well, my dear boy. You're here, so you'll act as my assistant." He then paused for a moment, as if in deep thought, like he wasn't quite sure what to say to me. "I hate the phone, so you'll always take my calls. I'm never here to anyone, except my aunt, and a few assorted friends and colleagues whose names you will soon learn. My staff is either afraid of me or hates me but they pretend to be my friend. You'll accompany me to happy hour and remember what I say, and to whom. Most of it isn't important, but if I happen to promise something, like a cover story, let me know who it was. Then, if the person is un-deserving and most of them are, you can give some excuse when they call. Just say the *Star* covers are all assigned and that I must've made the promise by mistake, something like that, you'll get the hang of it."

"What about writing? What do you want me to write?" I asked.

"We'll decide that later. I want you to meet everyone on the staff and then tell me what you think. Make them think that you hate me and become their friends," he smirked. "Then they'll tell you what they really think and you'll tell me without letting them know. You'll let me know everything that's going on behind my back." He paused and looked about as if checking to see if anyone were listening. "Oh yes, this is going to be delightful."

"What should I do first?" I inquired, still standing there looking at his back.

"Pretend you're me. Stand here," he said, and moved out of the way. "Mindy answers the phone up front but if this phone rings, answer it. If anyone asks for me, take a message. I'm leaving. I'll be back by lunchtime, what time is it?" Anthony asked, looking at the clock over his desk. "Actually it's nearly lunchtime," he said, answering himself. "So I won't be back until after the lunch hour, whatever that may be." Anthony then patted me on the shoulder and quickly walked out of the room. I stood frozen.

Pretend to be Anthony Deerpark, now that was a job. As soon as I walked up to his desk the phone rang. I hated answering phones because I never liked talking on the phone, to me it was so impersonal yet some people could go on forever, but since I knew that no one would be calling for me I felt prepared to tackle the task at hand.

"Anthony Deerpark's office, may I help you?" I said, as professionally as I could. I had never actually answered phones for anyone but many times had pretended to be my own secretary at my former magazine so I did have a little practice. Surely all it would require was a pleasant greeting and then I'd swiftly take a message.

"Who is this?" said a voice as deep as an announcer's and authoritative as I'd ever heard. I almost expected an announcement of the world news.

"This is Jamie. Mr. Deerpark's assistant," I said, trying to sound friendly yet in control.

"Stop it! Who is this?" demanded the voice. "Put Anthony on. Tell him it's Johnson Donne," bellowed the voice, like the voice of OZ, commanding and all knowing.

"He's not here," I said meekly. "Would you like to leave a message?" Message taking wasn't as easy as I thought.

"No, I don't want to leave a message," he shouted. "I don't know who you are, and I don't know what game you're playing, but I'm going to get you. You won't ever forget it when I do, so be prepared. You have no idea who you're speaking to, do you?" The caller asked without waiting for an answer. "I'm Johnson Donne and I'm the money behind that sleazy tabloid. Consider yourself fired and tell Anthony that I'll see him later." The line went dead and I stood holding the phone until the sound of the busy signal filled the room. I slowly hung up the phone and looked around. Standing in the doorway was Mindy Morgan surrounded by her gang of beautiful boys and planted on her face was the biggest smile her mouth could produce. Obviously, she had been listening in on the other line. Could it be true, that my new job had ended before the end of the first day?

"You can still come to my Oscar party darling," Mindy said, with pure smugness. "And do wear the tails."

SIX

Just A Party

Anthony returned just in time to save the day or at least my job. My job, which had next to nothing to do with writing, consisted of taking messages, following him around, spying on the rest of the staff, and making sure he got home safely after he had a few too many cocktails. And every night he had too many cocktails.

Eventually I met the motley crew known as the *South Beach Star* staff and they were all, without exception, very wary of me and thinking that I had sights on their jobs. Not really an insecure group but the type that hangs out with thieves and knows to watch their wallets. Most of the crew warmed up to me a bit when they realized that I was just Anthony's gopher and probably had no hopes or practical abilities that would take me any higher. They didn't bother to ask about my credentials as they thought I was another transient. One staffer even warned me that not one of Anthony's previous assistants had lasted longer than two weeks. He pulled me aside and told me that one assistant had disappeared after the first day of work and never returned. Not a supportive voice among the group, but for the most part they were a friendly lot. Even Mindy Morgan, the wicked witch that guarded the front door, warmed up to me after I made an appearance at her Oscar party wearing tails. In reality, I think she just came to the conclusion that this timid writer from

Virginia was no threat to her or anyone else since I had followed her orders and wore tails. All of Anthony's previous assistants had been duds, so why should I be any different?

My days were spent in the *Star* office acting as Anthony's faithful servant and while I yearned for an opportunity at writing again, I was content because I felt needed. It was actually a joy not being the boss and responsible for an entire publication. The *Star* was published weekly and the content was riddled with misspellings and grammatical errors. The first time that I was allowed to observe during production, I was shocked at the entire process. The actual layout was done on boards in the front-room with the articles, photos and ads pasted down by Jack Garfield; a handsome young blond stud that I later discovered was a former porn star and who also had served as Anthony's driver. When I picked up a board and started marking the copy for errors, Jack yelled at me. He said it was way too late for corrections as the boards had to be at press in a couple of hours. When I mentioned it to Anthony, he laughed and said, "We can't let a few misspellings get in the way of journalism." Later I think he also said something about not letting a few lies get in the way of the truth but I completely blocked that out. I shouldn't have.

And then there were the photos in Holly Sanders' nightlife section. I understood that these photos were taken "out and about" but most of her photos were out of focus. I couldn't understand how anyone could have taken such photos and chosen them for publication until I met the photographer. One afternoon this middle-aged blonde bombshell (and I use that description very loosely) stumbled into the office yelling for Anthony. At first I thought she had wandered into the wrong office. Mindy had asked me to watch the office and snuck out right after Anthony had gone to lunch.

"Anthony, are you here? Hello, is anyone here?" shouted the voice from the front office. I rushed out to find this woman going through the papers on Mindy's desk. At first I thought she might be one of Anthony's drinking companions who I had caught ransacking our office, but then remembered that most of Anthony's drinking buddies were young boys.

"Hello, can I help you?" I politely asked the disheveled lady standing before me. This was not the typical character that you might meet in the *Star* office. Most were attractive young men or distinguished older gents who preferred the company of attractive young men. There was also the occasional advertiser that had dropped by to pay a bill or complain that their ad was placed in the wrong position. This lady looked like she might have been a beauty in her day, which was decades ago, however she still dressed as if she were twenty and a sleezy twenty at that. I hate to jump to such conclusions but if this had been a movie, this woman would have been cast as an over the hill call girl who was still displaying her wares as if it was fresh baked bread. In fact, her breasts were so pushed up and on display she was a walking illustration of a boob job and I certainly no expert in that field.

"Who are you?" slurred the blonde.

"I'm Jamie, Mr. Deerpark's assistant. Can I help you with something?" I said, trying to be polite to this woman who was obviously inebriated way too early in the day, even by South Beach standards. In one hand she held an Instamatic camera and in the other was a large Styrofoam cup with a straw that she clumsily held while trying to hold a stack of copies of the *South Beach Star* under her arm.

"Oh, you're Jamie, I've heard so much about you," she said, as she moved closer. "You're cute," she said, with a big smile. "I'm Holly, Holly Sanders. You must know my 'Out with Holly' photo columns. I'm just here to pick up some more film. Can you be a doll and take the film out of this camera? I'm such a klutz." And she handed me the camera and walked into the back office screaming. "I need to use the john, I'll be right back." So this was the other woman on the staff of the *South Beach Star*. Holly was the Ying to Mindy's Yang, the lightness to Mindy's dark side and while I found this woman more pleasant, I still felt uncomfortable. Like the part in a movie where you know something really bad is going to happen, like a murder, and the murderer just entered the room.

I turned and watched Holly walk away and then realized I was holding Holly's little Minolta Instamatic camera. The very instrument that produced those out-of-focus photos for her 'Out with Holly' photo pages and yet while even a child should be able to produce clear photos with this camera, more than half of Holly's photos were either too dark or blurry. Now that was a talent. Not one useful to a photographer but a talent none the less.

"Why haven't I seen you out?" Holly screamed, as she walked back into the front office. I was still standing in the exact same position where she left me, still holding the camera in the air. "Did you take out the film? No? Just pop that little button on the bottom, I just had my nails done and I've broken too many already using that stupid camera." Those were definitely the words of a photographer that had never bonded with her camera.

"Here's your film," I offered, with the film in one hand and the camera in the other.

"Oh no, give that to Jack. He'll process it for me and I'll be back later to pick my shots. By the way, you're going to be my date tonight. I just ran into Anthony at LINCOLN and told him I needed an escort for Tasha Simon's annual birthday gala at The Forge. It's a hot ticket so Anthony told me to take you," she said, while paging through the last issue of the *Star*. "Shit! They put my photos in the back again! I'm going to kill Jack," she screamed. "Those photos are from a party at The Living Room, it's one of the hottest places on the Beach. I'm trying to get them in as an advertiser." Then sweet as honey, she turned to me and said, "You're cute, we're going to make a lovely couple." Holly then wrapped her hand around the back of my neck and stared into my eyes. "Wear something sharp; I'll meet you at LINCOLN at nine. Don't be late. Oh, and bring a pad and paper. I want you to take notes of who's at the party. Everyone will be there and since you don't know anyone you can ask for names. Bye love." And then she kissed the air on each side of my face and rushed out the door, in a blur, just like one of her photos. I was going to say that people come and go so quickly here but thought not. It would be too easy. I was still in shock from my first air kiss.

 Mindy Morgan had been complaining all week that she hadn't been invited to Tasha Simon's birthday party. It was the event of the year and she couldn't believe that she hadn't been invited. Mindy kept screaming announcements about how much she hated Tasha and how everyone in South Beach knew that Tasha was a phony bitch. Now if that wasn't the pot calling the kettle black. I had yet to meet anyone more deserving of the title phony bitch than Mindy and that was being kind. Earlier she had even threatened to crash the party, but I couldn't imagine that even Mindy Morgan would crash Tasha Simon's exclusive VIP birthday party at The Forge. The Forge was an old Miami restaurant and watering hole of the rich and famous. Decorated with fake antiques, fake stained glass and fake brick walls, it was known for its excellent cuisine and world class wine cellar as well as its very active bar scene. The crème de la crème of all walks of life had dined at The Forge, from famous celebrities to mobsters and everyone else in between. Cheap suits and fake tits were the norm but the lights at The Forge were very low.
 Holly would be covering the party in photos but no one from the *Star* would be covering the party in print. Since the former nightlife columnist Lonny Matthews had left to promote parties, the *Star* didn't have a regular nightlife columnist. A party of this caliber should be covered in the *Star* and given that Holly would be

covering the event with her trusty Instamatic, I saw this as an opportunity to cover the party as a writer. I didn't see myself as a nightlife reporter but I was eager to write something and according to Mindy and Holly it was the hottest party of the year. Anthony wasn't even invited. I was also really excited because I was finally going out without having to follow Anthony around and remember everything in case he forgot. Not only would I write about Tasha Simon's birthday party but I'd take my camera. It wouldn't hurt to have a few photos that were actually framed correctly and in focus. I'd never covered nightlife but surely there would be something interesting to write about. Besides, it was an opportunity that I couldn't pass up. Finally I'd be able to contribute something to the *South Beach Star* and hopefully Anthony would like it.

what's HAPPENING?
by KIDD

QUEEN OF THE NIGHT CELEBRATES: When Ms. **Tasha Simon** celebrates a birthday (who knows which one) the world comes to pay tribute. At least it seemed so, the other night at The **Forge**, a glamorous but dark old-world eatery filled with lots of old furniture & guests just as old. Socialites (from every stratosphere), paparazzi, club-kids, the rich and not-so-rich, the beautiful and the cosmetically-enhanced, all gathered for this fashionable event to bow at the feet of Ms. Tasha Simon. While I had never met the lovely lady who writes the weekly **QUEEN OF THE NIGHT** column in the **Herald**, I stood in the well-dressed receiving line with the rest of her well-wishers and hoped for an introduction. When I arrived at the front of the line, the seated Ms. Simon stood and took my gift (you don't arrive at a Queen's birthday party empty-handed) and placed it to the side in the pile with the others. She smiled graciously as I told her my name. Tasha lit up (or maybe it was the flash from someone's camera) and greeted me with a couple of air kisses." Artist **Aaron Von Powell** had gifted Ms. Simon with a beautiful painting (of the diva herself) which was hung on the wall above where she stood. Among the other notables that mingled, air-kissed, and posed for photos at The Forge that night were **Shareef Malnik** (The Forge's owner), **Danilo de la Torre** (the talented drag performer **Adora**), artist **David Rohn**, **Karla** (Roses by Carla), **Chris Paciello** (owner of the hot new club **Liquid**), **Sofia Vergara** (MTV), **Ingrid Casares** (Chris Paciello's partner and girl-pal to **Madonna**), **The Scull Sisters** with son **Michael** (the legendary artists always wear brightly colored costumes and travel with their son - not sure which sister is the mother), promoter **Mary D.**, **Pat Swift** (**Plus Models**), **Eric Newill** (Managing Editor of *Ocean Drive Magazine*), designer **Scott Hankes**, performance artist **Andrew Summers** (TOP SECRET), DJ **Ursula 1000**, **Brigitte Andrade** (publisher of *The Adventures of Bibi & Friends*), publicist **Susan Garfinkle**, writer **Brian Antoni**, publicist **Howard Miller**, **Charlotte Baron** (Rose's), **Crispy** and **Larry Callendar** (821), designer **Peter Page**, **Nayib Estefan** (son of **Gloria & Emilio Estefan**), designer **Sam Robins**, **Elkin Zapata** (Words on the Beach), **Jason Binn** (*Ocean Drive Magazine*), **Anna Claria** with **Sonny** (Caterer to the Stars), **Merle Weiss** (Merle's Closet) and attorney husband **Danny**, haute couture designer and club promoter **Gerry Kelly** (BASH), photographer **Manny Hernandez**, and the list goes on and on. Someone spotted **Sylvester Stallone**, who is known to show up late night at various South Beach hot spots like **Bar None**, but I didn't see him (and I only write about what I see, there's not enough room to write about what I hear). Two beautiful young boys barely dressed at all, but wearing all blue (interesting headgear with horns and blue short-shorts with exposed buttocks called **Rubio & Kidd Madonny** stood on a platform as if they were going to perform but just posed as did most of the crowd.

EVENT OF THE WEEK: Tasha Simon's birthday party at **The Forge**. It was an event like I've never attended before; everyone was camera-ready and almost demanded to have their photo taken. I didn't get a piece of cake but there was a lot of dish.

TREND OF THE MOMENT: If Rubio & Kidd Madonny have any influence on fashion, we'll all be wearing sequined short-shorts with exposed buttocks. Then everyone will really have to watch where they sit.

QUOTE OF THE WEEK: "I'm only interested if it concerns me."

NEXT WEEK: If you see this column here again, then you'll know that the nightlife gods have blessed me. This is the premiere of my column in the *South Beach Star* and hopefully you'll be reading it weekly.

The Morning After Madonna's Party

SEVEN

My New Friend

Wide awake, I rushed into the *Star* office hoping to avoid talking with anyone as I needed to write my column. Madonna's party last night had been incredible and I had not yet been to bed. First there was the coke that I found in the back of the limo and then when I met Celia later at the Delano, she introduced me to her friend Tina, which I learned later was actually crystal meth. Celia stuck it up my nose without telling me what it was and of course you can't say no to Celia. It burned a little at first but it gave me the most incredible high. I felt great and so confident and couldn't stop talking about the party. Celia tried to seduce me again but I politely declined. We still had a great time and we sat on my bed talking all night. When I realized that it was nearly eight in the morning, I kicked Celia out. I quickly showered and dressed because my column was due today and I hadn't written one word.

"Why if it isn't blondie, our star columnist, if you'll pardon the pun," screamed Mindy, as I walked by her at the front desk. "No hello,? No I had a great time last night? No Madonna said hello?" She continued her rant.

"Morning Mindy," I said, apologetically hoping she would stop her ranting and let me get to work. "I haven't written my column yet and it's past due."

"Well, stop the presses," she screamed. "Nothing is more important than your column. In fact, and I quote the current *Ocean Drive* Magazine, 'a party is not a party unless Kidd is present.' You have seen the new issue, no doubt?"

"No I haven't, what are you talking about?" I asked. I only used *Ocean Drive* as a reference for names as it was filled with pages and pages of party shots of people at events. I kept a stack of past issues next to my desk in case I couldn't remember the name of someone that I photographed at an event. I never read the columns so it wasn't a surprise that there was something in one of the issues that I hadn't read.

"Here you are listed as one of the fabulous top ten people to invite to a party. I can't bloody believe it. I was a formidable South Beach hostess giving parties long before you arrived on this beach and now it's you who gets invited everywhere. Aren't you even going to tell us how fabulous Madonna's party was and who was there?"

"Mindy, I'm behind schedule so you'll just have to read about it in my column just like everyone else and by the way, it was one of the best parties that I've ever had the pleasure of attending. And Madonna definitely did not send any greeting to you," I said, trying to see if I had any phone messages but wouldn't dare get near Mindy's desk. "Certainly you know how she feels about you after that scene you made a couple of weeks ago at Liquid?"

Mindy had confronted Madonna in the VIP section and demanded that she pose for a photo. Of course Madonna would have no part of it and the bouncers promptly pounced on Mindy and escorted her out of the club. Is it any wonder that she isn't invited anywhere?

"Mindy we'll talk later. I have to write my column," I said, as I quickly rushed into the backroom to my desk.

"I hate you, you bloody stinker," Mindy yelled, at the top of her voice causing those in the office to look up for a moment before returning to their work. Mindy's rants and dramatic outbursts were the norm. Mindy's yells were like thunder, you could hear them but unless you were nearby you knew you were safe from being hit by lightening.

Mindy Morgan's hate tirade for me began the morning after Tasha Simon's birthday party when she had discovered that I had not only gone to the party but had taken photos and written a column covering the event. The news had leaked back to Mindy that there was a reporter from the *South Beach Star* at the party with Holly Sanders and was taking photos with a real camera, not a little Instamatic. I had taken Tasha Simon a birthday gift and even introduced myself when I gave her the present. I was certainly surprised when Tasha greeted me like an old friend and introduced me to her party guests as she posed for photos.

After that first column was printed with Tasha Simon's photo, it became Mindy Morgan's mission to undermine and destroy me. She immediately went to Anthony and claimed that she should be the one writing the nightlife column not me. Anthony backed me in every way and seemed to take great relish in Mindy's pain. When my "What's Happening?" column was voted the "Best Nightlife Column" in the local *City* paper, Mindy nearly went insane.

"Come back in here this instant," Mindy screamed. "I have your telephone messages and I think you might want to see them, you bloody asshole." The office went silent. When I didn't answer she started screaming again. "If you're not in here in five seconds I'm going to rip up your phone messages into millions of little pieces, including the ones from Versace and Miss Tasha Simon herself."

Slowly I walked back to the front and stood in front of Mindy's desk. "Thank you for taking my messages," I said, as civilly as possible. "I would have gotten them when I came in but you seemed a little busy." Actually she was a little crazed and I was afraid of having my arms eaten off.

"Here are your bloody messages," Mindy screamed, as she threw them up in the air.

"Thank you very much," I said, and bent down, picked them up, then walked calmly back to my desk.

"You bloody..." she screamed after me but I shut the door behind me. Her ranting was still audible since the wall that separated the front and the back offices didn't go all the way to the ceiling, but it gave me a feeling of power to slam the door.

Back to the task of writing my column, the column that now appeared weekly in the *South Beach Star*. Who knew that I would ever write a nightlife column, me being a foreigner to the whole nocturnal world of nightclubs and parties? I had hopes of being a serious novelist, not a nightlife columnist. Sure, I like going out occasionally but I certainly wasn't prepared to face the nightly schedule of openings, galas, nightclubs and events that I was expected to attend. After Tasha Simon took a liking to me at her party, Holly took me under her wing and made it her mission to introduce me to everyone, and I mean everyone in the nightlife world. Since that night Holly and I were joined at the hip, going out every night. After I learned which clubs and weekly parties were hot I started going out without her because I always felt like I was babysitting Holly which was the feeling I had when I had to go out with Anthony. They both had love affairs with Jack Daniels. One of the phone messages was from Holly, and since she wasn't invited to Madonna's party, she wanted all the dirt. The world would never learn the craziness and debauchery that were part of Madonna's party, not from me anyway.

"Kidd, phone call line one," yelled Mindy, from the front. While it irked Mindy to answer the phones and take messages, she felt it gave her some kind of power to control the *Star's* phone lines. Especially my phone calls. "It's Holly, one of your girlfriends," Mindy announced sarcastically.

"Kidd, here," I said quickly into the phone. "Hey Holly, I just got in and I have to write my column. Can I call you back later?" I said, hoping she wouldn't want a complete rundown of Madonna's party. "Yes, it was incredible and I'm sorry I didn't meet up with you afterwards but I had to meet Celia. Okay, I'm sorry and I'll call you as soon as I finish my column. Bye."

Holly wished Celia were dead. Holly had laid claim to me as her party escort, even though she always wandered off looking for a new man du jour. Then I met Celia and my life was no longer my own. One night I had ended up in a club called SWIRL, populated mostly with drug dealers, drag queens and those looking to purchase one or the other, sometimes both. In fact, the night I met Celia at SWIRL I thought she was a drag queen but she's definitely all woman and we've been inseparable since. Holly couldn't understand why I would rather go out with anyone else but her and she took it very personally. In fact, Holly had begun to resent me a bit since I didn't need her to get into the clubs anymore. She still hoped that I'd throw Celia to the curb so she could retain her place by my side. Until that day, and she hasn't given up hope, she still called me if there's a hot party or if she can't get on a guest list or needs help with a potential advertiser.

Celia, on the other hand, doesn't have any negative feelings for Holly. Celia just doesn't have any place in her world for anyone who doesn't love Celia. And Celia's world is full of stylists, makeup artists, designers, drug dealers, hot gay boys and a revolving buffet of handsome men who seek her attention. Why Celia chose me as her steady companion, I'll never know. Sure I love her but it's a high maintenance relationship that wears me out but we do have fun. Somehow we clicked and our nocturnal adventures became infamous with many being documented in my column.

Before South Beach, I had never been one to experiment with drugs but found that if I wanted to keep up with the hectic nightlife schedule and still make an appearance in the *Star* office everyday I needed a little help. Coke was the drug of choice on the beach and my column had made me quite popular with not only the club owners but also every promoter, doorman, performer, and club kid who hoped to be mentioned in my column, which also included drug dealers. Honestly, I don't know how I would have been able to make the rounds nightly, hitting an event or two and sometimes half a dozen clubs without a little help. The mornings always dragged a bit but a bump or two of coke had me up in no time. Today was different. That Tina stuff Celia gave me had me bright eyed and raring to go. I felt like I could write two columns, clean the office, call everyone I knew, and plan my schedule for the rest of my life. For some reason I felt like chatting with everyone, even Mindy.

"Kidd, phone call line two," announced Mindy, sounding like a raving housewife talking to her cheating husband. Well, maybe I didn't want a chat with Mindy after all. "It's Celia, your other girlfriend. Pick up you asshole," she screamed. Great, it was Celia. I had to tell her how wonderful I felt and that I definitely needed some more of that Tina stuff. This was the perfect drug. I hope it wasn't addictive.

What's HAPPENING?
ramblings on South Beach nightlife
by KIDD

BLONDE AMBITION: Now I can say I've experienced the ultimate party of excess that could only be topped by designer **Gianni Versace**, who happened to be one of the guests at **Madonna's** party. While the term party seems hardly a fitting term for the celebrity-filled event at Madonna's house, I now know how Cinderella felt when she went to the ball and met Prince Charming. The event was truly a Madonna production with Madonna photos everywhere and the music was all Madonna. Madonna was a beautiful and gracious hostesses, there were lots of "Prince Charmings" including the handsome **Rupert Everett, Christopher Ciccone** (Madonna's brother), **Chris Paciello** (owner of Liquid), **Ingrid Casares** (prince to Madonna), **Sylvester Stallone** with a beautiful model on each arm, drag diva **Paulina DeSota** with a group of muscle-bound go-go dancers (who performed later that night), and a bevy of beauties including **Helena Christensen,** promoter/club kid **Kevin Crawford,** models **Joel & David Fumero, Marcus Schenkenberg,** and a colorful group of local drag divas that included **Paloma di Laurenti, Sexcilia, Taffy Lynn, Brigitte Buttercup,** and **Damien Devine.** The paparazzi waited by the gates all night.

AND THE PARTY CONTINUES: After the Madonna party I stopped by **LINCOLN.** The usual suspects were in varying degrees of inebriation and holding onto something for support, either the bar or to the nearest person. Next stop was **Liquid,** where most of the crew from Madonna's party had gone at the invitation of **Chris Paciello** (drinks on him). **Helena Christianson** was seen dancing by herself surrounded by a group of handsome men who pretended to be dancing with her.

SEEN SHOPPING FOR WHITE PARTY: Rupert Everett, (at **Zoo 14**), Christopher Ciccone (at **Cabana Joe**), and makeup guru **Kevyn Aucoin** (at **MARS**).

WHITE PARTY UPDATE: The search for **"Mr. South Beach" Competition** continues with another preliminary at **Warsaw** on Friday night. The contestants just have to parade around in swimsuits before the judges (no tipping allowed). Judges included **Henrietta** (the oldest drag queen on the Beach) and **Paloma** (the queen of the Beach) and me. One contestant was disqualified because his girlfriend wouldn't let any of the drag queens touch him.

EVENT OF THE WEEK: Back Door Bamby opens at the new Washington Avenue club **KBG** this Thursday night with hot promoter **Mykel Stevens** (now sporting a shaved head) at the helm. His feisty sidekick is the fabulous artist **Attila Lakatoush** (whose team does he really play for?) who has promised us a series of exciting Thursday nights. Can you say **Debbie Harry** with a whip? Have you ever experienced public bondage with an open-bar? Do you enjoy watching drag queens mud-wrestling while lip-syncing to **Madonna**? It'll be another night of beautiful people (they pose and smile while the rest of us talk about them) with assorted hipsters and maybe a few drug dealers. Entrance to Back Door Bamby is not in the back.

TREND OF THE MOMENT: Sex instead of a resume.

CLUB OF THE WEEK: Liquid, which happens to be Madonna's favorite South Beach club, is always packed with lovelies of both sexes and there's a lovely girl (actually she's a boy) who walks around selling lollipops.

BARTENDER OF THE WEEK: Dotty (formerly of **West End**) is now at **821.** She's also an incredible masseuse if you need another way to relax.

QUOTE OF THE WEEK: I wouldn't mind meeting a Cuban Drug Lord. (Overheard at The Forge.)

NEXT WEEK: White Party Madness begins and I've bleached my hair white for the occasion. Until then, see you out

EIGHT

The Power of the Press

The days and nights had started to blend together and while Celia was the main woman in my life, Tina had become my new best friend. During the day I made my appearance at the *Star* office for as long as necessary, making phone calls, writing my column, setting up interviews, or meeting with ad reps. As soon as my column became popular, I no longer was expected to follow Anthony around as his assistant and my weekly salary was doubled. Since doubling salaries wasn't something that Anthony normally did, he asked that I keep the deed secret.

Advertising revenue had increased at the *South Beach Star* as a result of my column. Even though Anthony wouldn't admit it, the ad reps all told me it's what sold the ads. Oddly enough, what made Anthony realize how popular my column had become was a phone call from one of his bar "trades." Remember Anthony's best friend was Jack Daniels and Anthony liked to socialize all over town with his friend served on the rocks. Anthony had trade accounts at his favorite bars so he never had to pay for cocktails although he always tipped generously. One of his "trades" called one day about his account and it seemed that he had consumed nearly double the monthly agreement but the bar was willing to erase the debt and start from zero if the writer for the "What's Happening" column would start writing about them. So important was this trade transaction, it was the first order of business out of Anthony's mouth when I entered the office.

"Morning blondie, your roots are showing," yelled Mindy, as I walked in. Of course there were no visible roots since my friend Michael was very meticulous about the upkeep of my bleached hair. Michael knew that people asked me about my hairdresser and he certainly didn't want to ruin his reputation with a client of my visibility showing his roots. I always wore caps during the day anyway so there was no way that Mindy could have noticed roots even if I had them.

"Thanks Mindy," I said, as I passed her. "Your fangs are showing."

"Anthony, Kidd is here!" yelled Mindy. Something was up because my entrance wasn't usually announced.

"Morning Anthony," I said, as I cleared my desk before sitting. Mindy had thrown a stack of phone messages on my desk so she wouldn't have to hand them to me.

"Kidd, I need to talk to you about one of our accounts," started Anthony. I walked over to his work area since it seemed serious. "You know TWIST? They've been one of our accounts since I started this paper. They called me and pointed out that you never write about them," he added, like I had done the world a great disservice by omitting them.

"You know I never write about a bar or club if I have to pay for a cocktail and they've never offered me a free drink unless I happen to be there with you," I said, a little smugly since I knew where this conversation was leading. I couldn't believe that I had become such a shallow reporter writing about only clubs that offering me free cocktails. When I had run my magazine in Virginia I wouldn't even let the food critic accept a free dinner. I also couldn't believe that I was standing up to Anthony. It was the Tina talking. Tina gave me the confidence to do anything, including the energy and motivation to clean my apartment.

"You know we have an account at TWIST and it seems to be overdrawn," Anthony said, as if it were of utmost importance. "However, they've stated that they'd be willing to wipe our account clean and even increase our monthly allowance if you start writing about them." Anthony paused before he added, "Of course your name will be added to the account immediately."

"That's good news, I'll drop by tonight and start mentioning them in my column," I smiled broadly and tried to act humble with sincere gratitude like he had just given me a prize.

Actually TWIST was on my itinerary of stops, especially late night stops, and was located next door to SWIRL where I made an appearance every evening no matter how many events were scheduled. I knew about the trade account with TWIST and knew my name wasn't on it, even though Anthony's driver was, so I rarely mentioned TWIST in my column. Many of the TWIST bartenders were fans of my column so I never paid for cocktails but I certainly never told Anthony that. It was kind of a contest with me to see how long it would take before my name was added to the TWIST trade account. Still I found it odd how Anthony measured the value of things. It made more of an impression on Anthony that TWIST would erase his drinking debt and double his trade account if I mentioned them in my column than the increased advertising revenue my column had generated. I was quickly realizing that things were measured differently in South Beach or at least at the *Star* office.

"Seems everyone's reading your column these days Kidd," said Anthony. "Good job," he added, dismissing me with the wave of his hand. "Back to work." Then as if he had a sudden brainstorm or a snap decision Anthony added, "One more thing." Of course Anthony knew exactly what he had planned to say. "Do you think you could increase your column to a full page? You could cover more events and list more venues. The ad reps say that helps them sell ads," he said, while pretending to look at work on his desk so it seemed as if what he was saying wasn't that important. God forbid that Anthony would credit me with the increased advertising revenue.

"I'd also get my salary doubled if I double the size of my column. Correct?" I stated, strongly and proud. It was definitely the Tina. I could never have been so aggressive about money matters without the confidence that Tina gave me.

"What do you mean double your salary?" Anthony whispered, realizing that Mindy probably had her ear to the door listening. Silence. I looked at him and waited. He turned and looked me right in the face. "Of course your salary will be doubled," he said, in hushed tones. "But don't you dare let anyone else know how much I'm paying you. You're already making more than any of the other writers. A lot more."

"Thanks Anthony, I won't tell a soul," I whispered and walked quietly to my desk. My first thought was to call Celia because I needed more Tina but I couldn't tell her about the raise unless I wanted everyone in town to know. Celia had been my middle-man, or lady as you will, since I really didn't want anyone else knowing that I was doing crystal. Who did I think I was fooling? Celia's reputation as a drug-whore was big enough for both of us and we were always together. I didn't have a drug problem like Celia did but if I didn't have Tina I'd never make it through a night of multiple events, multiple cocktails and remember any of it. Tina was necessary for me to do my job or at least that's what I thought.

Tonight Celia and I were going to the opening of a new club named SPIT and Celia's friend Anderson Laurent, a very handsome and talented artist, was one of the promoters. Anderson was one of the men that Celia had fallen madly in love with and Anderson had fallen for her but Celia had become obsessive and had demanded sex. While Anderson still played the part of a straight man in public he was a practicing homosexual so Celia would never find herself in his bed, at least not without another man there. Anderson, like most of Celia's gay male friends, remained a devoted friend as Celia was beautiful and well connected, which was important to a nightclub promoter and artist. Celia had promised Anderson that she would bring me to the opening night so I would cover the event in my column. Celia and I had planned to arrive for the opening and walk the red carpet for the photographers. That had been the plan but it wasn't in the stars.

NINE

Fashionably Late

Two years after my devastating breakup, I was still single and emotionally crippled with a personal barrier that permitted entry to few. However, the bond between Celia and I had grown even stronger because of Tina. While I could see Celia's addiction to the drug, I completely denied my need for the illegal substance even though I depended on it to get me through every night. The drug had also reignited my libido and I began a secret affair with a handsome preppie guy who was also the boyfriend of a publisher of a very successful local glossy. Our late night/early morning trysts seemed more exciting because we were both cheating; I on Celia, he on his boyfriend.

Because of Celia, Tina was always available and I never had to buy the drug although I came in contact with drug dealers every night. Giving my job as the reason for my use of Tina, I depended on it to get me through each night of events as well as making me alert the following day. Normally not a drinker, the amount of alcohol I consumed nightly would have had me on my butt, but with Tina I was able to function and maintain an appearance of sobriety, or so I thought.

Apparently Celia's use of the drug had escalated and often her actions were a bit extreme. One night Celia called me and told me to pick her up at her apartment. She would be waiting inside the front door. I cabbed over to her place and had the cab wait while I went to the door to retrieve her. When I got to the door I saw Celia rushing down the hallway to the back door so I got back in the cab and told the driver to swing around the back. When I got to the back door, Celia was rushing down the hallway to the front door. I knocked on the window hoping that she would see me but she opened the front door and stepped outside. I got back in the cab and told him to go around the block once again to the front of the building. When I got there Celia was nowhere to be found. I buzzed her apartment but there was no answer so I got back in the cab so we could drive to a pay phone. This was pre-cell phones, which would have prevented this whole ordeal.

When Celia finally answered her phone she was crying hysterically. She started screaming at me and asked why I hadn't come by to pick her up. I explained that I had been there and saw her running down the hall each time to the wrong door. Still sobbing she explained that she had forgotten which door she was supposed to be waiting at, so she kept running from door to door hoping to see me. After running back and forth, Celia eventually wore herself out and had gone back to her apartment to change clothes. I told her to go to the front door and wait for me and I'd come back and pick her up. Apparently Celia had gotten dressed too early and helped herself to a little too much Tina, which caused her to act paranoid and frantic, two traits that she didn't wear well. I promised myself I'd never let myself get that way.

Always looking fabulous, Celia's preparations, often with the assistance of stylists and make-up artists, for a night on the town were feats unto themselves. I had endured too many nights watching and waiting for her to get dressed. No matter how wonderful she looked, if Celia didn't have a stylist to tell her she looked beautiful, and often she did, she would change outfits repeatedly not able to make up her mind on her own. Finally I told Celia that I would no longer sit and wait for her to dress but would only show up at her door when she was completely dressed and ready to leave.

Celia had promised to meet me at the Living Room for cocktails before we headed up the block for the opening of SPIT. The Living Room was a beautiful restaurant/bar owned by the very handsome and very French Milon brothers, now one of the hottest nightspots on the Beach and a favorite of models like Kate Moss and Helena Christensen. Eric Milon, a former model himself, was an excellent host who discreetly handpicked guests for his private affairs in the backroom. The first time that Eric took me in the back I felt so out of place among all the beautiful models until he sent over a handsome male model with a glass of champagne. Because of the nature of the goings-on in the backroom, members of the media were never invited but somehow I had become more like family than press. It was like Las Vegas, what happened late night in the Living Room's backroom stayed there and was never repeated. TMZ would have gone crazy and one night's adventures would have filled a week of segments with a couple hour long specials thrown in.

As I waited at the bar, I watched the parade of beautiful models enter and the Euro-trash that followed them. South Beach clubs treated the models like royalty because they attracted a wealthy clientele that would spend outrageous amounts of money to be near the beautiful girls. Tweaking a bit and quite impatient as a result of the Tina, I finished my drink and headed out the door. Luckily there was a pay phone just on the corner.

When Celia answered, I immediately demanded an explanation. Celia knew that I hated waiting and that I hated to be late for an opening. Arriving "fashionably late" was the norm on South Beach. However I preferred arriving on time to avoid the crowds. Celia explained that the stylist was a nervous wreck and taking a little longer to dress her since she wanted to look especially beautiful for the opening of her friend's club. After a little pleading, Celia convinced me to meet her at BASH, another hot club a favorite of European clubbers, located just a few doors away from SPIT, run by fashion designer Gerry Kelly. The six hundred block of Washington

Avenue was wall-to-wall clubs with the exception of a pizza parlor and a hardware store. Since the club was so close to SPIT, I agreed to meet her there if she hurried. I could already see a mob forming at the door of SPIT. Although I was always pulled through the crowd at the velvet ropes, I hated being in the middle of any screaming group especially if they had been waiting long to get in.

At BASH I was welcomed by the dapper Gerry Kelly who was standing at the bar. Gerry, originally from Ireland, had landed in South Beach by way of Ibiza where he had worked his magic promoting "over the top" parties. While a successful nightclub entrepreneur, Kelly was also known for his couture fashions. Always fashionably dressed, Kelly was a handsome Irishman who was always photo-ready.

"Welcome Kidd," Gerry said, with his arms outstretched. "It's always a pleasure to have you visit my club." After a hug and double air kisses, Gerry led me to the bar where a vodka cranberry sat waiting. The bartenders knew me at BASH and always took care of me if Gerry wasn't around. Gerry had been featured on the cover of the *Star* many times and was a regular fixture in my column. I called him the most photographed man in South Beach. Gerry was an excellent host and made everyone feel important.

"Celia's meeting me here and we're going to the opening of SPIT," I told Gerry while finishing my cocktail. When he asked if I'd like another vodka and cranberry, I realized that Celia was late again. I'd learned to sip my cocktails so they'd last longer which meant I'd also drink less but the Tina had made me thirstier than usual. I usually limited myself to one cocktail per stop and often, if the owner wasn't standing next to me, dumped the cocktail or left it sitting on the bar. Gerry's witty conversation had made the time fly but I looked at my watch and frowned. Gerry, as perceptible as ever, noticed my concern.

"Would you like to use my office phone and call Celia?" he offered graciously.

"Thanks," I said gratefully. I didn't want to spend the night running from pay phone to pay phone. Gerry led me to his office which was located behind the stage, the location of his infamous weekly over-the-top fashion shows. Gerry told me to make myself comfortable and he'd wait for me at the bar. I dialed Celia's number and hoped she wouldn't answer because that meant she was on her way.

"Hello is this Kidd?" said the heavily accented male voice on the phone, apparently one of Celia's stylist friends.

"Yes, this is Kidd," I snapped. "Where is Celia?"

"Celia is being dressed. She told me to tell you that she's almost ready and please have another cocktail and she'll meet you soon and she's very sorry," said the voice apologetically. Celia was smart to have someone else answer the phone as she knew I'd be yelling at her at this very moment. I loved her dearly but she always did this. At least I wasn't sitting there watching her getting dressed. Sometimes I thought that she changed clothes just to put on a show for me.

"Tell Celia to get in a cab now and meet me here at BASH or I'm going to the opening without her," I screamed into the phone. "Sorry," I said trying to compose myself. "Who am I speaking to?"

"This is Juan, I do her make-up," said the voice. "Miss Celia wants to look beautiful for you and she will be there soon. Bye now." And he hung up.

Taking advantage of the privacy of Gerry's office, I did another bump of Tina and tried to compose myself. I shouldn't have let myself get so worked up but Celia was always making me late for events. The club was starting to fill with people and Gerry was greeting friends. I made my way back to my spot at the bar where there was another vodka cranberry waiting.

"Kidd, I'd like you to meet Sean Penn, he's one of the owners of the club." I had heard that the actor Sean Penn was one of the owners of BASH but celebrity owners are usually out of sight as it's their name that is used to promote the club. "Sean is just here for the weekend and stopped by to see how the club is doing. Sean, this is my friend Kidd, who has been one of the club's supporters and has given us lots of press in his column."

"I've heard all about you. Apparently you're friends with my ex-wife," he said, as he offered his hand.

"So glad to meet you," I said, as I accepted his firm handshake. I can't believe Madonna would have thought to mention me to her ex-husband. I knew that Madonna must have given me the mark of approval, otherwise Sean wouldn't have acted so gracious. Sean Penn was known to hate the press and his battles with the paparazzi were documented in tabloids as well as in the courtroom.

"Shall we have a drink," Gerry offered. "Let's move to the VIP section so we won't be bothered. Gerry noticed my hesitation and added, "Kidd, why don't you take a photo of Sean and me for your column?"

That was an offer that I couldn't refuse. While I considered the local club owners, promoters and performers the real celebrities of the South Beach nightclub scene, Sean Penn was a double celebrity since he was a movie star and one of the owners of BASH. Safely behind the velvet ropes of the VIP section, I snapped the photo of Gerry and Sean. A waiter led us to a table where an open bottle of champagne awaited with three glasses, each with a strawberry. For the moment all thoughts of Celia had vanished from my head as well as attending the opening of another club. The very sly Gerry Kelly knew that sharing a bottle of champagne with Sean Penn at BASH certainly trumped attending the opening of SPIT.

Gerry and Sean chatted away like old buddies and included me like I was their best friend. The party was interrupted when a waiter tapped me on the shoulder and told me that there was a phone call for me at the bar. It had to be Celia. I said my apologies and went to the bar to take the call. It better be Celia telling me that she was on her way.

"Hello, is this my former friend Celia?" I said, flippantly into the phone receiver.

"Is this Kidd," asked another accented voice. Celia had an entire brigade of hot young Latin boys who loved dressing her up. Celia was their Barbie doll and they loved to make her beautiful because they knew she'd be photographed and they'd take the credit for her look.

"Yes, this is Kidd," I snapped. "Where is Celia?"

"Oh, Mr. Kidd, I love your column. You are the most famous writer on South Beach. Everybody read your column, you fabulous," he spat out quickly without stopping. "Celia almost ready, she so beautiful. Juan is doing make-up now, she look very beautiful. Mr. Kidd will be so happy. Please meet her at TWIST in five minutes."

"At TWIST!" I screamed, to no avail. Celia's messenger had already hung up. I walked back towards the table but saw it was empty. Gerry and Sean had disappeared; apparently they had retreated to his office for some privacy. I headed to the door and out through the waiting crowd onto the street. I heard my name shouted a couple of times but my head was spinning and I was in no mood to chat. How dare Celia do this? TWIST was five blocks away but it was only a half a block from her apartment. Celia only had me meet her at TWIST when she didn't have cab fare and unfortunately my pockets were also empty as I had given her my last bit of cash earlier for our nightly supply of Tina. So I walked the five blocks to TWIST and tried to cool off. Miami nights can be hot and sticky, especially when you're tweaking on Tina. It didn't help that I was wearing a black suit jacket but I always wore a jacket when I went out at night. If Celia valued her life she had better be there waiting.

After walking the five blocks to TWIST, I thought to myself, I really need a drink. Oh no. I never had felt the "need" for a cocktail before. Sure, there were times I wanted a drink but this was a moment I really needed a drink. Actually, I needed a little alcohol to calm me down and something cool to drink to quench my thirst from the walk certainly wouldn't hurt my mood. My heart was beating fast, not so much from the walk but from the Tina that pumped through my veins. The typical gay crowd filled TWIST and I felt overdressed for the club, since I was wearing a black Thierry Mugler suit while everyone else was decked out in tight jeans and t-shirts. I eased up to the bar and while I was feeling tense and angry I still smiled at the bartender. Frankie, a hot Latin muscle-boy who also manned the door at Liquid on Sundays, stood before me with a huge grin.

"Well, if it isn't my friend Kidd," he said. "What's up? Are you slumming tonight? You're all sweaty darling, you look like you could use a cocktail. A big one coming right up." South Beach was filled with hot Latin boys like Frankie, but I still had a thing for blonds.

"Thanks Frankie," I said, still breathing hard. "Have you seen Celia? She's supposed to meet me here."

"No darling, I haven't seen Celia. She hasn't made her entrance yet," he said, as he placed a very large vodka cranberry in front of me. "Here, drink this. You know how Celia is." Unfortunately, I knew full well about Celia. I glanced at my watch and noticed that it was almost two hours past the time that Celia had promised to meet me at the Living Room. I had lost count of how many cocktails I had consumed while waiting for her and now I was all sweaty and we were missing the opening of SPIT. I looked for a vacant seat at the bar because I really needed to sit down. Celia had better walk through that door *real soon*.

Luckily I found a seat at the far end of the bar and sat down. My camera, hanging from my right shoulder, was beginning to feel heavy and cumbersome so I shifted it to the other shoulder. TWIST was not the place to wear a suit or carry a camera. TWIST was a well known gay nightclub with two floors and five bars. The crowd was friendly and very casually dressed, some without shirts.

I felt very out of place sitting at the bar dressed for the opening of SPIT, which was promoted as the next hot club of the moment, but now I was certainly not in the mood for facing another opening-night crowd. Through the crowd I thought I saw the singer Ricky Martin holding on to a big muscle guy. While lots of guys looked like the Latin heartthrob, very few would turn and run so quickly like this one when he saw me with my camera.

"Mr. Kidd, is that you," came a familiar sounding voice. I looked up and saw a handsome young Latin boy smiling at me. "I was hoping I would find you here," he said. "I talked to you on the phone earlier. I'm Luis, Celia's stylist. She sent me to keep you company while you wait. Celia's on her way. She so beautiful," he gushed. Celia was the clever one, sending this hot Latin boy to keep me company. Celia still had no idea that I was having an affair behind her back so she thought this little stud would keep me happy.

"Hello, would you like a cocktail," I offered, with a smile thinking that this Luis would be better looking without the makeup. While someone my age might have considered a little makeup to hide the obvious signs of over work, late nights and too much of everything, this Luis, who couldn't have been older than twenty-one if that, needed no cosmetic enhancements. The makeup made him look too pretty and even girlish, but he was still adorable.

"Jes, thank you. I'm big fan of your column Mr. Kidd," he gushed.

"Please, it's just Kidd. No Mr." I corrected him. I already felt old and out of place wearing this suit. I didn't need a little Latin twink calling me Mr. Kidd.

"Sorry. Celia talk all about you. She love you so much. She look 'specially beautiful for you tonight," he rambled, obviously directed by Celia to keep me occupied until her arrival. This gorgeous young boy would never look twice at me otherwise.

"So, you're a stylist?" I asked, trying to make conversation.

"Jes, I try. Celia say she will set me up with agencies. She so beautiful. We take pictures of her in my clothes. I hope to get job," he continued, attracting the attention of almost every guy that passed.

"Kidd, look who just walked in," announced Frankie. I looked up and standing in the foyer of the club was none other that Celia with another young Latin boy at her side. The crowd seemed to part and she looked my way and smiled. She walked towards me as if she was starring in a one-woman fashion show and the entire bar was her runway.

"My darling Kidd," she slurred, as she grabbed my hand. "What do you think," she asked, apparently referring to her ensemble as I know she didn't really want me to say what I was thinking at the moment.

"You look lovely my dear," I said, and I meant it. While she could barely stand, obviously she'd had her share of cocktails while she was being dressed, she did look fabulous. "Would you like to sit?" I got up and offered my seat.

"No darling, we must be off. We don't want to be late for the opening," she announced, as if I were the one at fault here. "Here, I brought you a present," she said as she handed me a small pink bundle of tissue paper with a bright red bow. "Open it now," she purred with that ruby red puckered Marilyn Monroe mouth of hers.

"Oh, it's a piece of chocolate," I exclaimed. "Celia you know I don't eat chocolate." I had given up chocolate years ago when I had gone on a diet to lose the extra weight I had gained in Virginia. I had no self control and couldn't stop with one chocolate so I banned them from my life.

She grabbed the chocolate and held it up. "I'm so sorry, it's a beautiful piece of Godiva dark chocolate. I guess I'll have to eat it myself." And the chocolate disappeared in her mouth followed by a gigantic smile. "I love you Kidd," she slurred. "Let's go."

"Okay Celia, let's go," I said, and let her take my arm for support, which she certainly needed. I looked around and both the young Latin boys had disappeared, they had done their jobs and left. Celia and I were off to the opening.

"Kidd, let's take a cab please," Celia pleaded.

"Sorry darling, I gave you my last bit of cash today," I announced sadly. Luckily I don't have to pay for cocktails and most of the bartenders refuse my tips so I'm able to party all night without a penny in my pocket. Excuse me, I meant I'm able to cover a long night of events for my column without a penny in my pocket.

"Kidd, isn't it fabulous? Here we both are, dressed in designer labels, both looking fabulous and we don't have a penny to our names. We can get in any club in town and we are walking down Washington Avenue just like everyone else but we're going to another fabulous club opening." Celia had a way of putting things in perspective, not always a logical one, but it always made sense in an odd sort of way.

"Celia, it's nearly three a.m. The opening was five hours ago. Do you really think anyone will still be there?" I smiled down at her as we walked, thinking how incredible she looked even if she needed help staying steady.

"Who cares?" Celia slurred. "If nobody's there, then it's not a hot club. My friend Anderson will be there and all that matters is that we arrive together." As usual, we made a dramatic entrance, wandered through the crowd, saying our hellos and eventually made it upstairs to where Celia's friend Anderson waited. Celia introduced us and I took their photo. (The photo was featured in my column along with a paragraph noting the details of the fabulous opening of SPIT.) Another bump of Tina and I felt like a new man. I left Celia with Anderson and I walked home alone knowing that I'd have a blond waiting for me in my bed. I wondered how long I could keep this illicit affair a secret.

what's HAPPENING?
ramblings on South Beach nightlife
by KIDD

ANOTHER OPENING: Lately it seems like there's a new club opening every week. This week the opening was the new Washington Avenue club **SPIT** that not only boasted two floors but an impressive roster of promoters hosting weekly parties. SPIT's opening night party was scheduled at 10 p.m. but I arrived a little late after several stops. First stop was the **Living Room** (no sign of **Eric Milon**), next was **BASH** (where the infamous **Gerry Kelly** hosted and introduced me to the famous ex-husband of **Madonna, Mr. Sean Penn**), and finally **TWIST**. My date of the evening, **Celia**, made a spectacular, however quite late, entrance but we did make the opening of SPIT. A typical opening night crowd filled the club and the party had peaked just prior to our arrival. The downstairs dance floor was still packed with thrashing bodies while upstairs the hipsters and fashionistas were more mellow. Seen at SPIT: promoter **Mykel Stevens**, artist **Anderson Laurent**, **Ash Rana**, *Miami-Herald* columnist **Tara Solomon, Kim Green, Kevin Crawford, Leslie Quick** with **Boss Model Ryan** and drag sensation **Kitty Meow**.

SALVATION: Billed as a new circuit party, the **Do Ask, Do Tell** event at **Salvation** was a mega-hit. Stars and stripes decorated the club and drag diva Kitty Meow (wearing stars and stripes) was walking decoration. Hot dancers were barely dressed in various red, white, and blue but go-go boy **Boris** was dressed as a patriotic cowboy (wearing red, white, & blue sequins and riding an imaginary horse). South Beach legend **Louis Canales** passed through the crowd with his camera, promoter **Samuel Nunez** greeted the crowd (and passed out drink tickets), **821** owner **Larry Callendar** modeled his new club fashions, **Richard Trainer** of **TWIST** partied with an entourage, and **Henrietta** (the oldest drag queen in South Beach) stood at the bar watching the go-go boys.

LUA AGAIN?: Everything old becomes new *again*. This past Sunday night I attended the third-anniversary party for **Hercules** (a roving party) at **Lua**. But wait, didn't Lua close? I remember going to a week of parties for Lua's closing and even recall attending the opening party for **REX** (the new name of the club after minimal redecoration) but now it seems that Lua has returned. So Hercules has found its new home (at Lua) with the party produced by **Mark Leventhal, Bill Spector & Conrad.** Seen at Lua: **Holly Leventhal** (wife of Mark Leventhal), **Cristina** (Camel/KBA rep), **George Nunez** (owner of Lua), **Bruce Braxton,** and **Donna Cyrus** (Club Body Tech).

EVENT OF THE WEEK: Friday night is the end of the drag race at **Lucky Chengs.**

TREND OF THE MOMENT: Wearing gym shorts from local high schools. The trick (and I use that word loosely) is to convince a willing high school student to give up their shorts. The prize could be more than just the shorts but a visit to jail. Get their shorts from willing students who prefer skipping gym.

DRINK OF THE WEEK: The Cosmopolitan. This is Queen of the Night **Tasha Simon's** favorite cocktail and it's now all the rage thanks to **Cheryl Cook** who runs the bar at **821**. She pushed the drink on people and now whips them up by the dozen.

BARTENDER OF THE WEEK: Crispy at 821. Serves her drinks with a bit of sassy wit.

SEEN OUT: Mother at **LINCOLN, Madonna** at **Liquid** (exiting out the backdoor surrounded by photographers), **Andy Bell** of **Erasure at the Church,** Kitty Meow, **Elaine Lancaster** and **Kevin Aviance** at **Testament.**

QUOTE OF THE WEEK: My boyfriend is out of town, so wanna be my revenge?

NEXT WEEK: He's from Mexico, his name is **Alex** and he's one of the newest go-go boys at **Escuelita** where he performs (the safest way to say it) on the bar. Carumba!

TEN

Trouble in Paradise

Justin Cartier disliked me from the first day he laid eyes on me in the *Star* office, but now that my column was hot he was pretending that he was my best friend. A former model who acted as phony as his name, Justin could sell anything and talk his way out of a paper bag (Tiffany of course). While the ladies all fell prey to his manly charms, it was only the boys that he cared about. As advertising director of the *Star*, Justin did quite well for himself but supporting a lazy boyfriend from Brazil and two drinking habits was quite expensive. In fact Justin was one of the *Star* employees who trashed my resume after promising to pass it on to Anthony. I discovered that Justin had hoped to get his Latin boyfriend a job at the *Star* even though said boyfriend had no skills (out of the bedroom) and could barely speak English. I had discovered that office skills and the command of the English language were not necessary to work at the *Star* but the fact that Justin's boyfriend was an illegal alien put a damper on the situation, as Anthony felt that he was already harboring his share of fugitives.

On most occasions Justin and I managed to avoid each other but for some reason Justin had made an appointment to take me to lunch. For the life of me I couldn't think of a logical reason for the invitation and honestly I was a little scared but also intrigued. From the day that I started working at the *Star*, Justin had tried to get me fired even though my job was no threat to his. As head of advertising, Justin should have been pleased when the popularity of my column began attracting advertisers but he was furious. The conflict was that my column was attracting advertisers that he hadn't generated and ones that he couldn't control. Many of his advertisers were trade accounts, and unknown to Anthony, were used primarily for the benefit of Justin and his boyfriend.

Dreading the day of my lunch appointment with Justin, I avoided going to work until nearly noon. Celia had given me some type of sleeping pill the night before so I had slept like a baby. While I hoped that everyone would think that my energy came from the giant café con leches that I drank, not one person on the "been there, done that and even got arrested" *Star* staff was fooled. Spelling and grammar might have eluded some but not one *Star* staff member could be fooled when it came to drugs.

"Good morning fuckface," was the greeting tossed to me by Mindy as I entered the office. "Avoiding the sun all together or just morning? I have a stack of messages for you, love," her voice dripping with sarcasm and she stuck out her tongue as she handed them to me. Why did she keep doing that? Her face was scary enough without a tongue jutting out of it.

"Thanks love," I said, trying to avoid looking at her as I grabbed the messages and rushed to the backroom.

"Justin called," Mindy yelled. "He wants you to meet him at El Rancho Grande at two for lunch." This time Mindy actually got up from her seat at the front desk and followed me to my desk. "What's up? Did hell freeze over? I thought Justin hated you. In fact, I know he hates you because he's said it a million times. This is like the forces of good and evil having a lunch date," she added, standing in front of my desk with her arms folded.

"No Mindy, that would be you and me having lunch," I said, hoping that would shut her up.

"Something's up and I want to know what it is," she demanded, even though I ignored her. Mindy could not stand that something was happening without her knowledge and the idea of me having lunch with Justin infuriated her to no end. She was right. Justin and I were like two magnets repelling each other. Something was definitely off kilter here and I imagined that I was innocently walking into some sort of trap. My innate curiosity had gone into overdrive and I had played the possibilities and scenarios of our lunch meeting in my head and none of them made sense.

"Can't two staff members have a meal together without cause for reports on the wire service?" I added, hoping she'd go back to her desk. I picked up the phone praying she'd get the hint and leave me alone.

"Don't you dare try to ignore me," she screamed, and grabbed the phone out of my hand. "Tell me what you two are plotting and tell me now." I was actually enjoying the distress that this lunch was causing Mindy.

"Mindy stop it," I said, and grabbed the phone back. "Justin just wants to go over a few advertising accounts. That's all, nothing more. Now please, let me get some work done. I have to return all these calls and check my schedule for tonight." I pretended that she wasn't still standing there and started to dial a number but she still didn't move.

"Fuckface, I'm not going anywhere until you come clean," she announced. I felt like I was in some B-movie and I was being interrogated.

"Mindy stop it," I said, exasperated. "To tell you the truth, I have no idea what Justin wants and I've tried to avoid meeting with him, but Anthony said I must. Surely it's something to do with advertising." I paused a moment to think about the absurdity of the situation. Here I was having a conversation with Mindy Morgan but the topper was the fact that Justin and I were having lunch together. "I can't imagine what else Justin would want from me," I added. "I'll tell you as soon as lunch is over."

Mindy looked at me and smirked. "If I were you, I'd be a little scared. Justin is up to something and you'd better watch your back." Mindy smiled at me as if she had just heard good news that she wasn't sharing. She turned and walked calmly back to the front office then walked back in the doorway for another announcement. "Oh, by the way, Anthony told me to schedule a meeting on Thursday with all the ad reps. He wants to introduce them to the new investor and nobody knows who it is, including Justin."

"Thanks for the info, Mindy, I really need to return these calls," I said, pretending the information meant nothing to me. The *Star* had survived this far without investors, the money deposited into the company by Anthony's best friend Johnson Dunne didn't count. Johnson never met with advertisers or had any say in the way Anthony ran the *Star*. Sure he liked to pretend that he had power, like my first day of work when he fired me on the phone. But in reality, he was just a silent partner and had no say whatsoever. This new investor, however, could mean that major changes were on the horizon. Should I be concerned? My column was bringing in ad revenue so I was safe, at least I hoped so. Maybe that's what Justin wanted to talk about? Certainly he was not afraid of losing his job and if he was why would he be meeting with me?

"Kidd, it's girlfriend number one on line two," yelled Mindy. That meant it was Celia. Celia had claimed number one position while Holly was still my number two. While Celia and Holly remained my loyal nocturnal companions and I seemed to have a million friends who all wanted to be mentioned in my column, at the end of the night I usually ended up alone. My affair with the cute blond prepster ended abruptly when I told him that I couldn't deal with another secret affair. I had a history of secret relationships ending badly so I stopped this one before I got hurt. So, I was alone again, unless you count my other best friend Tina. South Beach had become an international playground for singles and

South Beach's nightclub scene was ripe with sexual activity, and I had witnessed innumerable scenes of sex. One night I had walked into the men's room of Warsaw just in time to witness one of America's most virile actors, who played a rugged action hero in most of his top grossing films, down on his knees servicing a drag queen named Silver. Everyone was having sex in public these days, even the material girl who I watched getting way too intimate with a hot Latin dancer. Surely it was research since the muscular go-go boy later appeared in her metal covered sex book. While all of South Beach was hooking up, I still thought about my former boyfriend in Virginia even though he had left me broken hearted and broke. Call me crazy, but I missed him and would probably take him back in a minute.

"Hey Celia, what's up?" I asked, trying to sound happy but suddenly the grim reality of my life hit me in the face.

"Finally! I've been trying to get you all morning. I've got a hot news flash for you," Celia said smugly like she was the cat that ate the mouse. "Did you hear what happened to Justin last night?" she quickly asked, not waiting for a response. "He got arrested in Flamingo Park and you know what that's all about." Flamingo Park is a little park located in the heart of South Beach and has become the late night meeting place for gay boys. While public sex has never been my thing, the trees and bushes of Flamingo Park are rampant with late night orgies. Every now and then Anthony proudly makes the announcement at LINCOLN that I'm still the only *Star* staff member who hasn't gotten arrested in Flamingo Park. With Anthony, I learned to take such comments with a grain of salt since it really wasn't a compliment as I believe he was proud of the fact that he had a staff filled with guys who had been arrested in Flamingo Park.

"Justin must be out already," I announced. "I'm meeting him for lunch and he called to change the time from one to two." How interesting. I wondered where

Justin's boyfriend was when all this had transpired. Being an illegal alien, he certainly wouldn't chance getting arrested for sex.

"You're having lunch with that pompous ass?" Celia questioned. Justin was not one her favorite people since he never gave her the time of day. Justin totally baffled Celia because gay men usually loved her. Justin was that rare breed of gay man who had no place for women in his life and his only female friend was a butch lesbian. Of course Justin was able to put on the charm for female advertisers and they all loved him but all he loved was their money.

"Yes, but it's probably about advertising," I stated, knowing full well that Celia needed to know every detail. Justin had made the lunch date last week before he was arrested for sexual deviancy and because of Anthony's announcement I know this wasn't his first arrest. "I'll call you when I finish lunch and give you all the dirt. We're having lunch at El Rancho Grande so I can run upstairs before I come back to the office. I'll need to visit Tina anyway. That reminds me, I need to put in an order for tonight," I added, remembering that my crystal supply was low.

"Kidd, I'm beginning to worry about you," Celia said. "You're might be depending too much on Tina. You're starting to do just as much during the day as you do at night," she added, acting too much like a mother. Celia just didn't like being excluded since we always shared our drugs when we were out at night. "You're doing too much baby. I get to sleep all day. You have to give your body some rest."

Now if that wasn't the pot calling the kettle a junkie. "I got a good seven hours sleep last night thanks to you and your little pills," I retaliated. "My body gets plenty of rest." I said it, but knew it wasn't true.

"Oh sure and how many bumps have you done today?" she added, knowing full well that I never came to the office without a bump.

"Celia, I have to go. I have to get a little work done before I leave for lunch," I said, quickly hoping she'd drop the subject. "I'll call you as soon as lunch is over." How dare she call me on my drug usage, Celia of all people? Sure I'd heard the horror stories of crystal addiction but I'd never let that happen to me. Sex parties and three day binges were not a part of my lifestyle. Tina was my friend and helped me work. Shit, it was already one thirty. I'd have to finish these calls after lunch so I'd have time to stop by my apartment for a bump. After all, this was a business lunch.

ELEVEN

A Nose for News

While it seemed that my weekly nightlife column had made me the toast of the town, I was also now hated or at least the cause of tension by most of the *South Beach Star* staff, even the man who had hired me. Anthony had been my savior, the man who saved my life, my biggest supporter who always watched my back, but lately he seemed to resent me, especially when he gave me my weekly paycheck. Apparently the *Star* was in big trouble financially and Anthony resented anything or anyone that took money from his pocket. If Anthony only knew about Justin's scams and trade ads. It was obvious to everyone but Anthony that Justin was stealing him blind.

"Morning fuckface," chimed Mindy, as I walked in the office. What was refreshing about Mindy was that she hated me to my face and didn't pretend to be nice. In fact I knew the moment I saw a smile on Mindy's face that someone was in trouble or she had just dumped on someone big time.

"Morning sunshine," I pleasantly replied, not wanting to wreck my good mood.

"Here's your messages and an announcement of the mandatory *Star* staff meeting on Friday," said Mindy, handing me a stack of messages and a sheet of paper. The announcement was on *South Beach Star* stationery which was interesting since I had never seen anything printed on *South Beach Star* stationery. I didn't even know there was such a thing. "Read it, sign it and give it back, so Anthony knows you read it. If you miss the meeting you're fired," Mindy said, looking at me with a big smile. "Don't you have something else to do on Friday?"

"Well I was flying to Paris but I guess I'll have to cancel my flight. I wouldn't miss this meeting for the world, even if it wasn't mandatory. To see the entire *Star* staff together in one place where alcohol isn't being served will be a historic occasion," I said, as I signed the paper and gave it back to Mindy. Never had we ever had to sign a paper for a mandatory meeting. This was getting scary.

"Certainly everyone will run to LINCOLN immediately after the meeting," quipped Mindy. "In fact I think I'll sneak over to LINCOLN and get a quick drink before the meeting, otherwise I'll freak." Now that wouldn't be a pretty site, I couldn't imagine Mindy freaking out. I thought it was her calling to push others over the edge.

"Come on Mindy, you're an adult or at least can offer a passable simulation of one better than most of the staff," I added. What was wrong with this picture? Mindy and I were throwing quips back and forth like we were buddies. "Getting a cocktail before the meeting might be a smart idea. I heard that Anthony is putting a stop to all trade accounts so I guess the staff will be buying their own cocktails from now on," I said, as I gathered my mail and headed to my desk in the back room.

"Hey, does that mean you too?" Mindy yelled at me, but I ignored her. "Kidd, don't you ignore me. Does that mean you too?" She screamed louder this time but luckily the phone rang. "*South Beach Star*, this is Mindy Morgan, how can I help you?" Mindy said, using her sweet as pie voice that only fooled strangers on the phone. She couldn't fool people in person since it was so unbelievable to hear nice words coming out of that face. "Kidd, no he's not here, you just missed him," replied Mindy, to the caller loud enough so I could hear. "I can take a message, but I have to warn you, he rarely returns

87

his calls……okay, I'll give him the message, bye now." There was silence and the sound of typing.

"Mindy, was that call for me?" I asked, stepping back in the front office.

"No, Kidd. It was actually a wrong number," she said, looking at me with a giant grin on her face which was scary in itself as Mindy had one of the few faces where a smile made her look scarier. I didn't want to squabble so I started to walk out, then I turned around and took out my wallet and handed her a stack of drink tickets from various clubs and walked away.

"My God Kidd," she screamed. "These are like gold. Drink tickets from SWIRL, Liquid, TWIST, and LINCOLN. I didn't even know LINCOLN had drink tickets. Oh, you can have the TWIST tickets back, I don't go there. On second thought, I better keep them in case. Kidd, come back," she screamed. "Thanks darling, what's with the change of heart? Are you leaving town?"

"Just a token of appreciation from one alcoholic to another," I said, standing in the doorway that separated the two offices. "Don't you dare tell anyone I gave them to you and remember to tip. Also, I just wanted to straighten something out. I've never been mean to you, Mindy. You're always screaming at me from the moment I walk in and doing whatever you can to break my balls. Like not taking a message for me when the phone just rang," I added, amazed that I was talking to her like I actually cared.

"Oh that," Mindy said, in a soft tone I had never heard her use. "That was just a joke to get back at you for ignoring me. I called line one from line two and pretended it was a call for you. I would never not take a message from a real caller. You know that. Sure I sometimes give callers a hard time but a girl's got to have a little fun," she smiled. "And how should I treat you, asshole? This nobody walks in from West Virginia, gets a job as Anthony's assistant, starts writing a nightlife column that makes him the toast of South Beach and gets invited to every Goddamned party in town after I've sat here at this fucking desk for two years answering phones and reviewing films. I worked this town up and down. Of course I hate you," she screamed. "But you know what?" She turned and looked around like she was making sure that no one was listening. "I really don't. I'm proud of you. You're the first writer who has worked here who really cares about what he does. Of course I'm jealous," she added quietly. "You did what I wanted to do and you've helped this paper a lot but if you tell anyone I said this, I'll kill you," she added quickly.

"Greetings children," said Anthony, as he rushed into the office. "Mindy, my messages please and have you finished that list of advertisers I asked for?"

"I'm trying to work but Kidd won't leave me alone," Mindy replied. "Fuckface, get back to work, I've got things to do," she snarled at me. "Here's your messages, Anthony and your mail."

"Thanks. Nice to see the children bonding," Anthony said sarcastically as he rushed to his desk in the back office.

"Oh Kidd," Mindy said, grabbing my arm. "Thanks," she said, quietly looking me straight in the face.

"No problem," I said, giving her a little smile. "And I'm from Virginia not West Virginia." I walked back to my desk marveling at the conversation I just had with Mindy. Of course she'd deny ever having said those things or acting nice to me if I ever brought it up again but it made me feel good. Sometimes you never know how people really feel about you and I guess some people pretend to hate while others act as if they're your best friends. Which is worse?

"Kidd, I need to talk to you about some things," growled Anthony, as I sat down. "Are you free for lunch?"

"Anything for you, Anthony," I said politely, knowing his mind was filled with money worries. "I'll just be here at my desk working. Let me know whenever you want to go."

"In about an hour, and could you make a list of all the contacts you have at clubs and other potential advertisers. We need to talk money," Anthony added, speaking as seriously as I've ever heard him sound.

"Sure thing," I agreed. Wow. I had never known Anthony to be so concerned with advertising and money. Sure he yelled about ads and money all the time but it was just part of his weekly tirade. If there wasn't enough revenue flowing in from the ads, he always managed to get money from somewhere. Usually it was from his millionaire aunt or his best friend Johnson Donne who played the part of the wealthy socialite to the hilt but in reality was just an aging homosexual with lots of rich friends.

Life is full of surprises and on South Beach nothing should be taken for granted. For example, my lunch with Justin had completely thrown me for a loop. Just when I thought that Mr. Head of Advertising was going to soak me for client leads or pull some other prank to try to get me fired, he asked me to be his partner in promoting a new weekly gay party night at one of the clubs. Justin poured on the charm and told me that with all my contacts I'd be a perfect partner since I could promote the party in my column and we'd both make a fortune. Of course I had to say no. I told him as a nightlife columnist, I could not put my name on anything and had to cover all events fairly. Journalistic integrity was not a concept that he was willing to accept, but after I told him I would write a cover story on him as promoter of the party and pump up the event without any compensation he was satisfied.

Justin completely avoided the subject about being arrested the night before so I finally had to ask. Celia would have killed me if I didn't get the scoop, and what kind of reporter would I be if I didn't try to find out what had happened? It wasn't something that I could print but I had to be informed if anyone asked so I waited until Justin paid the check, which also shocked me, then casually asked about the arrest. Justin turned red and looked away a moment and then let it out. "Miguel left me and went back home," he said sadly. He had never talked to me about his boyfriend so I knew this was hard for him. "He was afraid of being arrested and was tired of living off me. I finally met someone who wanted to work and didn't expect me to support him and he couldn't work legally so he left. I was so upset and didn't want to face the crowds in the bars so I went trashing in Flamingo Park and got arrested." Justin tried to make light of the whole incident but I could tell he was troubled by the whole ordeal. "Luckily I have an attorney on retainer that's helping me with this party so I was out in no time. How did you find out?" he asked. "Does everyone in South Beach know?"

"Celia told me," I said. "Apparently one of her little Latin boys was also arrested and shared a cell with you. He called Celia when he got out. I haven't told anyone," I added. I knew that the news of another arrest in Flamingo Park certainly wouldn't help Justin's reputation with selling advertising however I've heard party promoters are used to being arrested. I guess that's one of the reasons he has an attorney on retainer.

"Thanks," he said. "And don't tell Anthony about the party. I need to get a few things worked out before he finds out."

So this party was just another secret enterprise that Justin was keeping from Anthony. Hopefully Justin had got it together this time and really planned on letting Anthony know, but just in case, I knew it was wise not to mention it at lunch. I didn't want to get in the middle of anything that was happening between those two and I had a feeling that Justin would soon have much more to worry about than some party if Anthony started checking the books. Once Anthony figured out how much scamming Justin had been doing, something was going to hit the fan and it wasn't going to be drink tickets. Luckily I brought some Tina with me as I definitely needed a bump before this meeting with Anthony.

"Kidd, are you ready to go," Anthony yelled.

"Sure, let me run to the bathroom first. You know how I hate public bathrooms," I said, as I rushed to the bathroom. Anthony was the one person who had no idea of my relationship with Tina.

"Kidd hurry up, let's go," yelled Anthony. "And don't forget to wipe your nose," he yelled, at the bathroom door.

I guess he knew. Oh, shit. So much for my drug-free reputation with Anthony.

TWELVE

I Think I'm In Trouble

That night I started to drink, I mean really drink. There's an endless list of famous writers like Ernest Hemingway and Truman Capote known for being alcoholics but my drinking had nothing to do with writing. Anthony had taken me to lunch earlier that day to tell me that the *South Beach Star* was in big trouble. The *Star* was in debt and unless Anthony cut corners big time, he would have to shut down. Of course no one would ever imagine such a thing since Anthony dined out every day, drinking expensive bottles of wine, and always tipped like a millionaire.

Apparently the amount of trade ads had exceeded the actual ads sold for cash and the *Star* was cash poor. Not only cash poor but deep in debt and his cash cows had run out of milk. Anthony had painted such a dismal picture of the financial state of the *Star,* I actually thought I was going to lose my job. While Anthony swore that no one would be laid off, he did cut my salary and ask if I'd consider selling advertising. I told him I'd mull it over, even though I really thought it was wrong for a writer to sell advertising. Anthony always said that I was the only one on the *Star* staff with ideals and integrity; however the tone with which he said it made it clear that it was not a compliment. I had always stood by my principals but if I couldn't pay rent, or worse, couldn't afford to buy Tina then I'd be forced to change. Anthony painted such a dismal picture of the whole situation which really scared me. I might have to start selling ads after all or even worse, get another job.

After changing into my typical evening uniform, black jacket, black t-shirt, black pants and black boots, I headed out to LINCOLN where Celia was supposed to meet me. Our relationship had turned a little sour since she started to mother me and monitor my drug use. I should have been the one monitoring her. I'd also stopped waiting for her, unless she was bringing me some Tina, and to top it off, she said that I was becoming jaded and didn't actually care about anyone but myself. When she really wanted to stick the knife in, she'd remind me that I had completely neglected the book I had planned to write. She was right about that, nearly a year had gone by without working on my novel.

Celia had said she would meet me at midnight but I arrived an hour early because I needed a dozen cocktails to make me forget about my lunch with Anthony. When I walked into LINCOLN I was amazed that it was so packed, until I remembered that there was a performance scheduled by the drag diva Joey Arias. The crowd made it almost impossible to get to the bar and luckily David, one of the bartenders, saw me and brought me my usual vodka cranberry.

"Some crowd," I remarked, as he put down my drink.

"Yeah, we're packed every time that Joey Arias sings," said David. "Haven't you ever seen Joey Arias perform?"

"No, I haven't but I hear she channels Billie Holiday and is simply incredible." I couldn't believe that I had forgotten that Joey Arias was performing at LINCOLN. I had been looking forward to that show since I heard it announced but the craziness of my life had blocked out everything.

"Yes, Joey Arias is unbelievable. Gotta go," David said, and rushed off to attend to the screaming crowd, all yelling for cocktails.

"Hey baby," came a voice from behind as two hands wrapped around my waist. The voice sounded a bit like Celia but it was much too early for her. "Gotta bump for a lonely friend?" whispered the voice in my ear. I turned and found myself looking into the eyes of a very drunk Celia. Oddly enough, we had both decided to tie one on without alerting the other. I had never seen Celia look such a mess, even at the end of a very long night. Celia always looked fabulous with perfect makeup even if she was wasted but tonight she looked like she'd been drinking for days.

"Hey baby," I replied smiling. "What brings you out so early? Are you okay?" Celia immediately grabbed me and started bawling.

"I'm getting evicted Kidd," she wailed. "And I haven't got any money. If I don't come up with the rent by the end of the week they're going to throw me out." Now that was an opening statement that deserved a cocktail.

"Wait a minute," I said. "You can't get evicted so quickly. That process takes at least 30 days."

"I'm behind three months already," Celia whined. "They served me with eviction papers over a month ago. I don't know what I'm going to do, Kidd," she bawled, and clawed at me like a little baby. People were looking at me like I had done something to her.

"Why didn't you say something before?" I asked.

"I really thought something would happen and I would get the money," replied Celia, in her little girl voice. "You know how I am with money." Yeah, she never had any.

"I know, you never like to think about money but this is something you can't just ignore and hope it will go away," I said a little too loudly.

"Don't scream at me," she wailed. "I thought you'd be more considerate than that and be on my side. Lately everything is about you and you have no time for me," she screamed, and started to walk away.

"Wait Celia," I said, as I grabbed her arm. "I'm having money problems too but maybe I can help you."

"Can you lend me the money?" she asked.

"I would if I could but I don't have it, Celia," I said. The reality of all this money madness was really hitting hard. If things didn't work out at the *Star*, then I might find myself in Celia's position.

"Forget it Kidd, you're getting too big for your pants," she screamed. "I thought you were my friend. Go hang out with your famous buddies." She looked at me hard, then turned and pushed her way through the crowd.

Everyone in the area had been watching our little screaming match and I tried to compose myself. Luckily the lights were suddenly dimmed and a bright spotlight came on, illuminating Joey Arias, who was standing on top of the bar at the other end. The crowds screamed and yelled as the brunette drag diva worked her magic. I became an immediate fan and almost forgot the confrontation with Celia. I stood amazed and couldn't believe that voice was coming from a man dressed as a woman. The critics were right, it really sounded as if Joey were channeling the voice of the late Billie Holiday.

As the famed drag performer sang, I threw back cocktails like there was no tomorrow which was very unlike me. Upset about Celia and the financial state of the *South Beach Star*, I felt a sadness come over me like I had not felt in some time. What Celia said reallly hurt me. I needed my friend Tina to cheer me up or at least pick me up.

Unfortunately I did not have my supply of crystal for the evening because Celia did the drug shopping and I paid her instead of a dealer. Actually, it was one of the ways she made extra money because many of her friends gave her the stuff and she would turn around and charge me for it. Just when I was about to leave I spotted Denny, one of Celia's friends, who was in the corner talking up Joey Arias so I wandered over to say hello.

"Hey Denny, have you seen Celia?" I asked, hoping he would know what was happening with her. "She just threw a fit and stormed away from me."

"Sorry Kidd, Celia's avoiding me. She's overdrawn at the Denny bank," he said smiling. "Is this your first experience with Storm Celia?" Denny said smiling. "Celia is famous for her mega-tantrums and all I can say is take cover. Hopefully you won't become one of her fatalities like many of her ex-friends. Forget about Miss Celia. She's a survivor and knows how to take care of herself. Have you met my dear friend Joey Arias?"

"I haven't but I must say I was floored by that incredible performance," I raved, as I held out my hand to Joey.

"Thank you darling," purred Joey. "Join us for a cocktail or whatever." The performer was quite charming and didn't act the diva like some drag queens that possessed much less talent.

"Speaking of whatever," I whispered, into Denny's ear. "Do you know where I can get some Tina? Celia usually gets it for me."

"You're in luck, my good friend," Denny announced, with a big smile. "I'm the one that introduced Tina to Celia so consider yourself in good hands."

"I've had a day from hell and with my little encounter with Celia I would really like to see Tina," I said softly. "Besides, I think I've had a little too much to drink."

"Here, this should hold you over," said Denny, as he slipped something in my pocket. "We'll take care of business later. I'll give you my number so you can call me whenever you need to see our friend. I rarely venture out but I braved the crowds tonight to see the fabulous Joey Arias perform."

"So, how long are you in town?" I asked Joey.

"Just for tonight darling," Joey said, looking seductively into my eyes. "The sun is too bright in Miami so I'm flying back to New York tomorrow morning. You must come up and see me sometime."

"Do return soon, you're too talented not to share yourself with us," I whispered, in her ear. "Ciao to both of you," I said smiling. "I must run and energize a bit. This is but my first stop of the evening. It might not look like it, but I'm working." I kissed Joey on both cheeks and hugged Denny after he gave me his card then squeezed through the crowd and out the door.

"Kidd, did you get a photo of Joey?" asked Lawrence Freely, owner of LINCOLN. I had completely forgotten to take photos and my camera hung limply on my shoulder. I couldn't believe how wasted I was.

"Sorry, I forgot," I said, as he came up and gave me a hug.

"Well you can't leave without taking a photo of me and Joey Arias for your column," Lawrence added. "Look at this great crowd. Wasn't the show the best? Joey Arias is a legend."

"Yes, the show was unbelievable. Can we take a photo of you and Joey outside in front of the window, it's too crowded in here." I couldn't believe that I had completely forgotten to take photos of Joey Arias singing or anyone else for that matter. I was in a daze because of the money turmoil and the incident with Celia didn't help things at all. Tonight the trendy bar LINCOLN was filled with an A-list crowd that included most of the club owners in town as well as model legend Lauren Hutton and designer Patricia Field. And I didn't get their photos. Well, at least I'd get Joey Arias' photo. Lawrence brought Joey over and we rushed outside.

"My apologies for pulling you outside for a photo," I said to Joey. "I couldn't leave without a photo for my column." Lawrence looked at me and smiled since it sounded much better that I asked for a photo than if he had demanded a photo with the star performer.

"Anything for you darling," purred Joey again. "I hope I see you out later."

I quickly posed Joey and Lawrence in front of LINCOLN and snapped away. The crowd started pouring out of the bar and some even screamed for photos but I rushed up Lincoln Road away from the madness.

Walking towards my apartment, I realized how drunk I had become and was happy that I lived just a block away. I stumbled up the stairs to my apartment and could barely fit the key into the door. Once inside I ran to the bathroom so I could get out the treat that Denny had slid in my pocket. I grabbed it and was about ready to open the tiny bag when a wave of nausea hit me. I sat down on the toilet and opened the bag and did a couple of bumps.

Tina always made me feel great but my head was still spinning from all the alcohol. I never had been a very good drinker and this evening was proof. The nausea subsided but I still didn't feel so terrific so I did another couple of bumps. I took a couple of big breaths and splashed water on my face before I dared look at my reflection in the mirror. Luckily the wattage on my bathroom light was dim so I couldn't see how bad I really looked. I was all sweaty so I needed to change clothes before I went back out for my evening rounds.

When I couldn't decide what to wear I did another bump of Tina and started rearranging my clothes in the closet. Next I decided I'd just straighten my bathroom up a bit and before I realized what I was doing, I had all the cleansers out and was scrubbing my bathroom floor. I never understood the power of Tina and when I did too much I always started cleaning and rearranging my apartment. If it wasn't for Tina my apartment would be a mess. I always thought that Tina was the perfect drug for husbands to give wives since it made you horny as well as want to clean everything in sight. Or so I hear.

My phone rang and I looked at my watch. It was 5 a.m. and I was still cleaning. I was supposed to have gone out and I knew I had missed at least two events. When I answered the phone no one was there. I did another bump and wondered who had called. I hoped it was Celia looking for me. I called her but there was no answer. Her answering machine didn't even pick up and her phone just rang and rang. I did another bump and started working on the rest of my apartment. Tina would not let me stop cleaning.

At 6 a.m. I looked around to find that I had completely cleaned my apartment. I was wired and knew I'd never get to sleep. It was way too early to go into the *Star* office so I had no idea what to do. After cleaning for hours I was in no mood to wander into a crowd of people at one of the after-hours bars. I found Denny's card on my counter and decided to call him. It was early but maybe he was still up, but if not, I'd just leave my number on his answering machine and thank him for the little present.

"Hello, you're caller number two and you're on the air, what's your name please?" said the voice on the phone.

"My name is Kidd," I said timidly, thinking that I had dialed the wrong number.

"Welcome to Denny's talk-a-thon," said Denny, who was doing a pretty good imitation of a radio announcer. "If you answer this question correctly you'll win our grand prize. Have you been up all night?"

"Why yes I have," I said, wondering how he knew. I guess it was pretty obvious but I wasn't really thinking clearly. "I've been cleaning and just finished but couldn't sleep so I thought I'd leave you a message."

"Congratulations, you've won the prize. Now get in a taxi and get your butt over here and join the party," ordered Denny.

"You're having a party at 6 a.m.?"

"The party never stops at Denny's or as I prefer to call it, the House of Denny's. So get over here quickly," Denny said, like he was disappointed that I wasn't already there.

"I'll be right there," I replied. I couldn't believe that I had agreed to venture out so early in the morning. The sun was coming up and I really needed to make an appearance at the *Star* office soon. I usually only went to parties for work but obviously this wasn't a party that could be even be mentioned in my column. I really didn't know Denny that well but now he was my new link to Tina so I couldn't say no. Oh God, maybe Celia was right and I did have a problem.

what's HAPPENING?
ramblings on South Beach nightlife
by KIDD

JOEY ARIAS OR BILLIE HOLIDAY: LINCOLN became a late-night cabaret the other night as drag performer **Joey Arias** took center stage on top of the bar and sang her heart out. This diva doesn't lip-sync but actually channels the voice of the late **Billie Holiday**. The crowd was wowed and included model legend **Lauren Hutton, Crispy Soloperto, Greg & Nicole Bilu Brier, Digby Liebovitz (SWIRL)**, promoter **Mary D., Andrew Delaplaine (WIRE)**, designer **George Tamsitt**, writer **David Leddick** (*My Worst Date*), **Lawrence Freely** (owner of LINCOLN), promoter **Mykel Stevens** and drag divas **Taffy Lynn, Bridget Buttercup, Shelly Novak, Sexcilla** and **Daisy Deadpetals**.

GROOVE JET CELEBRATES: **Greg & Nicole Bilu Brier**, owners of **Groove Jet**, celebrated the two-year with an invitation-only party. The VIP Lounge was packed like a New York subway at rush hour. The only difference being that this crowd was more attractive (every third person was a model) and had cocktails. Among those that braved the crowd were **Tasha Simon, Louis Canales, Michael Landau, Morgan Craft** (Moe's Cantina), supermodel **Bridget Hall, Terry Delano** (Bar 609), **Jacquelynn D. Powers** (Senior Editor of *Ocean Drive Magazine*), **Tara Solomon, Tommy Pooch**, photographer **Jesse Garcia, Bobby Radical, Chyna Girl, Gilbert Stafford, Orejona Ashton** (Irene Marie Models), **Renzo Rosso** (Diesel), and **Stephanie Sayfie** (SoBe on TV). At one point two people even climbed up the tree in the VIP Lounge to find a place to sit. **Wanda** (the tallest drag queen in South Beach) came in and sat on the bar. At 3 a.m. I made my way exited to find there was still a line of people waiting to enter. I took the next train downtown.

WEEKLY STOPS: Berlin Bar, The Living Room, LINCOLN, TWIST, SWIRL, BASH, Liquid, Café Torino, Kremlin, Warsaw, Salvation, The Beehive, and the Delano.

THE SWIRL BEAT: DJ JoJo Odyssey and his music packed the bar and outside patio of **SWIRL** making it almost impossible to enter. **Holly** (formerly of **Salvation**) guards the door. Inside were **Michael** (Hannah & Her Scissors), **Nicole** (Elite Models), artist **Bobby Radical**, drag diva **Ash Rana** (Lucky Cheng's/Back Door Bamby), and makeup guru **Kevyn Aucoin**, as well a group of beautiful models.

LOCAL BOY MAKES GOOD: Check out the new **Versace** campaign in publications like W, Vanity Fair, Interview, and OUT. The campaign features the beautiful ex-**TWIST** bartender **Brett** (no last name needed).

RUPAUL RETURNS: RuPaul, the spokesmodel for **Bailey's Irish Cream**, will be in the area this week. The beautiful diva will be performing at clubs in Ft. Lauderdale and also will be the guest of honor at a **Louis Vuitton** party at the **Delano**. Color me impressed.

SEEN: **Calvin Klein** and **Barry Diller** at **Amnesia**.

EVENT OF THE WEEK: Larry Vickers' monthly **Astor Place** Chef's table that has a Gilligan's Rasta Island theme.

FASHION TIP OF THE MOMENT: If it's too tight to wear, wear it. You'll just have to find someone to help you take it off.

BARTENDER OF THE WEEK: Andy of SWIRL. He even gave me his **Camel Lights** when there were no more at the bar.

DRINK OF THE WEEK: A Zipless-Fuck. A drink I concocted and named after a phrase stolen from writer **Erica Jong**. The ingredients are **Absolut Kurant, Chamborg** and a splash of soda. Tastes delish, but hits you right between the eyes.

QUOTE OF THE WEEK: "I'm so upset now that I have to work for a living."

NEXT WEEK: Find out about the new hot spot where drinks are free (for some). At this exclusive club time stands still and it never closes. Find out the details next week.

THIRTEEN

Out With the Girls

Halloween in South Beach was one of those redundant experiences, as costumes were the norm for every night of the year. Everyone always dressed in costumes, or so it seemed, and I'm not just talking about the drag queens. Club kids dressed to shock instead of to impress and the gays tried to outdo each other by either wearing the tightest or skimpiest outfits imaginable. Not being a fan of dressing up, even on Halloween, I was quite comfortable in my usual "costume" of black everything, jacket, shirt, pants, and boots. I often quipped that it was hard enough to dress up as me, why would I want to dress up like someone else? South Beach always celebrated Halloween with a week of parties, costume contests and scary encounters which would usually culminate on the actual date of Halloween, unless it landed on a Friday night or late in the week and then festivities would continue through the following weekend.

Celia had literally disappeared from my life and had not answered any of the dozens of phone messages that I had left for her. When I finally dropped by her apartment I discovered that she had moved out and I had no clue where she was living. Just like that, my best friend, or so I thought, had vanished from my life. I was already depressed from the money situation at work and I really missed Celia. I felt a little empty and didn't really feel like going out since Halloween was Celia's favorite holiday and she had planned our costumes weeks in advance. We had planned on going as the famous lovers Cleopatra and Mark Anthony. Celia had one of her stylists make us the costumes and she looked gorgeous as Cleopatra. While I felt quite uncomfortable wearing the Mark Anthony costume, I promised to wear it for Celia who believed that we were guaranteed to win prizes. Now with Celia out of my life, I had nothing to wear and frankly had no desire to mingle with all the goblins, witches and drag queens.

"Kidd's here," yelled Holly, as I walked into the office. "I'll ask him to go out with us," she screamed into the phone before she hung up. Holly was sitting at the front desk where Mindy Morgan usually sat and was at the office suspiciously early.

"Morning Holly," I said, surprised to see her. "What's the occasion to get you here so early?"

"Mindy's sick and can't come in so I'm subbing for her," she said, a little louder than necessary. "Actually she met someone and wanted to stay home and play house today," she whispered.

"So you're Mindy for the day. Any messages for me?" I asked, hoping to avoid further conversation and head back to my desk.

"Yes, your friend Kim called and wanted to know if you had any plans for tonight," Holly said, with a big smile on her face. "So I suggested that the three of us hit the town together."

"I'm not sure what I'm doing tonight Holly. Celia and I had planned on going out but now that she's disappeared I don't know if I'm going out at all. I really hate Halloween." What had happened to the chipper Kidd that remained optimistic and never accepted depression as part of his life? What had happened to Jamie Kidd, the one who wanted to be a respected novelist by the age of thirty, he's the one I was really worried about.

"You've got to go out!" Holly squealed. "How could you not cover Halloween for your column? It would be a disgrace and besides it's one of the best party nights of the year."

"Well, I don't know. I guess I should go out but I don't have a costume so if I do go out I'm going as me," I said unenthusiastically. I couldn't deal with the idea of finding a costume at the last minute and really didn't want to wear some stupid outfit anyway.

"You can't do that," Holly replied. "I'm dressing up as Jayne Mansfield and Kim's going as Marilyn Monroe. You have to wear a costume, Kidd. I'll help you think of something. It'll be so much fun," she said, looking at me with a big smile as the phone kept ringing.

"Okay, I'll go out with you two, now answer the phone," I said, knowing I wouldn't hear the end of it otherwise. "I'll call Kim back and tell her that I can't say no to Marilyn Monroe and Jayne Mansfield." I then rushed to the back office while Holly answered the phone.

Holly was right. Halloween was a night that I needed to cover for my column but I had no clue what I could pull together for a costume. I wasn't in the mood but with Holly and Kim by my side I was guaranteed an interesting evening. Holly normally dressed like a modern day Hollywood bimbo so I couldn't imagine what her Jayne Mansfield costume would look like. With the help of numerous trips to the plastic surgeon, Holly looked like she was about thirty-something in club lighting but I knew her real age was fifty-something. Holly also fit the "dumb blonde" category to a tee and thought that every guy, gay or straight, wanted her body. South Beach was overflowing with young beautiful model so Holly often had to settle for the n'er-do-wells and castoffs, or those hoping to live off a wealthy older lady. Holly was not wealthy but always had "blow" and never had to pay for a cocktail so she was usually guaranteed male companionship as long as supplies lasted. Whenever she had a problem getting a cocktail for free she'd whip out her little Instamatic and offer to take a photo for her "Out With Holly" column in the *Star*.

Work was the farthest thing from my mind and luckily Anthony wasn't in the office. I wandered back to the bathroom for a little bump so I could energize for the day. I knew I should call Kim since Holly had made arrangements for the three of us. Kim had been calling me for weeks and I hadn't returned any of her calls.

Kim was a perky little blonde from New Jersey who studied at the University of Miami but at night hit the club scene with a vengeance. Apparently her older brother was a promoter in New York City and she'd been going out since she was sixteen. One night in SWIRL, the place where I've met most of my good friends, Kim came up to me and started raving about my column and asked why I never wrote about her. I had never even seen her before or so I thought but she went on about how we'd hung out several times. Kim told me that she worked with Wilhelmina models, so one day I decided to call her at the office and see if she wanted to go out. I was a bit put off when the receptionist told me that nobody by the name of Kim worked there. When I ran into her again I told her about the phone call and she looked at me like I was crazy and announced that she was a model with Wilhelmina and didn't work in the office.

Now Kim was attractive, but not what I'd call model gorgeous and since she was about six inches shorter than most working models, I never in my wildest dreams thought she was a model. I apologized for the mistake but later realized that ninety per cent of what came out of her mouth was a fabrication but she was fun to hang out with as long as the supplies lasted.

"Hello Kim, it's Kidd," I said, into the phone. "Holly tells me that you two have a big night planned for Halloween."

"Well, hello Kidd, It's about time you called me back. Yes, it's going to be so much fun," Kim screamed. "I'm dressing as the actress Marilyn Monroe. You've heard of her right?" Was she serious?

"Yes, I know who Marilyn Monroe is," I said. Kim was always saying things like that because she was always talking about movie stars that she thought no one knew.

Movie stars from the old days like the seventies and the eighties. Kim was twenty but had a fake I.D. and told everyone she was twenty-three. No one believed her.

"You have to dress as someone fun like Elvis or the Incredible Hunk," she said.

"It's the Incredible Hulk not hunk," I said laughing. "I don't think I could pull either one off but I'll find something. Let's meet at LINCOLN around eleven and we'll go from there," I said, knowing that if I left it up to Holly and Kim, they'd never make a decision. I was surprised that they knew what they were wearing.

"Sounds great, Kidd," she squealed. "Hugs and kisses until tonight."

Completely baffled as to what to wear, I needed a little help from Tina. Since I was alone in the back office I forfeited going to the toilet and did a couple of bumps at my desk. Filled with illegal confidence and energy, thanks to my bag of crystal, I quickly returned all my calls and set up appointments for the rest of the week. Buzzing with energy, I decided I'd leave so I could pull together a costume for the evening. What I really wanted was to stay home and hide from all the craziness and wallow in my depression but I couldn't. I had a date with two beautiful women so why did I feel so alone? Guess.

Known for my punctuality, I had always yelled at Celia whenever she arrived late but tonight I walked into LINCOLN just minutes before midnight, an hour later than my scheduled meeting with Holly and Kim. Somehow I had pulled together a suitable costume but it took me a while to get up the nerve to walk out of my apartment dressed as Groucho Marx. While Groucho Marx had starred in movies with both Marilyn Monroe and Jayne Mansfield, I was convinced that Holly and Kim wouldn't have any idea who Groucho was. Wearing a black wig, oversized jacket and pants, and the Groucho glasses with nose and moustache attached, I was sure that no one would recognize me. Sliding up to the end of the bar, I stuck a cigar in my mouth and expected to surprise whoever waited on me. Milton, one of my favorite bartenders at LINCOLN, was on duty and was dressed as a clown. He came over and handed me my normal vodka cranberry.

"Hey Kidd," he said, leaning over the bar. "Cute costume. Holly called four times and said that she and Kim were on their way, but you're lucky. They just walked in a few minutes before you did and they're in the bathroom."

"Thanks," I said. I was a little surprised that he recognized me with my wig and glasses. I was sure that my costume would be the perfect disguise.

"Kidd, there you are," screamed Holly as she and Kim rushed for me with open arms.

"You look adorable," squeaked Kim. "Who are you?" she asked.

"I'm Groucho Marx," I announced. "You've certainly heard of the Marx Brothers. He was a great comic wit who said things like, "Women should be obscene and not heard." It was obvious that both girls had no idea who Groucho Marx was. Holly was certainly old enough to have at least recognized his name but seemed totally clueless. I wouldn't have had that problem if I had come as Brad Pitt, George Clooney, or Ricky Martin, but if I could have pulled off those impersonations my life might have been a little cheerier.

"You don't know who Groucho Marx is?" yelled Holly. Apparently the two had done a little coke in the bathroom as they were both more energetic than normal and normal was usually more than perky enough.

"Who cares," said Kim. "You look adorable. Let's party." Kim was always happy as long as there were cocktails and coke and she never paid for either. She was the perfect party girl until she got too wasted or the drugs ran out and then she magically disappeared. Although Kim and Holly were supposed to be dressed as Marilyn Monroe and Jayne Mansfield neither of them looked like they were wearing costumes. In fact, they didn't look much different than they usually did. So I felt like I was the only one wearing a costume but at that point I didn't care. I had done enough Tina before I left my apartment to energize me for the entire night and I felt like I could almost fly. At least I wasn't dressed like Mark Anthony but I did miss Celia and I didn't feel happy at all. Oh well, it was Halloween and I was out in glamorous South Beach and I had Marilyn Monroe and Jayne Mansfield at my side. It brought to mind one of Groucho's famous quotes, "I have had a perfectly wonderful evening, but this wasn't it."

what's HAPPENING?
ramblings on South Beach nightlife
by KIDD

A SCARY NIGHT OUT: On Halloween night everyone looked "fierce" or at least thought they did and wanted to be photographed (over and over). At **LINCOLN**, bartender **Milton** was dressed as a clown and the first to recognize me behind my **Groucho Marx** costume. My companions **Holly (Out With Holly)** and **Kim (Wilhemina Models)** were dressed as **Marilyn Monroe** and **Jayne Mansfield** (don't ask who was which) and together we roamed the scary streets and clubs of South Beach. Our first stop was **SWIRL** where the costumes and decorations were in direct competition. Bartender **Andy** was dressed as a mobster (or so he said) and owner **Digby** dressed as a groom (although he already has a husband). At **Warsaw** there was a block-party with a block of Espanola Way blocked off for outdoor fun since the club was over-packed. The costumes were incredible and there were so many men in drag (hopefully for the last time) and muscle men in leather pants (without shirts). Speaking of no shirts, drag diva **Paloma Di Laurenti's** gorgeous all red (see-through) costume was flawless. She looked like a Vegas show-girl vampire. Seen at **Warsaw**: **Elaine Lancaster** (dressed as herself), **Kitty Meow** (dressed as a cat), artist/promoter **Anderson Laurent** (dressed as a devil), **Damien Devine** with chiropractor **Dr. Hal Kreitman** (wearing matching zebra print costumes & alien ears), **Leslie Quick** (wearing an alien costume that won first place costume award) with **Ryan** (her personal **Boss Model**), and **DJ Shannon** (dressed in fifties garb). After Warsaw I stopped at **Liquid**, which was packed with a very straight but friendly attractive crowd of strangers (very few drag queens and musclemen costumes) I lost the girls. The real drag queens were waiting by the office door (it was payday). Seen at **Liquid:** Liquid owner **Chris Paciello** (dressed as a mobster-imagine that), performer **Power, Madi Madness, Girlina**, and promoter **Jack Benggio** (dressed as a cowboy).

HOW MANY BARTENDERS DOES IT TAKE TO MAKE A BALL? All of them. **Camel/KBA Marketing** produced a giant extravaganza **Bartenders' Ball** at **Rezerection Hall** (the old **Paragon**) filled with bartenders, waiters, bar owners, doormen, promoters and DJs. KBA Marketing reportedly spent over $80,000 for this event for the 43 venues in South Beach that sell Camel cigarettes. The party (decorated with life-size camels, giant packs of cigarettes, a four-screen slide show, table lights designed as giant hands holding lit cigarettes) hits the road as Camel produces a similar party in 27 cities. The South Beach party featured performances by **Planet Soul** and **Funky Green Dogs** and open bar all night with trays of food that never stopped coming. **SEEN AT THE BALL:** Promoter **Tommy Pooch, Tommy** and **John Turchin, Nick Van Tarsch** (owner of **Lua**), **Terry Delano** (Bar 609), **Gerry Kelly** (**BASH**), **Kevin Crawford** (**Liquid**), designer **Jennifer Stein, Digby** (**SWIRL**), door god **Gilbert Stafford, Lawrence Freely** (**LINCOLN**), door host/promoter **Roy Hansen**, photographer **Jesse Garcia**, promoter **Mykel Stevens**, artist **Attila Lakatoush**, DJ **Gigi**, and **Greg & Nicole Brier** (Groove Jet).
CLUBS OF THE WEEK: **Liquid** on Monday, **BASH** on Tuesday, **Lua** on Wednesday, **KGB** on Thursday, **Warsaw** on Friday, **Salvation** on Saturday and (if you're still standing) **Groove Jet & Amnesia** on Sunday.
EVENT OF THE WEEK: Thursdays at **Kremlin** with Go-Go boys, music by **DJ David Knapp**, and **Adora** as your hostess.
TREND OF THE MOMENT: Giving up cigarettes. Don't tell the Camel/KBA folks.
DRINK OF THE WEEK: A Hollywood. A **Cosmopolitan** made with cheap talk, cheap vodka, and garnished with a smashed cherry.
QUOTE OF THE WEEK: "I knew I wasn't going to make it on time so I decided not to show up at all."

FOURTEEN

All Dressed Up But

The South Beach nightlife scene had totally consumed me and my lifestyle included a whirlwind schedule of events, parties, openings and morning parties. My dream of being a successful novelist by the age of thirty had passed me by as had my thirty-fifth birthday. Instead of just covering the nightlife scene, I had become a component of the party crowd and work often seemed secondary. The tension at the *South Beach Star* mounted as Anthony blamed his financial troubles on the entire staff daily. Anthony had cut everyone's salary including mine and my spending had exceeded my income. My life wasn't so fabulous anymore as I found myself broke and realized I needed to find a way to supplement my weekly paycheck but I still couldn't bring myself to sell advertising. Things were looking so grim that I feared that I had better start selling advertising fast because I couldn't fathom looking for another job.

After yet another staff meeting where Anthony threatened us with the reality that the *South Beach Star* could close any day if we all didn't get out there and sell advertising, I decided I had better hit the streets. Walking down Lincoln Road I had hoped to find someone to buy an ad but felt hopelessly out of my league where advertising sales were concerned. I had sold advertising for my magazine in Virginia but that was a whole different world.

Lincoln Road was thriving once again now that the remodeling was completed and lots of new boutiques and stores had opened. I stopped to look in the window of MODE a new shop on Lincoln Road that featured hot designer fashions for both men and women, selling labels like Dolce & Gabbana, Versace, Claude Montana and Thierry Mugler. Since I never could afford such fashions, I was doubly afraid to even enter shops like this, but I loved to window shop.

"See anything you like?" said a striking blonde woman standing in the doorway. I hadn't noticed her before but she was looking right at me so I couldn't ignore her.

"Everything's beautiful," I remarked.

"So why don't you come in and try something on?" the blonde said.

"I'm just window shopping," I stammered. "My budget doesn't include designer clothes but I do like looking. Oh, I'm Kidd by the way. I work around the corner at the *South Beach Star*."

"I know who you are," said the blonde who was suddenly standing by my side. "I'm Arlene and this is my boutique. I've seen your photo in all the local magazines and I'm a fan of your column. You should have someone dressing you. Why don't you step inside," she said, as she guided me with both hands into the shop. "I think we should talk business."

I wasn't prepared for this little exchange but was thinking that maybe I was on the way to landing my first advertising client. Not only did I sell her a series of ads in the *Star* but I walked out of MODE with a new Thierry Mugler jacket. Arlene had asked me to stop back by the store at five to meet her husband. She had also asked if I was interested in doing a bit of marketing and promotion for the boutique. Since she thought I was so visible on the nightlife scene, the target market for MODE, she thought I'd be the ideal publicist for the store. Her offer was exclusive of the advertising contract and when she offered to compensate me with half cash and half clothes I was immediately convinced, since I was in desperate need of both. Arlene said she just wanted her husband to meet me and give his nod of approval.

At five o'clock I left the *Star* office and walked the half a block around the corner to MODE to meet Arlene's husband. When I arrived at the shop the door was locked so I knocked on the door but the store seemed empty. I put my face close to the glass of the door and tried to see if I could see anyone inside. The shop looked deserted but I knocked again, this time a little louder. Suddenly I saw movement in the back of the store and saw Arlene running to the front with her arms waving wildly.

"Sorry, we were in the backroom," said Arlene, as she opened the door. She was out of breath, like she had just run laps instead of running the short distance to open the door. "Come in, I want you to meet my husband."

Stepping into the shop I felt like I was walking into some sort of trap and felt very nervous about the meeting. Suddenly a very tall man stepped out from behind the curtains that acted as a door to the backroom. A sterner face could not have been placed on any man and his eyes bore into me like I was indeed the enemy.

"This is my husband Niklas," said Arlene, as she guided me back to where he was standing.

"Hello, I'm Kidd," I said, while I held out my hand. Instead of taking my hand, he looked down at me for a moment then glanced at his wife before turning his eyes back on me.

"So you're homosexual?" he asked, as if he were interrogating me in a lineup.

"Excuse me," I said, looking at Arlene. "What does that have to do with anything?" Her husband had an endearing way of making me feel totally uncomfortable and I felt like running out of the shop. His German accent also made me feel uneasy. Hitler had hated homosexuals just as much as he hated Jews so maybe homophobia was a German trait. What really was the purpose of this meeting and why had they turned the music up so loud?

"Good, it's true," continued Niklas, and his German accent seemed more pronounced. Apparently my questioning response had answered his question. Suddenly a smile appeared on his face and he completely changed. "My wife told me all about you. You must understand I'm most concerned with men who work with my beautiful wife. I'm a successful business man and very careful. I'm an extremely jealous man and I don't want anger." He looked at me smiling but I still felt like running out of the store. His smile had not put me at ease at all.

"Niklas is very protective of me but I told him all about you," cut in Arlene, trying to break the tension. "I assured him that you were the perfect person to help us market our shop since you know everyone." They both stood side by side looking at me like I was a new car that they had just bought. I felt very uncomfortable and didn't know what to say.

"Thank you," I finally said, then let Tina take over. "Your shop is beautiful and you have a great collection of designer fashions so it will be easy to market MODE. There are many ways we can promote your shop and I've written a proposal that includes several of my ideas," I continued, hoping that all was well. I really needed this account and had already told Anthony that it was a done deal.

"No business now," snapped Niklas. "Let's go for cocktails and talk. Become friends. You talk business with my wife later." Suddenly we were headed out the door to Au Petite Bistro, the little French café down the street on Lincoln Road. Niklas took control and ordered a bottle of wine. Before I could say anything, Niklas started grilling me about the people I knew. Luckily I was friends or at least casual acquaintances with everyone whose name he mentioned. I was really frightened that if he named someone that I wasn't connected with the deal would be off. By the end of the second bottle of wine, this couple had adopted me into their lives and it was obvious that I had no say in the matter.

The three of us became a social trio, out all the time and they always paid. Niklas liked the fact that everyone welcomed me with open arms and of course I introduced them as my close friends and the owners of MODE.

Arlene and Niklas had become friends of a sort but most importantly MODE was my first advertiser in the *South Beach Star* and for the time being my only client. Arlene and Niklas also hired me as the publicist for their shop so they pretty much felt like they controlled me. If I had an important event to attend, Arlene would dress me in fashions from the store so I could mention that my clothes came from MODE whenever I was photographed. After a couple of months promoting MODE the press started to take notice and the shop became popular with stylists who used their clothes for fashion shoots for national fashion publications. Suddenly I was no longer just a nightlife columnist but also publicist/advertising rep.

When Arlene was asked to organize a fashion show for a big annual charity luncheon I knew I had done my job. This charity luncheon was a very prestigious event and I knew the press coverage would be incredible. MODE would not only provide all the clothes for the fashion show but Arlene would be the emcee and commentator for the fashion event. The Tenth Annual South Florida Bowl Charity Luncheon was a publicist's dream and I had already sent out press releases naming Arlene as the emcee and MODE as the fashion sponsor of the annual charity event.

Just when I thought all was going well, I received a frantic call from Niklas at the *Star* office telling me I had to rush over to the store immediately. Without a clue as to what was wrong I walked over to MODE and entered to find the store deserted.

"Hello," I yelled, after entering the shop. "Is anyone here?"

"Kidd, I'm in the backroom," screamed Arlene. "Lock the front door and come back here." It was strange that she wanted me to lock the front door and it made me a little nervous but I did as she wished and walked through the curtains to the backroom. Clothes were scattered everywhere and Arlene was sitting on a small stool so tiny it looked almost like she was sitting on the floor.

"What's wrong?" I asked. "Are you okay?" Clearly she was distressed and her eyes were big as saucers.

"Is the front door locked?" she asked quickly. "No one else is here?" What could have happened for her to be so frantic?

"The door is locked and we're alone," I replied, looking down at her. Then I noticed that there was a distinct smell of something burning.

"I'm freaking out about the show and want to ask you to emcee the show with me," she said quickly. "Please, you have to do this for me. I've been crazed with planning the show and that would take a big load off my mind. Everybody knows your column, Kidd. You're a local celebrity anyway. And you're funny. I'm not. Say you'll do it."

"Sure," I said. Of course she wasn't really giving me a choice as I had to keep my one and only account happy. "I'd love to do it," I added, with a fake smile. Something was wrong with this picture and I could smell trouble. That distinct odor should have been a major clue.

"Thank you, thank you," she said quickly, and then stood up revealing that she had been holding a pipe the whole time we were talking. Apparently she had been smoking something. I wasn't sure what it was and I really didn't want to know. If she did drugs that was her business but she really shouldn't be smoking anything illegal in the back of her store. I really wasn't anyone to point fingers but I was afraid that the trouble I smelled was rock cocaine. Some people called it crack and I didn't want to think that I was working for someone who smoked crack, but she might not want someone working for her who did crystal meth. So I let it slide.

"I think we'll work well together at the podium," I added, pretending that I didn't notice that she'd just relit the pipe. "We should make cards describing all the fashions because I'm not as familiar with all the designers, especially the women's fashions."

"No problem," Arlene said, waving her hand. "I'll take care of that. Why don't you go upstairs and pick out a suit to wear for the event. Of course you should be dressed head to toe in clothes from MODE so you can describe what you're wearing during the show. And unlock the front door in case we get any customers," she added. "I'll be out in a minute."

The next two days I spent most of my time at MODE as Arlene pulled the clothes for the fashion show. Arlene described the clothes as she put the outfit together but kept running to the back room while I was expected to keep an eye on the store and check-out the models after they had changed into the clothes. I greeted customers and even sold a few things while she was secluded in the backroom, and hoped that no one noticed the smell from her pipe. Arlene was a bit of a mess and I was worried about how she was going to act in front of a crowded ballroom for the charity luncheon. I had to admit she was acting a little cracked out.

On the day of the event I arrived at the Intercontinental Hotel dressed in the Claude Montana suit that I had selected from MODE. It was beautiful and I felt that I looked great in it but knew that I'd have to return the twelve hundred dollar suit after the event. The charity luncheon was being held in one of the larger ballrooms that came equipped with a stage. A rehearsal with all the models was scheduled an hour before the event and the models were all standing around backstage when I arrived. I had suggested we have at least one rehearsal before the day of the event but Arlene waved the notion away as nonsense. I had been in the store when most of the models had been fitted but there was one that I had missed. Celia was standing in the middle of the group of models and she looked away as I walked closer. More tension, that's all I needed. Arlene was nowhere to be seen and Niklas was pacing back and forth.

"Where's Arlene?" I asked, walking up to him.

"Kidd, good you're here," Niklas said, like I was there to save the day. "Arlene is not feeling very well. She's in bathroom. You're going to have to emcee fashion show without her." He was staring at me like I was the blame for whatever had happened and I looked at him like he was crazy.

"What do you mean emcee the show?" I asked. "It's Arlene's event. I don't know the clothes. She's supposed to be the main commentator; I'm just her sidekick." Obviously it wasn't the time for humor. All the models were staring at me and looked confused. Suddenly Celia spoke up in my defense.

"Kidd, you'll be great," Celia said. "You can do it. We all know what we're wearing so we can do a quick rehearsal." Celia looked at me and smiled. I was glad to see her and happy that she was on my side. It was the first time I had seen her in months and what a strange situation this was. Now I just had to find the cards that Celia had made with the descriptions of the clothes.

"Niklas," I yelled. He was walking towards the stage door exit and I was afraid he was going to disappear. "Do you know where the cards with the fashion descriptions are?" I asked, trying to take control of the situation.

"I know nothing," Niklas said. "Go in the bathroom and talk to Arlene," he said, as he pointed towards a door on the side of the stage. "I'm going outside for a smoke. I'll be back before the show starts," he announced, and strutted off without looking back. I stood there speechless. We had less than an hour before the luncheon was scheduled to begin and I had no idea what was going on.

Suddenly Candy Apple, one of the local drag divas, came through the door with an entourage of hairdressers.

"Hello kids," she yelled. "I'm here to make you all look beautiful, so line up for hair and makeup." Candy then walked over to me and looked me up and down. "Kidd, what are you doing here?" I felt I had just had my face slapped.

"I'm taking Arlene's place as emcee," I replied.

"Good, I thought Arlene might have gone crazy and stuck you in the show. You'll be fine as the emcee." Slap on the face number two. "We can't do anything to make you look better anyway." Then she turned and started directing her crew to work on the models.

While the models were busy in hair and makeup I walked to the bathroom door and knocked. I was hoping that Arlene would come out.

"Arlene, are you in there?" I yelled. No answer. "If you're in there I need to talk to you about the fashion show. We have less than an hour before people start arriving." I waited for a response but when none came, I started banging on the door. "Arlene, open this door now or I'm leaving!" Apparently those were the magic words and the door opened and she pulled me inside.

"I can't come out," Arlene said, looking like a crazed maniac. "They're all expecting me to be wonderful and charming and beautiful but I can't do it," she chanted, like a speed demon, not letting me get a word or even a thought in edgewise. "You're going to do it by yourself and you'll be great. Please Kidd, I'm freaking out. You have to do it. You're great with words and people and you're funny and people love you. Please, Kidd. You have to do it." She finally stopped to take a breath and looked at me with such a frightened expression that I wanted to put my arms around her and make it okay but I knew all she wanted was her crack pipe.

"Okay, I'll do it," I quickly said. "I guess I really don't have a choice as you're not in any condition to get out there in front of a crowd. Now where are the cards with the descriptions of the clothes? I guess I can just read your commentary as the models come out. Just give me the cards and I'll go work with the models," I said, looking at her. She froze and kept staring at me with those big saucer eyes that started filling with tears.

"I got so busy with everything else I forgot to make cards. I'm so sorry Kidd," she said sobbing. She forgot to make the cards but I saw the pipe sitting on the bathroom sink. She didn't forget that.

"Arlene, pull yourself together," I said, trying to compose myself at the same time. "I'll just write down the designer names during rehearsal. I'll figure it out. Now pull yourself together. Splash some water on your face and calm down," I said, hoping she'd stop crying. I grabbed her and gave her a big hug. "Don't worry, I'll take care of everything. You know you'll have to at least make an appearance at the end of the show." I looked at her and smiled. She had stopped crying and had lit a cigarette. "And Arlene, please put that pipe away."

"Oh my god, I forgot it was there. I'm sorry. Thanks Kidd," she said suddenly, and smiled but tears were streaming down her face. "You better hurry, they're going to open the room in forty-five minutes," she said, looking at her watch. Arlene sounded as if she was the captain once again but she'd be steering the ship from the bathroom and I'd be at the podium. I walked outside and took a deep breath. What had I gotten myself into?

"Attention everyone," I announced, as I walked backstage where all the models were waiting. We're going to do a quick dress rehearsal. Everyone get dressed and as each of you pass by me on the podium tell me the name of the designers of the fashions that you're wearing. They will be opening the ballroom in less than forty-five minutes so we have to work fast. I want everyone dressed in ten minutes and ready to go." I turned and walked out front to check out the podium but also to try to compose myself. I couldn't look at any of the models directly in the face as they'd realize immediately that I had no idea what I was doing. I stood at the podium and looked out at the empty ballroom which would soon be filled with nearly five hundred ladies expecting a professional fashion show. Oh my god, how was I going to pull this off?

"Hello, hello," came a voice from backstage and then a sprightly little brunette lady dressed in a pink Chanel suit came out with a clipboard. "Are you Kidd? I'm Betsey Saunders, the event coordinator for the South Florida Bowl Charity Luncheon." She held out her hand and smiled broadly.

"Yes, I'm Kidd. Nice to meet you," I said. I had never seen a perkier person in my life.

"Arlene told me that you'll be doing the honors as emcee. We're so honored to have you here today. The ladies are so excited about the fashion show. We have a special plaque to give to Arlene and her husband at the end of the event. I'll give it you so you can present it to them as they come out at the end of the show. Now I'll let you get back to your rehearsal," she said with a smile and disappeared behind the curtain. It actually seemed that she had known that I was going to be the only emcee for some time.

My mind was spinning and the next hour was but a blur. I barely remembered speaking at all but I recalled writing down the designers names with a number as the models came out in rehearsal. As soon as the last model left the stage, the sound guy announced that they were opening the room and I should go backstage. I was freaking out as all I had written down on the cards were the designers' names and had no idea what I was going to say. This would be a true test of my skills as a writer, since I'd be writing the dialogue as I spoke it.

I rushed back to the bathroom where Arlene had secluded herself. She pulled me in again but this time she looked great. Candy Apple had applied her makeup and she was dressed and looked fabulous. I thought if she could pull herself together that fast I had better pull it together too because this show was being reviewed for the *Miami Herald's* fashion column. Luckily I had brought a bag of Tina with me. I made a quick dash to the men's room, since the show was just about ready to begin. It there was ever a time that I could use a little illegal courage, this was it.

"Good afternoon ladies, I want to introduce to you our master of ceremonies for the Tenth Annual South Florida Bowl Charity Luncheon," said the perky little voice of Betsey Saunders. "He's a nightlife columnist and photographer with the *South Beach Star*. Today he will be introducing you to the fashions of MODE. Let's give a big welcome to our emcee Kidd."

That's all I remember hearing and I was suddenly standing at the podium. I remember the models walking the runway and my mouth moving. I heard the music in my ears and heard laughter and applause as I spoke but had no idea what I was saying. Before I knew it there was massive applause and the models all walked out and stood on the stage. Betsey Saunders came out smiling and took the microphone.

"Now that was one of the most interesting presentations we've ever had for one of our Charity Luncheons," said Betsey. "Kidd, your descriptions and patter were so refreshing. You made us feel like you were describing a wonderful party instead of a fashion show. Now if you'll introduce the owners of MODE, I'll let you present them with their plaque."

"Lovely ladies of the South Florida Bowl Charity," I announced. "May I introduce you to the owners of MODE, Arlene and Niklas Krautt?" Arlene and Niklas came out arm in arm and passed right by me without a nod and walked down the runway. When they returned, the couple stood like statues in the middle of the group of models while I announced that the South Florida Bowl Charity was giving them a plaque to honor their contribution for this grand charity event. When they didn't move to come accept the award I grabbed the microphone for one last announcement. It was obvious they were both out of it and too mortified to move.

"While designer fashions always look fabulous on lovely models like you've witnessed today, fashions found at MODE also look great on normal people like myself. Today I happen to be wearing a beautiful Claude Montana navy suit which Niklas and Arlene graciously gave me for emceeing this event." I noticed Niklas' expression change a bit as he looked my way but Arlene kept smiling like her face was frozen. Giving me the suit was the least they could do. I deserved it for saving their butts today.

"And now ladies, you're in for a treat," I announced, giving the audience the biggest smile I could muster. "The lovely Arlene Krautt will share with you her personal fashion forecast for the upcoming season. Here's Arlene from MODE," I said, as I handed the microphone to her. I briefly got a glimpse of her shocked expression as I turned and waved at the audience. I signaled for the models to follow me and we all walked backstage leaving Arlene and Niklas standing alone on stage.

The fashion report in the *Miami Herald* the next day raved about the fashion show and particularly about my commentary. I was completely shocked. The writer compared my comments to one of my nightlife columns. He wasn't as kind to Arlene. "Kidd has quite a fashion wit about him," wrote the fashion reviewer. Frankly the whole experience was like a bad dream and I couldn't remember a word I had said. Celia had told me that it sounded like I was reading from one of my columns the way I described the fashions. I never spoke to Arlene or Niklas again and the store closed a couple of months later. I had never emceed an event before and decided I would stick to writing but I did get a great suit out of the deal.

what's HAPPENING?
ramblings on South Beach nightlife
by KIDD

CLUBLAND: The winds of change have hit Clubland once again. The **Icon** party returns to **Glam Slam**. Promoters **Jeff & Carlos** are moving **PUMP** back to **Zen**. **Beige** (from New York) comes to the **Raleigh Hotel** this Thursday night (hoping to attract the "elite" of the club scene. Opening in a location between **Berlin Bar** and **The Living Room** is a **Video Arcade** (very Times Square) attracting an underage crowd not allowed in any clubs (unless they're models). **Liquid** has acquired a space in New York and it's rumored that another South Beach space is being sought out by Liquid's dynamic duo **Chris Paciello & Ingrid Casares**. The infamous performer **Power** (of **Salvation** fame) will be hosting his own night at **SPLASH** next Thursday. While Power is currently the Entertainment Director at Salvation, rumors are flying about the future of the club (could it be true that **Gloria & Emilio Estefan** are turning the club into a recording studio?). Promoter **Roy Hansen** starts a new special party in the VIP-VIP Room at Glam Slam on Saturdays.

FASHION COVERAGE BY KIDD: This past Saturday I had the honor of being the emcee for the **Tenth Annual South Florida Bowl Charity Luncheon Fashion Show** held at the **Intercontinental Hotel**. The fashions, from the boutique **MODE**, included designers **Thierry Mugler, Valentino, Armani, Raymond Dragon, Fendi, Agnes B,** and **Claude Montana**. The models were flawless with makeup by **Candy Apple**. Owners of MODE, **Arlene & Niklas Krautt**, received a lovely plaque for their contribution to the charity. I received a Claude Montana suit for my job as emcee.

MODELS & MORE MODELS: The Chili Pepper hosted a party for up and coming models (which I think is redundant because all of South Beach is a party for model hopefuls). The event was sponsored by **Fashion Spectrum** with publicist **G. Jack Donahue** at the door.

CLUB OF THE WEEK: KGB: where I spotted promoter **Mark Lehmkuhl, Roman Bekman,** publicist **Susan Scott,** photographer **Iran Issa-Khan, Eric Ormores (BASH), Gerry Kelly (BASH), Kevin Crawford (Liquid),** performer **Michael M, Chris Paciello (Liquid),** artist **Attila Lakatoush,** and artist **Aaron Von Powell.**

EVENT OF THE WEEK: Funky Melange of Mustached Mona Lisas at SWIRL.

TREND OF THE MOMENT: Shaving your head. South Beach guys have been sporting shaved heads for awhile (I thought it was the land of **Daddy Warbucks** when I first arrived). Now women (and wannabes) are shaving their heads. The other night at **LINCOLN,** drag diva **Bridgett Buttercup** shaved her head as part of her show. Yesterday I saw four women with shaved heads walking down Lincoln Road but I think they were part of a cult.

FASHION STATEMENT OF THE MOMENT: Sometimes you have to pay a hefty price for free fashions.

RESTAURANT OF THE WEEK: YUCA (young urban Cuban Americans) gets a standing ovation for not only its food and **Gospel Brunches** with **Maryel Epps** but for bringing entertainment like **Herb Alpert** and the famed Latin performer **Albita**.

NEW RESTAURANT: St. Tropez on Espanola Way. Good luck, **Roberto** & staff.

BARTENDER OF THE WEEK: Taffy Lynn (who serves up cocktails and sass at the upstairs bar of LINCOLN). Make sure you tip well as she controls her bar area with a strong whip and tongue. "Drink this. Give me a bigger tip or never come back. Go downstairs and get it yourself." The Taffy Lynn experience is not recommended for those weak of heart or under medication.

QUOTE OF THE WEEK: "You mean you work for a living?"

NEXT WEEK: It's **Octopussy** in the **Lounge at Liquid** and **Venus Envy** at **Starfish.**

FIFTEEN

I Thought We Said Goodbye

The MODE fiasco proved to be an excellent training ground for what not to do when dealing with advertising clients. Now that I had lost them as clients, I was back to square one and broke. My first instinct was to announce that I would never ever attempt to sell advertising or take on freelance public relation clients again. However, I needed to supplement my scaled down salary somehow. Hopefully I could meet with Anthony and formulate a plan of attack to sell some ads for the *South Beach Star* without endangering my integrity. What integrity? As the publisher, Anthony felt that he had artistic license to step outside the codes of moral and artistic values and do whatever he wanted. Anthony could sell a three-page spread to a client and swear that the ad sale had no influence on his giving the client a cover story in the same issue. The pendulum also swung both ways as Anthony sometimes sold a full page ad to a customer and then insulted them in the very same issue with some slam in his editorial. Anthony had a reputation for speaking his mind, especially while drinking, and had at one time trashed almost everyone of merit in town whether he meant to or not. Luckily it was the South Beach way to forgive and forget, well at least to forget.

"Morning Mindy," I said softly, as I walked into the *South Beach Star* office.

"Morning was over twenty minutes ago," chimed Mindy, handing me my phone messages.

"Time sure flies when you're trying to sell ads for the *Star*," I lied. Actually I had just come from my apartment but I wanted it to seem like I had been out trying to sell advertising space.

"Just a word of warning, Morning Glory," Mindy whispered, and for a moment I thought I detected a bit of concern. "Anthony hired a new ad rep and he's a pisser," she added.

"Is he here now?" I asked, just as someone was opening the door to the back office.

"Morning Kidd," Mindy screeched, in her normal tone acting as if I'd just walked in. "Anthony wants to see you right away." She quickly went back to her work and ignored me. The door to the back office opened but no one stepped out at first, but then I was floored by the person that appeared. It was Jeffrey, the guy that I had secretly had an illicit affair with for several months. I broke it off because I was tired of secret relationships and told him it was either me or his boyfriend. At the time, I wasn't really ready for a full-time boyfriend but didn't want another clandestine relationship. South Beach is a small town but I never thought I'd run into Jeffrey in the *Star* office. Jeffrey was wearing a grey suit with a white shirt and tie. I had never seen him so dressed up before and knew something was definitely up.

"Oh, hello," said Jeffrey. "You're Kidd, aren't you? I've seen your photo in *Ocean Drive* Magazine. I'm Jeffrey Scott, the new advertising sales rep." He stood tall and switched his briefcase from his right hand to the left and held out his right hand for me to shake. I was completely speechless. Here was the guy that I had slept with at least three nights a week for over two months standing before me pretending that we had never met. Okay, I'll play along and see where this goes.

"Welcome to the *South Beach Star* staff," I said, as I took his hand and shook it. I looked him right in the eye to see if I could get some sort of reaction from him. "I've never known anyone on the *Star* staff to wear a suit and tie but there's a first time for everything. You do wear it extremely well." I finally had my chance to flirt with him in public but since he was pretending to be a stranger it was obvious that he had an ulterior motive and he ignored my flattering remark. Was the Universe playing with me?

"Advertising is serious business and I believe that appearance is important. No matter what you're selling, whether it be a vacuum cleaner or a luxury car, it is important to look your best and to believe in your product." Jeffrey stood almost at attention and I imagined that he was just spitting out some jargon that he had learned in school and I'm sure Anthony ate it up. This was not the Jeffrey that I had late night liaisons with, but a robotic facsimile. Whatever he was pulling here, I didn't like it.

"Well, good luck to you," I said, totally baffled by the whole situation. Here I was in yet another situation of having had a relationship with someone and couldn't tell a soul. No one knew, so no one would believe me if I said anything so I remained mute and walked into the back room. The fact that Jeffrey had decided that he wanted to work for the *Star* was way too bazaar. Was my whole life a big hoax that was being filmed for laughs? I didn't get it but I knew that Jeffrey wouldn't last a week as an ad rep at the *South Beach Star.*

"Morning Kidd, so glad you could grace us with your presence," greeted Anthony, from his perch in the back. While Anthony had made it clear to me that I had no set hours, he wanted me to spend time in the office. For some reason Anthony didn't feel this way about most of the other writers and actually preferred that they drop off their weekly articles in the writers' box up front. For some reason I had been chosen to be the go-between for Anthony and the world. In Anthony's mind I was probably still his assistant as he had never hired a replacement when I my ranking changed from gopher to columnist.

"Morning Anthony," I said, trying to sound cheerful although I certainly didn't feel it.

"I'm glad you met Jeffrey. Put your things down and come over here," ordered Anthony. That usually meant that he either had something very serious to discuss or didn't want Mindy to hear the conversation. Or both.

"So what's up?" I asked, standing in front of Anthony. Anthony's desk was built into a wall unit and was nearly a foot higher than other desks. A meeting at his desk meant that you had to stand since Anthony's stool was so high. If you sat in one of the regular desk chairs you felt like a little child looking up at a parent, a position that Anthony relished. I preferred to stand which forced him to look up at me, however I rarely felt in a position of power unless I was tweaking on Tina.

"You're well aware of the financial situation of the *Star,* so I felt it time to hire an advertising rep with actual sales experience." Anthony paused a bit and looked at me with a smile. "And this Jeffrey Scott not only has experience but has connections," he added, with a grin. I knew there was more. "Jeffrey happens to be the boyfriend of Gordon Chase, the publisher of *The Spectrum.*" Anthony paused again and looked at me as if he'd just won his hand at poker. It appeared that Anthony thought Jeffrey was some trump card since *The Spectrum* was the most successful magazine on the beach. Anthony regularly ridiculed the publication although it was probably because he was jealous of their ad revenues. Hiring the boyfriend of the publisher seemed an odd move, even for Anthony. I had no idea what he had up his sleeve and it made me a little nervous. Of course I had something up my sleeve but I wanted it to stay there. Obviously Jeffrey hadn't mentioned to Anthony that he knew me and I couldn't imagine the knowledge of our secret affair would help matters at all.

"If this Jeffrey is so good then why isn't he working at *The Spectrum?*" I asked. There was something terribly wrong about this whole situation and why did I feel that I was the one going to suffer the consequences?

"He can't work at *The Spectrum* because his boyfriend is the publisher," Anthony almost spat out. "Actually, I think Jeffrey came to me for a job to spite his boyfriend because he wouldn't give him a job at *The Spectrum*." Anthony gave me that Cheshire cat smile once again. Could it be possible that Jeffrey came to the *Star* to spite both me and his boyfriend? "Jeffrey lives with Gordon so he goes to all the *Spectrum* parties and hears all the dirt and has sworn that he'll share the information with me." That's interesting, I thought, but there has to be more.

"But does he really have advertising sales experience?" I asked, hoping to completely bypass the boyfriend business. In reality it seemed that Anthony was more concerned with getting revenge by helping Jeffrey get revenge. There was little mention of selling advertising. I understood the revenge scheme but hoped that I would be excluded from this whole scenario.

"Actually he's a communications graduate but he has experience designing ads," Anthony stated. "He's young, aggressive, and determined to show up his boyfriend by selling ads for a competitive publication." Yeah, I know what he thinks of his boyfriend and know that he's not to be trusted.

"Anthony, you don't really consider the *South Beach Star* as competition with *The Spectrum?*" I asked. The *Star* was not in the same league as *The Spectrum* but I knew full well that Anthony believed that advertisers were advertisers and if we could get a few of *The Spectrum's* clients to contract with the *Star* we certainly would be ahead of the game. Somehow I think that Jeffrey had a bigger game plan than just selling advertising.

"Has Justin met Jeffrey?" I asked, knowing that Justin didn't like anyone infringing on his territory. When I landed the MODE account I thought Justin was going to threaten my life. He swore that he had met with the owner of MODE, who had already made a commitment with him to advertise, so I should split the commission with him. Of course when I asked if he wanted to go with me to MODE and work it out, he suddenly got real busy. Justin had never even stepped foot in the store but still gave me grief about the account.

"Not yet, but I've scheduled a meeting with Justin and Jeffrey at four," Anthony answered. "Would you like to join us for the meeting?"

"Actually I have a meeting at four with a potential advertiser," I lied. I knew that sparks would fly at this meeting so I didn't want to be anywhere in the building. "I'll try to catch up with you all later at LINCOLN." I hoped to get Jeffrey alone so I could find out what was happening.

"Good, because I do have a few things I'd like to discuss with you after the meeting and I told Jeffrey that you would let him follow you around on some of your nightly excursions," Anthony said, and waited for my response. "He's a big fan of your column I might add." How interesting. Could it be that Jeffrey wants to get back together and has worked out a plan to make it all seem legitimate? I didn't think so.

"No! I do not need an assistant," I snapped. "Here I'm trying to get some advertising accounts of my own and you hire someone that you want to follow me around. That's not going to happen." I stomped back to my desk and sat down and loudly sifted through my papers looking at my phone messages. "And I don't care whose boyfriend he is," I shouted, not looking up. Why was this happening to me? I would never ever have any kind of secret relationship or affair again. It just wasn't worth it.

I couldn't believe that Anthony had hired Jeffrey to sell ads when I was now struggling to make ends meet. I knew Jeffrey had ulterior motives for working at the *Star* and Anthony didn't have a clue. Anthony had employed Jeffrey for all the wrong reasons and it was certainly going to create tension among the *Star* staff. I was extremely tense and Jeffrey had just started. I never yelled at Anthony like that. Working at the *Star* was no longer a joy. It was getting harder to make ends meet since Anthony had cut salaries. Jeffrey was being supported by his rich boyfriend and didn't even need a job. What was he doing here? I needed a bump and a new life.

SIXTEEN

Are You A Good Witch or A Bad Witch?

My life as a nightlife columnist at the *Star* was spiraling out of control with obstacles hitting me in the face daily. My salary had been cut in half and I had lost my one and only advertising account. I really needed to face reality and either get another job or sell some ads to help save the *Star* but more importantly so I wouldn't get evicted from my apartment. Like Celia, I had never been very good with money and had not saved a penny. When I had money I spent it, mostly on books and Tina, never anything huge or really frivolous but it was all gone. I thought my salary would keep increasing instead of being cut back to the bare minimum.

This was to be the day I had hoped to meet with Anthony and plan a strategy to sell ads, but when I walked into the office I found that he had hired a new young ad rep. It was not enough that he was the boyfriend of Mr. Gordon Chase himself, the publisher of *The Spectrum,* South Beach's most successful glossy publication but he was also the same guy who I had had a secret affair with. I knew for a fact that Jeffrey didn't need a job since he was living the life of luxury in his boyfriend's multi-million dollar penthouse condo that overlooked all of Miami. Apparently revenge was his motivation for taking this job and how could I compete with revenge? I just hoped I wasn't one of the targets.

Anthony had just left the office and was headed for a meeting which really meant that he was going to happy hour at LINCOLN. Before Anthony left he reminded me that he expected to see me there later so we could chat. Anthony held all of his meetings at LINCOLN or at lunch but I wasn't in the mood for any sort of meeting. When things weren't going well I usually turned to my best friend Tina and at the moment it seemed that my world was spiraling towards a crash landing. A visit to the bathroom for a quick bump certainly seemed in order.

"Kidd, come in here," yelled Mindy, from the front office.

"What's up?" I yelled back.

"Don't ask questions, just come in here," she screamed.

"Okay, just let me run to the bathroom first," I answered, knowing that it was impossible to ignore Mindy, a notorious ball breaker who rarely lost a battle. Mindy's hate campaign against me was a result of the success of my column so I suffered daily as a result. Recently her tirade against me had cooled a bit and some days she even acted civil to me. I first noticed the change when she stopped calling me fuckface and finally called me Kidd. That in itself scared the hell out of me and I was sure she would revert back to attacking me at any second.

"So, what's up?" I asked, all energized from my bathroom visit.

"You know that new kid, Jeffrey," Mindy asked, looking straight at me. "I'm giving you fair warning now. Watch your back!" What did she know? Certainly she had no clue that I had had an affair with Jeffrey.

"What in the world do you mean?" I asked. I was already worried enough about the whole situation of Jeffrey being hired. If he wasn't here to torture me then certainly he'd be running after all the new advertising accounts, which was indeed a form of torture. I wasn't very good at selling ads anyway and didn't need any competition. What had I done to deserve this? I just wanted to be a writer anyway, I never wanted to sell ads.

"Darlin' don't get fooled by that sweet baby face of his cause there's nothing sweet about him," said Mindy, like she had read his files and had discovered a demon in the making. "As soon as he walked out the door I was on the phone to my friend Sylvie who works in advertising at *The Spectrum*. She says he is a first-class user with a capital U and is taking Gordon for everything he can." Mindy took a big breath and I could see that she was enjoying dishing Jeffrey. "He wasn't hired at *The Spectrum* because everyone at that magazine hates him. Gordon is trying to pass him off as his nephew because he's still trying to pretend he's straight. Of course everyone in his office and most of South Beach knows he's gay and word travels fast in the gay world. One day after Jeffrey moved into Gordon's condo the little bugger walked into *The Spectrum* office and started acting like he owned the place and started ordering people around. Rumor has it that he has Gordon wrapped around his dick if you know what I mean?"

"If he's living with Gordon then why does he need a job," I asked. I had to pretend that Jeffrey was a complete stranger and I knew nothing about his life. "And why would he want to work at the *Star*?"

"That little bitch knows exactly what he's doing," Mindy quipped. "Sylvie says that he has big dreams and probably hopes to own his own magazine someday. He's smart and apparently wants to learn the trade but is real pissed that Gordon won't give him a job at *The Spectrum*. Sylvie says that both the Associate Publisher and head of advertising threatened to quit if little Jeffrey was given a job doing anything at *The Spectrum*." Jeffrey had only boasted about how well he lived and never told me anything about wanting to work in publishing.

"But I still don't understand why he would come here for a job. Couldn't he get a job anywhere else?" I asked. That's what I really wanted to know. Why had he come here? He knew I worked here and certainly knew there would be tension and I didn't need any more of that.

"Darlin' he won't be here long," smirked Mindy. "It's just a game with him. That little bugger knows that working at the *Star* will drive his boyfriend crazy. Gordon considers the *Star* a piece of trash and doesn't even acknowledge its presence. Gordon would go crazy if word got out that his boyfriend was working here. Having a gay boyfriend is one thing but having a gay boyfriend who works at the *South Beach Star* is another thing altogether." Somehow that didn't make me feel any better.

"So, you think that Jeffrey's time here will be temporary and I shouldn't worry about him?" I looked at Mindy hoping she would tell me that everything was going to be alright. Temporary would be good but there was still going to be tension.

"My guess is that the little bugger hopes this job is transitory but while he's here I wouldn't trust my pencil to him," she advised. "His kind is no good and he wants your job," she announced, looking right at me.

"What! My job?" I screamed. "Why would he want my job? His suit costs more than I make in a month and besides I thought he was interested in advertising." I started pacing back and forth not knowing whether to believe Mindy or not. That was totally ridiculous. Jeffrey would not want my job. In fact, at that very moment, I didn't want my job either.

"Before the little user left, he tried to warm up to me with that fake charm of his but he can't fool old Mindy," she continued. "He started asking questions about you. Yes, real specific questions. He wanted to know how many phone calls you get a day and if the invitations to all those events you cover in your column come to the *Star* office. He started asking about the celebrities that you know and if any of them ever called for you here at the office. You know, rubbish like that? You see, you have the high profile position. The money isn't important to him, he wants to make a big noise. What better way to get back at his boyfriend than getting a job as a writer for the *Star*? You know that pompous son-of-a-bitch is going to be furious when he hears that his little boyfriend is working at the *Star* anyway. Imagine if he gets a byline and starts spewing out revenge." Oh...my...god! This couldn't be happening. It's like waking up during your worst nightmare and realizing that it's real.

"No, that's not possible," I said, a little baffled at the thought of Jeffrey going after my job. His getting hired as an ad rep was a big enough blow. "Surely you're mistaken," I said. "Anthony would never let him write a column." Was Mindy just busting my chops again or did she really believe what she was saying?

"Kidd, this one is bad news," Mindy recounted. "Sylvie said that before he was banned from the office, sweet little Jeffrey demanded that Gordon fire two secretaries and a stylist. Gordon wouldn't do it himself but had his Associate Publisher fire them and tried to make it look like Jeffrey had nothing to do with it. Everyone at the office knew exactly what had happened and that Jeffrey was to blame. Jeffrey is hated by the entire *Spectrum* staff so don't underestimate this kid. Oh, by the way. He's called you twice already wanting to talk to you. Here's his number," she said, as she handed me the messages like she was holding something dirty. "I told him you were out but he wants to meet with you so I'd avoid LINCOLN if I were you."

"Shit, I'm supposed to meet Anthony there later," I said. "I might as well head right into the storm and see if I'm going to be dealing with a hurricane or just hot air. Thanks for the heads up Mindy," I said, looking at her with a forced smile. Maybe I was just being paranoid and Jeffrey was just interested in advertising and causing grief for his boyfriend. Right. I didn't believe it for a second.

"No problem fuckface, I'm just watching your back," she said. Mindy actually looked like she was trying to smile but the gruffness that controlled her face won. I guess I'm still fuckface after all.

"I'm going to pack up and head over to LINCOLN," I announced, and walked into the back office and turned off my computer. I grabbed my phone messages and put them in my backpack. Things weren't going well at all. I pulled out my bag of Tina and did a little bump since I didn't have much more. I desperately needed some confidence even if it was drug induced.

"Will I see you at LINCOLN?" I asked, before walking out the door.

"Listen fuckface, everything I told you about Jeffrey and the situation at *The Spectrum* is confidential," Mindy stated, like it was a life or death ultimatum. "Understand?" she snapped, when I didn't say anything.

"Yes, you never told me a thing," I replied obediently. "And thanks again for the heads up."

"Sure, now get out of here and go fight for your job," she shouted.

Once again I felt that I really needed a drink. Now I understood why Anthony drank so much. Paranoia often accompanied a crystal buzz and lately I seemed married to the feeling that everything was going wrong. I thought that the world hated me and Anthony was leading the parade. Maybe it wasn't just the Tina talking to me. Maybe it was actually true? My column had made me very popular and everyone knew my name, greeting me with hugs and kisses. I realized that most of them weren't really my friends; they were just kissing up to me so I would take their photo or mention them in my column. South Beach was very fickle and was probably the most superficial town in the world, even more so than Los Angeles. I wasn't stupid, I knew that if I ever stopped working for *the Star* or didn't get another visible media position that most of the people who claimed to be my friends would disappear. In fact I bet most of them would ignore me and wouldn't even give me the time of day. No, I was blowing things out of perspective. That would never happen.

SEVENTEEN

Too Drunk to Remember

An old friend once told me when all else fails get drunk. Last night at LINCOLN, I finally had my meeting with Anthony and thought it best to meet him on his level. I couldn't stomach Jack Daniels so I downed a couple of vodka cranberries and then, as an extra courage booster, had a couple of lemon drop shots. Anthony was holding court at the other end of the bar so I waved to him and waited for him to acknowledge me. By the time Anthony came over, he had already been drinking for a couple of hours so I wasn't sure if we'd even have our scheduled conference. Anthony was known for not remembering conversations or even people that he met while he was drinking, but he certainly remembered our meeting.

When Anthony sat down next to me at the bar he immediately started telling the story about how he had started the *South Beach Star*. It was a story I had heard many times and he always forgot that he had first told me the tale the day I met with him about a job in this very bar over two years ago. Anthony then told me how much he appreciated my work and involvement with the *Star* but the paper was now in big trouble financially and we had to do something fast or the *South Beach Star* was going to be history.

Anthony explained that hiring Jeffrey Scott was merely an attempt to save the *Star*. If by some miracle this new ad rep was able to bring in more advertising and put the paper on its feet, then Anthony said that he would be able to pay me my old salary again. Anthony confirmed the fact that he knew Jeffrey was a user and back-stabber but hoped he would parlay his position as Gordon Chase's boyfriend into ad sales. If nothing else, he would make a little noise and possibly help the other ad reps too.

Anthony had no idea that Jeffrey and I had been involved but somehow I think that wouldn't have made any difference. Earlier when I entered LINCOLN, I had walked right over to Jeffrey, who had just finished his little summit with Anthony, as I hoped to square things with him so there wouldn't be any pressure if we were going to be working together. He looked at me and smiled, the evil kind, and told me everything in one sentence. "Nobody breaks up with me, watch your back fucker." A chill went through my entire body. I knew I was in real trouble.

The *South Beach Star* had been around for quite a while and had witnessed the coming and going of dozens of other publications. Recently the Beach was inundated with so many new publications that were all fighting for advertising revenue and it was difficult to make a buck. The *Star* had always had a solid base of advertisers, complimented by a number of new clients, but its growth in advertising dollars didn't correspond to the increase of printing costs, office rental, and living costs. The *Star* was filled with trade advertising for services like food, laundry, massages, clothing, gym memberships and cocktails. In the beginning the trade ads were for Anthony's exclusive use, then later certain staff members were allowed usage of the bar trades as bonuses. Now the trade ads were out of control, many had been placed without Anthony's knowledge, which meant less cash was being generated. As Anthony repeatedly stated in advertising meetings, "man cannot live by trade alone."

Anthony had passed the performance stage of his inebriation and had entered the mellow serious phase. This phase we rarely were privileged to observe as he usually went home when he started to mellow out. For some reason, Anthony was treating me like I was his best friend and sharing all his concerns about the *Star*. I actually believed that he wanted my help. He kept saying that he was finally at a point with no solution and I certainly didn't know how to help. Then I thought about what I had done in Virginia to help boost the ad sales of the publication that I had started and shared the story with Anthony. A friend of mine, who was a television producer who worked at the local cable station, convinced me to produce a magazine format show. The weekly program became a great marketing tool for the publication and advertising sales went through the roof, in the beginning anyway, because we could do video segments for advertisers and even shoot commercials for them as well. My co-publisher (the other guy who I had a secret relationship with) acted as the cameraman and I was the on-camera host so we had no extra staff to pay. I was able to do video segments of our monthly cover stories and it was easy to incorporate both the magazine and the TV show. We had a magazine and a magazine cable show that cross-promoted each other.

Anthony nodded as I told him the story but he seemed immersed in his own thoughts so I wasn't sure if he was even listening. He convinced me that things were going to get better and I wanted to believe him. He said good night, waved good bye to the entire bar and was out the door. There I sat in a bar full of people yet I felt so alone. At that point I would have been drunk on my ass if I hadn't done bumps of Tina. I had always been a lightweight where alcohol was concerned and without crystal I would never have made it through the nights of multiple events with a cocktail at every stop. I never knew how Anthony could drink so much every night and show up bright and early every morning at the office. The mass consumption of alcohol had definitely gotten to me and I felt dizzy, so I stood up and waved goodbye.

When I walked in the *Star* office the following morning my head was still spinning from the previous night.

Breakfast consisted of a bump of Tina and an extra large café con leche but my blood wasn't really pumping until I heard the news of the day.

"Morning Kidd," bellowed Mindy, as soon as I walked in. "Wait till you hear the news. Anthony came up with the brilliant idea to produce a video version of the paper on cable and call it *Star TV*. He said he dreamt it or something. Can you believe it? And guess who he's picked to be the star host?" Mindy stared at me with a big "I told you so" look.

"You're kidding," I remarked. "Anthony's going to do a cable show?" I was in shock. Anthony usually forgot the conversations he had when he was drunk but this time had soaked up the report of my cable show in Virginia and spit it out as his own idea. "Is Anthony going to be the host?" I asked.

"Nope!" replied Mindy. "Anthony has cast none other than our bright new ad rep Jeffrey Scott as the host for *Star TV*. They're having a meeting right now in the back office. Here are your messages," she said, giving me that smug look of hers.

"I can't believe it. A cable show and Jeffrey's going to be the host?" I said a bit dumbfounded.

"Don't say I didn't warn you," Mindy whispered. "Jeffrey has started his takeover already and it's only his second day. And get this; I overheard Jeffrey say that he wanted to do a weekly nightlife segment."

I walked to the back office and sat at my desk. Anthony was leading a meeting in the back with Jeffrey standing by his side. I turned on my computer and tried to pretend that I was working while listening to every word spoken in this pow-wow. Anthony was going on about how the show would be a great marketing tool for the paper and both the *South Beach Star* and *Star TV* would cross promote each other. I was completely floored. It seemed like Anthony had recorded my conversation last night and was even spouting out some of my lines word for word.

"Morning Kidd," yelled Anthony. "Did Mindy tell you about my brilliant idea to produce a cable show with the same format as the paper?"

"Yes she did," I replied, with little enthusiasm. "Sounds like a great idea," I added. Brilliant idea, my god is he really going to try to pass the idea for the cable show his own? I guess he already had.

"Jeffrey here is going to be the main host," Anthony announced excitedly. "Maybe you can do a cover story on him in the paper. I have a strong feeling that this is going to pump some new blood into the *South Beach Star* and that ad sales will go through the roof."

"Through the roof?" I repeated. I remembered that those were the exact words I had used to describe the ad sales of the Virginia magazine after the launch of my cable show. "When did you come up with this idea?" I asked.

"It must have come to me in a dream," Anthony answered. "This morning I woke up and it was all formed in my mind. Amazing, huh?" said Anthony, smiling at me like a clever little boy. "You'll hear all about it. I'll have Jeffrey meet with you later." Jeffrey was standing next to Anthony with a bigger smile on his face, like he had won some contest. I guess he had in a way. It was only his second day working at the *Star* and he's landed the job as star host on a new cable show. I needed to learn to keep my mouth shut. Of course I never would have dreamt that Anthony would take my concept and resell it as his own, then cast my newest rival as the star. Now there would be no way I could get out of meeting with Jeffrey. I was cursed.

"Kidd, I'm going to be doing a nightlife segment on the show," announced Jeffrey. "I should really follow you around a bit to get a feel for the scene before we start shooting. Let's get together and talk after the meeting." Anthony started passing out papers to the ad reps so everyone's attention went back to him.

Obviously Anthony had not remembered that we had talked last night and clearly had no recollection of where the inspiration for the cable show actually came from. This wasn't the first time that Anthony took credit for an idea that wasn't his but this was the first time that it was my idea that was stolen. I hadn't even been invited to the meeting. Inside I was fuming, not only because my concept had been stolen but because he had assigned Jeffrey as the host. Since Anthony hadn't even asked me if I wanted to be involved with the cable show I decided to stay completely clear of the project and concentrate on selling ads for the *Star*. I had to make more money somehow, because my Tina habit was getting expensive and my work situation had just gotten worse. Just when I thought things couldn't get any worse, a new villain appears and threatens me to my face. Would anyone believe this if it was written in a novel?

what's HAPPENING?
ramblings on South Beach nightlife
by KIDD

MAKOS AND MCMULLEN AT LINCOLN: The popular & trendy **LINCOLN** is a fairly intimate bar so any event scheduled at this venue is packed. The **Christopher Makos**, who shot for *Interview* magazine during **Andy Warhol's** reign, and **Patrick McMullen**, also from *Interview*, Photography Exhibition sponsored by **Camel** cigarettes was no different. Luckily I arrived before the mob scene so I could actually see the art. The exhibition drew a "barely room to breathe" crowd. The impressive but motley crew, ranging from yuppies to drag queens, included **Eric Newill** (*Ocean Drive* Managing Editor), **Tonia Rahming** (*Ocean Drive*), **Laurie Scott** (David Barton Gym), photographer **Ren Dittfield**, artist **Attila Lakatoush**, promoter **Mykel Stevens** (Back Door Bamby), **Anthony Deerpark** (*South Beach Star*), **Jeffrey Scott** (*Star TV*), **Mindy Morgan** (*South Beach Star*), writer **Tom Austin**, writer **Brian Antoni**, **Glenn Albin** (*Ocean Drive* Magazine Editor), **Adora**, artist **David Rohn**, **Sexcilla**, **Taffy Lynn**, **Bridgett Buttercup** and photographer **Iran Issa-Khan**.

ANNOUNCING STAR TV: I've often quipped that nobody reads *South Beach Star*; they only thumb through the pages looking for their photo. Now *South Beach Star* offers an alternative, not a substitute, way to find out what's hot, what's new, what's happening, and where to go, called *Star TV*. It's a new cable show starring our own Jeffrey Scott. Now, you can read and watch yourself weekly. A Star TV is born.

SHADOW LOUNGE OPENS: Designer **Gerry Kelly**, one of the most photographed personalities in South Beach, shocked the nightlife community when it was announced that he was leaving **BASH**, the successful nightclub that he promoted for the past four years. Gerry welcomes everyone to his new venture **Shadow Lounge** which opens this Thursday night (Opening night gala is invitation only). Gerry handpicked his new staff which includes **Fernando Santos**, who worked with **Madonna** on her last European tour. The opening night gala promises to be a spectacular "over the top" extravaganza with entertainment by **Starseed Productions**, **RKM**, and choreography by **Jennifer Follia**. Guests expected are **Mick Jagger**, **Jennifer Lopez** and actor **Leonardo DiCaprio**.

ANOTHER OPENING: Promoters **Larry Vickers** and **Eric Vatel** opened their new bar **Zanzibar** in the light of the full moon. The streets of South Beach were packed as the crowds flowed into the clubs and bars. **Lorraina** (looking gorgeous) was at the door welcoming the guests (and keeping out the riff-raff). Among those enjoying the opening night celebration were **Jacky Vatel** (Café Paradis), socialites **Merle & Danny Weiss**, Eric Newill (*Ocean Drive*), **Jacquelynn D. Powers** (*Ocean Drive*), **Jason Binn** (*Ocean Drive*), fashion photographer **Thomas Heideman**, **Napoleon** (Rezerection Hall), **Alexis Ougrik** (BASH), promoter **Mykel Stevens**, and door god **Gilbert Stafford**.

EVENT OF THE WEEK: The opening of Shadow Lounge. Step into the night, step into the shadow and SEE THE LIGHT.

DRINK OF THE WEEK: A Bellini. Made with blended peaches, preferably from Georgia, and champagne, French of course.

TREND OF THE MOMENT: Booking an event and then canceling it at the last minute. How very South Beach.

BARTENDER OF THE WEEK: Phillip of **West End**. Congrats to Phillip and his lovely fiancé door goddess Lorraina, who have finally set the date for their wedding. Surprise! Phillip is straight.

QUOTE OF THE WEEK: "Let's work together on this."

CALL FOR WORK: Photographer available for extra work. Contact me.

NEXT WEEK: Another week of openings, parties, nightclubs, bars, galas, fundraisers and even a special dinner at **The Forge**.

EIGHTEEN

The Star is Wounded

Anthony's big new game plan was to have the *South Beach Star* and *Star TV* cross promote each other; however he had no idea that he had also created a battlefield with both staffs fighting for advertising as well as the attention of their leader. Cast as the star host of *Star TV*, Jeffrey Scott was indeed making sure that everyone knew that he was the star and his diva act was not winning him any friends. Anthony never asked me to get involved with *Star TV* and I definitely did not volunteer to help in any way, shape or form. Since Jeffrey was producing a weekly nightlife segment, he had become even more competitive. Suddenly my mail and phone messages began to mysteriously disappear, especially party invitations. I pretty much ignored Jeffrey's games and diva act until he blatantly alluded to the fact that he could do my job better. Those were words I promised I'd make him eat. I couldn't believe this was the same Jeffrey that had spent so many nights in my bed.

After *Star TV* had been on for a couple of weeks Anthony decided that the show needed a co-host. Anthony had a few people in mind for the job but announced that if any one from the *Star* staff was interested in the position they would have to audition. Mindy decided that she was the ideal person for the co-host job and broadcast the fact that she had both the personality and on-camera experience for the job. Mindy thought that she'd worked long enough at the *Star* office and that the job should be offered to her. Anthony told her that she had to audition like everyone else. Of course I knew how that was going to turn out. No matter how much experience or how good Mindy was, she did not have the right "look" to be an on-camera host for a South Beach cable show. The South Beach audience wanted to see beautiful, young and fit. It was all too obvious that none of those words could be used to describe Mindy. When the job was given to Jonathan Lucas, someone not even on the *Star* staff but a dear friend of Anthony's wealthy aunt, Mindy made a big scene and quit. With Mindy gone, I offered to take over her position at the front desk because I needed the money, Mindy had stopped doing the job for free, and I'd be certain of getting my phone messages and mail. Anthony gave me the job without blinking and I took over the controls of the *South Beach Star* office.

"Morning," I said, as Jeffrey walked into the *Star* office.

"Well, good morning Kidd," said Jeffrey, with a giant smile on his face but his eyes were hidden by his big sunglasses. "You look quite comfortable at the receptionist's desk," Jeffrey added, with a big smirk replacing the smile. Jeffrey had declared war and he had most of the weapons.

"You're here awfully early," I remarked. "Another big day of shooting planned for the star of *Star TV*? You don't have to wear your sunglasses in here Jeffrey. I'll protect you from your fans. I'm sure they follow you everywhere you go." I loved ribbing and making fun of him to his face but it wasn't as much fun as it should have been because usually the joke just went over Jeffrey's head. He thought I was serious. It took all the fun out of mocking someone if they didn't get it.

"Why thank you, Kidd," he said with false sincerity but I knew that he was the type that loved praise even if it was false praise. "Actually I had a little accident last night and ran into a door," he said, as he removed his sunglasses to reveal a big shiner under his left eye.

"Wow! Looks like that door had a strong arm," I said, knowing that his black eye could only have been caused by someone giving Jeffrey a punch in the face. My hat was off to whoever threw the punch. I would have loved to see something like that live on *Star TV*.

"Aren't you the sharp one?" Jeffrey said, as he put the sunglasses back on. "If you must know, my boyfriend and I had a little falling out," he said, lowering his voice. "Gordon is having a little trouble dealing with me being the star of *Star TV*. Boyfriends are so jealous. You're so lucky not to have to deal with that." Now that was talent, making me feel bad that I didn't have a boyfriend to give me a black eye.

"Being a star with a powerful boyfriend paying all the bills must be difficult," I said, hoping that would put Jeffrey in his place. But in case it didn't. "I can certainly understand how the publisher of South Beach's most successful magazine would be jealous of the host of *Star TV*."

"Yes, it's difficult," he replied, thinking that I was serious but the more he talked the more he realized that I might just be making fun of him. "My star is now growing brighter than his," he said, in a dreamy delusional sort of way that actually scared me. "Thousands of people now know my face and I've become the voice of South Beach," he said, but then stopped. He finally realized the absurdity of what he was saying.

"Yes it's true," I said, trying not to laugh. "You're the voice and the battered face of South Beach." Every day it was getting harder for me to hold my tongue and remain civil while Jeffrey played diva. Sometimes I just couldn't help myself. This was not the Jeffrey that I had been intimate with and at this point I almost believed it wasn't even the same person. Anthony had no idea what a monster he had created.

"Please hold all my calls, I need to plan the afternoon shoot," Jeffrey snapped, when it hit him that I had been making fun of him the entire time. He then turned on his heels and walked through the door into the back office as if he was walking towards the camera like Gloria Swanson did for her final close-up. Now Gloria Swanson would have been a perfect co-host for Jeffrey and I would love to have seen that duo fight over who was the biggest star.

Anthony seemed pleased that I had asked for Mindy's position at the front desk but questioned my ability to open the office every morning at nine a.m. It was my fifth day manning the front desk where Mindy once sat and I was questioning *my* decision to take this daytime job. While Mindy was never considered a receptionist, she answered the phones, took messages for everyone on the staff, separated the mail and made staff calls announcing meetings. Most of us didn't realize the importance or complexity of her position since Mindy seemed to control the dynamic and flow of the *Star* office so effortlessly.

Suddenly I had a newfound respect for Mindy, for not only being able to handle the responsibilities of organizing all the *South Beach Star* chaos but also the ability to just sit and watch all the craziness that surrounded the job. No wonder she called me fuckface. After the first day at her desk I felt like calling the entire world fuckface, especially if they called the *Star* office. Previously if there were any problems in the office, like a disgruntled reader or an angry advertiser or a drag queen who hated her photo, I was able to sneak out the back door or hide in the back office. Now I had to deal with each and every situation including complaints and requests from every staff member of both the *South Beach Star* and *Star TV*. While most problems were solved with a message to Anthony, Jeffrey was beginning to be a handful and treated me like I was his personal assistant. Now I was stuck to that desk eight hours every day except for lunch and bathroom breaks. Of course I couldn't have done it without Tina, who was now keeping me going day and night.

"Morning Kidd," shouted Anthony as he rushed into the office. "Have you heard from Jeffrey?"

"Actually he's in the back office," I replied, as I handed him his phone messages. "And he has a big black eye," I whispered. "Looks like he either ran into a disgruntled fan or he likes rough sex." I smiled when I saw Anthony's expression change from cheerful to worried.

"My word, I must take a look for myself," he said, starting for the back office. Anthony stopped and came back to my desk. "Good work, Kidd. You're doing a great job on the phones. This isn't interfering with your nighttime coverage is it?" Anthony was there for me.

"Oh no," I replied. "I've gotten my coverage down to a science and never stay more than a half an hour at one event. Since I have to open the office every morning, I've limited my alcohol consumption." Actually, I had also doubled my Tina consumption and it was the crystal that kept me going. So far this week I'd opened the office twice without having any sleep and I was even able to simulate cheerfulness.

"Good show and keep it up," he said before he disappeared into the back. I could hear him singing to himself as he walked back to his desk and then he screamed.

"This is not going to work," I heard Anthony scream before he peeked his head through the door of the front office. "Get Jonathan on the phone," he ordered. "Tell him he has to come in this afternoon for a shoot. Jeffrey is in no condition to shoot on-camera." A big smile came on my face and I thought of the German word *Schadenfreude* which means 'pleasure from other's misfortune.' I was getting much pleasure from Jeffrey's misfortune.

"It's not that bad," yelled Jeffrey, who was standing behind Anthony. "It can be covered up with makeup. I can do the shoot," continued Jeffrey. "It's my nightlife spot and Jonathan didn't go out to any of the events." Jeffrey almost sounded as if he were begging. If Anthony wasn't standing in front of me I would have been smiling from ear to ear but I had to act professional and concerned. Anthony ignored Jeffrey's screams and stood in front of me while I dialed the phone. I made a signal for them to be quiet so I could hear. Anthony turned and walked to the back office with Jeffrey trailing behind him.

Jonathan's roommate answered his phone and relayed the message that Jonathan was in bed with the flu and was too sick to even come to the phone. Yes! Another wrench thrown into the plot. Double *Schadenfreude*! This was so much more entertaining than any show, especially *Star TV*. I guess Jeffrey would have to do his segment with a big old black eye. I really didn't want to get in the middle of the situation but I was relishing the idea of sharing the news that Jonathan wasn't available. I calmly walked back to Anthony's office to give him the news.

"Why don't we have Kidd do the segment?" barked Anthony, after realizing that Jonathan wasn't available. He looked over to Jeffrey without even consulting me.

"Kidd! Oh no, not Kidd," came the quick response from Jeffrey completely ignoring the fact that I was standing right there. "Kidd wouldn't be good on-camera and we really should keep the staffs separate."

"Wait a minute," recounted Anthony. "I make the decisions here. And besides, you certainly didn't feel that way in the meeting this week when you suggested that you write an alternative nightlife column for *the Star* that reflects your nightlife coverage on *Star TV*? In fact you made it a point that you thought Kidd's coverage was lacking and you should be writing the nightlife column."

"But you shot down the suggestion," came Jeffrey's reply as he looked uncomfortably at me.

"And the reason was, if you'll remember, that I thought the nightlife coverage in Kidd's column was excellent and more than adequate coverage for the *Star*," announced Anthony. He looked my way and actually gave me a look that said 'I'm on your side.' "In fact it was Kidd's column that boosted advertising sales for the *Star*.

I think Kidd would be a great guest host for the segment since you are obviously wounded."

"It's my segment and I won't have anyone else doing it," screamed Jeffrey. "Makeup will cover the black eye and no one will even notice. I won't have Kidd doing the spot and that's final," he stated, before he played his trump card. He turned and gave me an indignant look before turning back to Anthony. "You still want me to cover *The Spectrum's* anniversary party, don't you?"

The Spectrum's anniversary party was the hottest party of the year and no one from *the South Beach Star* had ever been invited before Jeffrey was on the staff. Since Jeffrey was the boyfriend, although the battered boyfriend, of *The Spectrum's* publisher, the entire staff of the *South Beach Star* had received invitations to this illustrious event. Jeffrey had also received clearance for a camera crew to cover the red carpet where he would be interviewing celebrity guests as they arrived, and unlike the other parties that *Star TV* had covered, there would actually be real celebrities arriving at this event. Anthony had been talking about nothing else for days because he thought it would be a great opportunity to network with advertisers and would boost visibility of both *Star TV* and *South Beach Star*.

"Okay, then do the damn segment," said Anthony indignantly. Anthony did not like to lose and I knew Anthony would get back at Jeffrey somehow. At least I hoped he would.

There was silence. Anthony and Jeffrey realized that I was still standing there and they both turned and looked at me. Awkwardness had been taken to a new level and it was up to me to clear the air.

"I think Jeffrey will be fine doing the spot," I said with a smile, not wanting to cause further conflict. "I'm sure you're not the first battered actress that has used makeup to hide her bruises." I can't believe I said that but I'm glad I did. "I think I hear the phone ringing," I quickly added and rushed to the front office to the safety of my desk. The phone hadn't been ringing but I needed an exit line. Mindy was right. Jeffrey was trouble. I had no idea that he had actually requested his own alternative nightlife column for the *Star*. What nerve. Jeffrey had also just totally trashed me while I stood right in front of him so there was no telling what he would do in my absence. I had better watch my back. No, I had better get a gun.

NINETEEN

Could It Get Any Worse?

Anthony eventually apologized about the episode where he and Jeffrey were arguing about me doing a segment on *Star TV* while I was standing right next to them. Jeffrey, on the other hand, thought the whole incident a catharsis and no longer went through the motions of being civil to me unless Anthony was around. As if his ego wasn't big enough, Jeffrey started acting like he was actually a star and expected everyone to treat him that way. Now I know why his boyfriend hit him. Maybe he would hit him again.

Every day Jeffrey found new ways to terrorize me and made it a point to belittle me in the weekly meetings and usually announced that I didn't cover the most important parties in town. Of course, the parties that he was speaking of were parties that he was invited to with his publisher boyfriend. While Anthony was thrilled to have Jeffrey cover such events for *Star TV*, he knew that most of those events were not the sort of parties that he cared about or would have assigned to be covered for *the South Beach Star*. Anthony was only thinking about advertising and I'm afraid that he was beginning to side with Jeffrey. Maybe I was just being paranoid but it certainly seemed like I was being pushed out.

While some people imagined that their lives were hell, I was convinced that I was not only living in hell but also working there and was forced to answer the phones and take messages. I didn't understand why Jeffrey continued on his one-man crusade to make me miserable. I was miserable already but I still did my best to act the part of an eternal optimist but each day it became more difficult.   Every morning when Jeffrey entered the office I smiled and handed him his messages hoping that he would stop the tirade and start acting civilly towards me. Vindictive breakups were one thing but this was overly extreme. If he was acting this way towards me, I couldn't imagine what he would do if his real boyfriend ever broke up with him. That was a crime scene waiting to happen. Luckily my best friend Tina kept me alert and perky even if I hadn't slept in days. Still not admitting that I might have a little drug problem, and I really didn't, I did realize that my Tina consumption had steadily increased. Every morning I did a couple of bumps just to wake up, another before going to work and a big one in the office bathroom before I finally sat at my desk for my daily torture of answering the phones. No one would ever believe that I hated the job since I was friendly and very talkative to everyone who called. Okay, who was I kidding? I was becoming a male version of Mindy Morgan.

"*South Beach Star,* good morning," I greeted my first caller of the day. "No sir, no one from *Star TV* is in the office. I can take a message if you like. You're interested in advertising on *Star TV*? Just give me your name and number and I'll have someone call you. No sir, I can't help you but I'll have someone call you. Your name and number sir? No, I have no idea who will be calling you sir. Okay, could you repeat that number? Got it. Yes, thank you very much." Oh my God! I *had* become Mindy Morgan and I sounded just like her.

Star TV was finally attracting an audience and Jeffrey was milking its popularity to death. What had I done to deserve this torture? I was chained to this desk all day answering phones and taking messages for Jeffrey. I often disguised my voice when I answered the phone so people wouldn't recognize that it was me. Jeffrey was taking complete credit for the success of *Star TV* and rubbed it in my face every time he walked in. Oh, how I wanted to tell him that the entire cable show idea was really my idea. But then if I did, he'd just thank me for the vehicle that made him a star. In his mind, Jeffrey had become a giant celebrity and was so wrapped up in production, interviews, shooting, and attending parties that he no longer had the need to belittle me. He had finally put his "Torture Kidd Campaign" on the back burner or so I thought.

"Hello Kidd," chimed Celia, as she walked into the door of the *Star* office. Concentrating on trying to finish my column I had completely zoned out and didn't notice who had walked in but the unmistakable voice of my long lost friend brought me back to reality. Celia was standing in front of me smiling and looked as beautiful as ever. While I couldn't imagine why Celia was here or even awake at such an early hour I was very happy to see my former best friend. I really missed her.

"Well, good morning Celia," I said, a bit shocked. "What are you doing here and so early?" Nine in the morning was a time that Celia rarely saw, unless it was the end of a very long night. Celia and I had often partied all night, and most of the time she was still going strong when I left her apartment to go home and prepare for work. This bright and shining morning version of Celia was a person I didn't know. I hadn't seen her in months so I was overjoyed that she had finally come to visit me even though she really hadn't. The last time I saw Celia was at the MODE fashion show which I emceed. This morning, Celia looked like a stylist had dressed her for a glamorous luncheon or some sort of daytime society party. The Celia that I knew would never have dressed this way.

"I'm here to meet with Jeffrey Scott," she chimed. "I've been hired to do a weekly nightlife segment on *Star TV*. Jeffrey said I'd be doing the video version of your column, well not exactly your column but the same type of parties and events that you cover in your column." Celia stood erect and looked at me with a big smile not realizing that her words might not be exactly music to my ears. If it had been anyone but Celia I would have gone for their throat and blamed Tina.

"Jeffrey hired you to do what?" That's all I could get out. Jeffrey had hired my ex-best friend to cover my beat on *Star TV*. I had imagined running into Celia hundreds of times but never in my wildest of dreams could I have predicted this scenario. Celia was all smiles and pretended that everything was fine but surely she must comprehend that this whole situation made me uncomfortable. Celia wasn't that shallow or was she? I felt a fire grow inside me and tried to stay composed. Otherwise, I knew I would burst into flames.

"Isn't that great, Kidd?" Celia said, looking at me for approval.

"That's great Celia," I replied, giving her one of those false smiles I had perfected while sitting at the front desk. "When did you get hired?"

"I met Jeffrey last night at LINCOLN and we got to talking," she responded, with her typical innocent-sounding voice. "Jeffrey's so nice. At first he thought I was just another fan but I told him I was a nightlife veteran. Funny, but as soon as I told him that you and I used to be best friends, he warmed up to me and bought me a cocktail. We started talking like we were old friends," she added.

"Yeah, I'll bet," I said, trying not to scream. I knew where this plot was headed. I couldn't believe it. Jeffrey had devised a plan to drive me crazy and he didn't even have to be here. He was going to use Celia as his new weapon. Boy, was he good.

"It was when I told Jeffrey, that you and I used to go everywhere together, that's when he had the idea that I should do a nightlife segment. Jeffrey said I'd be perfect on camera," Celia squealed. "Isn't it great Kidd? Aren't you happy for me?"

Celia always managed to play the quintessential dumb blonde and she wasn't even blonde. She really hoped that I was happy for her, even though she knew she'd be competing with me. Could it be possible that she really didn't get it? Celia saw it as an opportunity for her to be on television and possibly be discovered. The only reason that Jeffrey had hired Celia was to give me grief, but I was really happy for her. Celia was perfect for the job, since she was beautiful and always camera-ready. She loved the limelight. I would much rather have had Celia doing nightlife coverage than Jeffrey any day, even if she was going to be covering my beat. Maybe it was fate bringing us back together, and we would become best friends again. I just hoped she didn't fall prey to Jeffrey's demands and become a pawn in his game of revenge.

"Yes, I'm happy for you," I replied. "I hope you become the star of *Star TV*." Of course Jeffrey would do everything in his power to prevent that from happening. He had made it clear to everyone that he was the only star of *Star TV* even though Jonathan Chase was credited as co-host and received equal billing.

Jonathan Chase, who was given the co-host position because of his friendship with Anthony's wealthy aunt, had no dreams of stardom. Hosting *Star TV* was merely a job for Jonathan even though he was just as vain as Jeffrey and loved the sound of his own voice. Jonathan had often asked me to do segments with him and had repeatedly suggested to Anthony that I should have my own weekly nightlife segment. Jonathan, unlike Jeffrey, was a warm giving and personable person, and it came across on camera while Jeffrey's false smile read shallow and insincere. Jonathan was the consummate professional and let Jeffrey take all the credit for the success of the show. All Jonathan cared about was doing whatever he could to make the show a success. He tried to stay clear of Jeffrey's political battles and ego trips, but it wasn't easy.

Celia stood smiling at me while I returned to answering the phones. Jonathan had just called in for his messages. Finally I stopped in mid-conversation with Jonathan and told Celia to take a seat. Celia smiled and took a seat across the room, but continued to smile and stare at me as if she was watching a movie. She was beginning to make me uneasy but I knew it was just Celia being nervous herself.

"Celia, what time is Jeffrey meeting you?" I asked.

"Jeffrey told me to meet him at ten but I thought I'd get here early to make a good impression," she said, still smiling. I had never seen anyone smile so much for no reason, especially Celia who usually saved her smiles for the photographers. I had to get rid of her.

"You're almost an hour early Celia," I replied. Okay, this bit of information made me believe that this wasn't the real Celia at all but a clone someone had sent in her place. Celia was infamous for being late. In fact, that was one of the things that drove me crazy about her. She was never ever on time, and it was completely out of character for her to be at an appointment so early. And smiling like an idiot. Something was up. Jeffrey must have told her there was a hidden camera in the office. There wasn't.

"Kidd, I wanted to talk to you and apologize," she said softly and then her smile disappeared. "I want to apologize to you for how I acted that night at LINCOLN. I was so awful to you." Tears began to stream down her face and suddenly she was bawling. "Please forgive me. I love you Kidd and I didn't want to take this job unless you'd give me your blessing. I was so mean to you and now you're being so nice to me. I hope we can be friends again," she added, wiping away her tears. I was a sucker for a woman's tears even though I had seen Celia cry a million times at the drop of a hat for no reason at all. One night she started crying while we were walking up Collins Avenue to a party. I asked her why she was crying. She said the wind was ruining her hair and her stylist friend had worked so hard fixing it. When I looked at her and told her that she looked beautiful, with the wind blowing her hair, she stopped crying immediately. She didn't really care about her stylist friend at all, just her hair. Now that was shallow.

"Of course we can be friends again," I said, bringing her a box of tissues from my desk drawer. "I've forgotten the whole thing long ago. I called you and called you, but you never returned any of my calls. I just wanted to make sure you were okay."

"I know. Then you'll forgive me?" she said, standing up and looking me straight in the face. Why had Hollywood overlooked this girl? She could fake sincerity better than anyone I had ever met.

"Yes, I'll forgive you," I replied, hoping the tears had stopped for good. "Now go in the back to the bathroom and freshen up. You want to look your best for your meeting with Jeffrey." I knew that would get her in front of the mirror.

"Thanks," she said, and gave me a little smile. "You don't mind that I'll be working with Jeffrey?" she asked.

"Of course not," I said. "I want you to be happy." If she only knew how I felt about Jeffrey. Of course it wouldn't matter to Celia. Celia was the star of her world, and everybody else were just supporting players.

"Well, you know I've always wanted to be on TV," she said, trying to act sweet. Celia could fake sincerity, cry real tears and charm the pants off anyone, but she couldn't pull off sweet. Not with me anyway. I knew that girl too well.

"Yes, I know," I replied. Truthfully, I wished the best for Celia but I knew that Jeffrey had it in his plans to use her in his vendetta against me and Celia played those roles so well.

That very night at SWIRL, the same bar where Celia and I had met, I walked right into a crew from *Star TV* led by Celia herself. Of course she acted surprised to see me and pretended she had no idea that I would be there. Celia didn't fool me for a second. She knew that I always started my evening at SWIRL. Jeffrey had always ignored me when we both happened to be at the same place, but Celia tried to include me in the shoot. When I declined, she stormed off and interviewed the owner of the bar, outside on the patio. I still didn't want to have anything to do with *Star TV,* even Celia's segments.

Although I was a bit put off by the confrontation with Celia at SWIRL, I tried to dismiss it and relax. It was still early and I had a whole night of events to cover. I stood at the end of the bar and sipped my vodka cranberry, as the bar filled up with the regular crowd of hipsters, drag queens and drug dealers. I was considered part of the family, and most of the regulars waved at me or yelled my name as they entered. I decided to wander through the crowd, back to the patio, just to see who was hanging out in the rear of the bar before I headed out for my nightly rounds.

When I returned to the front bar, I spotted Lady Bunny, a drag queen from New York City, famous for starting Wigstock, an annual drag festival held in Thompson Square Park in New York City, with non-stop performances of drag queens as well as bands like the B-52s and Blondie. Lady Bunny was a celebrity drag performer who was often booked at South Beach clubs, where she did her risqué and ribald show to packed crowds. Lady Bunny could only be described as an over the top drag diva of clown proportions with enormous hair and giant false eyelashes. Since she was a New York City drag icon, I wanted to introduce myself and get a photo of her for my column.

"Come here often?" I quipped, as I slid next to Lady Bunny at the bar.

"Not as often as you do, I'm sure," Lady Bunny replied.

"I had to come over and say hello," I added. "My name is Kidd and I'm a big fan."

"Just how big?" replied Bunny, looking me up and down. "I'm performing at Warsaw later, but I have a little time to spare."

"Actually, I was wondering if I could get a photo of you for my column in the *South Beach Star?*" Obviously Lady Bunny had misunderstood my approach.

"Oh, you're from the press," cooed Lady Bunny. "Of course, I'm very accommodating to the media," she whispered in my ear.

"Let me get a shot of you right there," I asked, as she posed.

"Hey Kidd," came a voice from the other side of the bar. It was Derby, the owner of the bar. "Can I get in that photo?"

"Sure, come on over," I replied, as I lowered the camera.

"Take my photo without him," snapped Lady Bunny. "I look better alone."

"But that's Derby, the owner of the bar," I replied.

"Take some of me alone, and then some with him," Bunny directed. "Then you'll have shots of me that you can use later."

Lady Bunny was right, so I took several shots of her alone, and then a few with Derby. It would be great promotion for the bar to have a photo of Derby with Lady Bunny in my column. SWIRL was always packed anyway, but a little publicity never hurt. Celia stood in the corner with the crew from *Star TV*. Celia loved to be photographed and when we went out together she would ask to be in practically every photo that I shot. I had to make sure that she stood on one end so I could cut her out, otherwise Celia would have been in almost every photo and that would have looked strange to everyone but Celia. Since I refused to be in her shoot, she certainly couldn't ask to be in one of my photos. I could see that she was fuming. I waved and motioned for her to come over for a photo, but she turned up her nose and walked over to one of the guys in the crew as if she hadn't seen me. I guess the battle was on.

Lady Bunny and I seemed to have clicked and the universe must have given us the same itinerary, since I kept running into the visiting drag diva at every stop I made. It had been a long night but I decided to make one last stop before heading home. I made my way to the upstairs bar at Liquid for one final cocktail. As I grabbed my vodka cranberry I felt a hand tapping me on the shoulder.

"Are you following me?" said a familiar but husky voice. I turned around to find Lady Bunny standing before me like she was posing for a photo. Later I discovered that her whole life was either a performance or a photo shoot. Bunny must have had some night as she wobbled a bit but stood her ground none the less.

"Greetings," I said. "I loved you at Warsaw. You put on quite a show. I tried to get near you to say hello, but you were surrounded by adoring fans."

"Yes, I'm always performing," she slurred. "I perform on the stage for crowds and in the dark for audiences of one." She paused a moment and then walked closer. "Do you like the dark?"

"Actually, I'm just heading out," I replied. "It's been a long night."

Lady Bunny turned and walked away without direction and with very little balance. Just as I was ready to make my exit, I ran into Denny, my dealer friend, who slipped a bag of Tina in my pocket. Lately Tina was my master so I slipped into the restroom for an energizing bump. I wandered through the club, upstairs and down, socialized with friends and chatted endlessly about nonsense. The hours flew and suddenly I noticed it was nearly five a.m. The club would be closing any minute so I rushed out the door because I hated being caught up in the closing-crowd as they dashed for the door.

The party still continued as if it would last forever, as I ran down the long staircase out to Washington Avenue. There on the sidewalk stood Lady Bunny, posing like she was being photographed for some glamorous red carpet event. With her back to me, Lady Bunny posed tirelessly as if there was a bank of photographers in the street, shooting her like she was a major star at the premiere of her newest movie. In reality, there was not one photographer in sight. I stood quietly and watched for a moment, enjoying the show. Lady Bunny was working it and was in her own fantasy world. If I thought it wouldn't break the mood, I would have gone over and taken a few photographs, but I didn't want to ruin the moment with a dose of reality. If only I was living in such a fantasy world, but my world was dosed with lots of reality and lately it wasn't so good. At the moment my reality was that I only had a couple of hours before I had to open the office of the *South Beach Star* and begin another day of answering the phones. This was certainly not the life I had imagined. My star was beginning to fade but I'd just do another bump and soon the sun would be up. As I walked home I thought about my book and realized I couldn't remember the last time I had written a word.

what's HAPPENING?
ramblings on South Beach nightlife
by KIDD

THREE ONE YEAR ANNIVERSARIES: Mezzaluna, SWIRL and CAFÉ TORINO all celebrated a one-year anniversary this past week. At Mezzaluna, there was a band and continuous food circulating throughout the crowd. A giant pizza was delivered to our table but no one ate. **SEEN AT MEZZALUNA:** Publicist **Susan Scott, Morgan Craft** (Moe's Cantina), *Fashion Spectrum's* **Michael Heiden**, the legendary **Louis Canales**, the **Scull Sisters**, artist **Bobby Radical, Dianne Thorne** (Image Models), producer/director **Itzik Feldman**, and model **Kim** (Wilhelmina).
A SWIRLING CELEBRATION: SWIRL's party was one of the best parties I've ever attended. If this celebration is any indication of parties to come, I hope this place lasts forever. Promoter **Larry Vickers** orchestrated the night with a "baby party" motif (baby bottles, pacifiers, and a dancer in diapers). **DJ Shannon** outdid herself with fabulous music and had everyone dancing. The never-ending food was provided by **Petunia's**. SEEN AT SWIRL: Steven Giles (BASE), Carlos (Mars), Richard Trainor (TWIST), Darren Beck (PRIDE), Chris Paciello (Liquid), Jack Benggio (Liquid), artist **Bobby Radical**, drag diva **Bridgette Buttercup**, J.C. Carroll (Art/Act), Mark Holt (Slave), Michael (Hannah & Her Scissors), Crispy (821), Milton (LINCOLN), door goddess **Holly** (Salvation), & makeup artist **Stacy Conde..**
CAFÉ TORINO TURNS ONE: Café Torino celebrated their anniversary with an incredible show of dazzling drag divas starring **Kitty Meow** (how does she get her legs so high in the air?). **Adora, Paloma DiLaurenti** and **Sexcillia**. It was an evening of breathtaking performances and delicious Italian food. **SEEN AT CAFÉ TORINO: Louis Canales, Kim Katsaris** (Burdines), **Jeff Bechtel** (Washington Avenue Assoc.), **Steve Porter** (ZMAX), artist **Aaron Von Powell**, photographer **Jose Antonio**, artist **David Rohn, Jonathan Lucas** (Star TV),
and the wonderful owners **Sondra** and **Mauro**.
FOLLOWING LADY BUNNY: It was one of those long nights with too many stops to remember but somehow I kept running into **Lady Bunny**. Bunny, as her friends call her, started the infamous annual Wigstock celebration in NYC. It's a drag version of **Woodstock** with performancers like the **B-52s** and **Blondie** as well as lots of drag performers. I first ran into Lady Bunny at SWIRL, where *Star TV* was filming. I photographed Lady Bunny and chatted with resident **DJ JoJo Odyssey** before making my nightly rounds. Next I stopped into **TWIST** for a quick cocktail before heading to **Warsaw** to see Lady Bunny perform but low and behold Miss Bunny was upstairs dancing by the DJ booth where **DJ Bugi** was spinning. Since Lady Bunny wasn't set to perform until midnight I took a detour and stopped at **LINCOLN** where I ran into editor/publisher **Anthony Deerpark** (*South Beach Star*) out later than usual. Promoter **Mary D.** was talking up her new party and bartender **Milton** was having fun despite the crowd. I entered Warsaw, drag diva **Elaine Lancaster** was at the door, just as Lady Bunny hit the stage. The crowd went wild for her very risqué show. After Warsaw, I was ready to end my evening but made one last stop at **Liquid** and ended up staying until nearly closing…again.
EVENT OF THE WEEK: *Star TV.* Watch it on Thursday night at 11 p.m. on Channel 3.
TREND OF THE MOMENT: Owning your own club. Seems like everyone on South Beach wants to own one and they do, for about fifteen minutes.
QUOTE OF THE WEEK: "I want to run someone's life."
NEXT WEEK: I promised myself I'd take a night off next week and get some sleep but I don't think it's going to happen. My calendar is full. Until next week, see you out.

TWENTY

Left Holding the Microphone

Everyone loves surprise birthday parties, especially if it's for someone else. Tasha Simon, the *Herald's* nightlife columnist, had planned a surprise birthday bash for party promoter Larry Lucas, South Beach legend and former nightlife writer for the *South Beach Star*. I was looking forward to the event but was afraid that the staffs of the *South Beach Star* and *Star TV* might collide. During the past few weeks I felt like I was in a Marx Brothers' movie dashing in and out of doors as I tried my best to avoid Celia and her crew from *Star TV*.

Recently when Jonathan, who had become my one ally on the staff of *Star TV*, had convinced me to go on-camera for a couple of interviews, both Celia and Jeffrey made complaints to Anthony. Jonathan thought I was a natural on-camera, and unlike Celia and Jeffrey, had no star ego. In fact, Jonathan had asked me to meet him at the Astor Hotel that night and he wanted me to interview Larry Lucas. Jonathan thought it was appropriate that I do the interview since Larry had previously written a nightlife column for the *Star*.

Jonathan rushed over to me as soon as I walked in the door of the Astor Hotel and announced that his cameraman was sick. Since no one from the *Star TV* staff had shown up he asked me if I'd do all the on-camera interviews while he manned the camera. Then he winked at me. Now what was up with that?

"Why don't you call Jeffrey or Celia?" I asked. "They would rush over and gladly do the segment, especially if they thought I was the only alternative."

"I didn't think of them," Jonathan said wickedly. I couldn't imagine what he had up his sleeve but I went along with it. The party was filled with the A-list of South Beach and almost every club owner and promoter made an appearance to celebrate Larry Lucas' birthday. This was the type of party that Jeffrey usually covered and bragged about the following morning, but tonight I was the on-camera host for *Star TV*. With the help of Tina and a couple of vodka cranberries, I was completely relaxed and had fun interviewing everyone of importance, especially Tasha Simon. The party was in full swing while Tasha waited by the door to announce Larry Lucas' entrance so we could all yell surprise.

"Surprise!" shouted someone behind me while I was interviewing Tasha. I turned quickly and saw that it was a very inebriated Anthony. He rushed up to me and grabbed the microphone and yelled "surprise" a couple more times while looking straight into the camera. Anthony handed the microphone back to me and wandered through the crowd yelling surprise. I had not seen Anthony that wasted in some time. Didn't he know that he was supposed to wait for Larry to show up before he yelled surprise?

After interviewing Tasha I thanked her and turned around and almost ran into Jeffrey who was staring at me. Jeffrey was standing with his boyfriend Gordon at his side and Celia on the other. The three of them were posed together like a fortress and there was no way to gracefully avoid them without making a mad dash in the other direction. I really wanted to fall through the floor but I just stood there holding the microphone. Talk about your false smiles.

"Well, look who has stepped from the shadows and into the spotlight," snapped Jeffrey, as if he was witnessing some impossibility. "Does Anthony know that you're doing the interviews for *Star TV* tonight?"

"Actually, he joined me on camera just a few minutes ago," I replied. Anthony had in fact yelled my name several times and given me suggestions on who to interview, so I knew he was aware of the situation. But would he remember? "Jonathan asked me to do the interviews for the party. He thought it fitting since I'm sort of following in Larry Lucas' footsteps, writing a nightlife column for the *Star*." I felt just like a criminal who had just confessed his crime and I didn't care what the consequences might be.

"I'm Gordon Chase and I'm a fan of your column," said Gordon, as he held out his hand. "I love your wit and I think your personality really came across in the couple of segments that I've seen you host on *Star TV*."

"Thank you, Mr. Chase," I said, as I shook his hand. I was honored to shake the very hand that had hit Jeffrey.

"Please call me Gordon," said the *Spectrum* publisher, who was suddenly being pulled away by an angry looking Jeffrey. Celia didn't look too thrilled herself, so I didn't want to sit at their table.

"Jonathan, I think you should let me take over," shouted Jeffrey.

"Surprise!" yelled Anthony from behind Jeffrey. As Jeffrey and his group turned to look at Anthony, Jonathan pulled me into the other room. I was ready to escape but Jonathan had other ideas.

"Larry is on his way, so let's hide," directed Jonathan. "Jeffrey is not doing this segment."

Before we had a chance to hide, Larry Lucas walked into the room and everyone yelled "surprise." Luckily Jonathan was prepared and got Larry's entrance on camera. We followed Larry through the crowd and gave his friends a chance to greet him before we pounced. I had only met Larry in passing so we weren't friends, but he was surprisingly friendly when he saw me.

"Hey Kidd, thanks for coming," said Larry, as he grabbed me for a hug. "You're doing a great job with your nightlife column," he added. "I look forward to reading it every week." Since Jonathan was posed with the camera I asked if we could do a little birthday interview. Larry agreed and we walked and talked while Larry greeted friends. Eventually we ended up in front of the big "HAPPY BIRTHDAY LARRY" banner by the bar. I had been a little nervous to interview this South Beach icon, but Larry completely put me at ease and we chatted like we were long lost friends. As fate would have it, we were just ending the interview when two waiters rolled out a four-tiered birthday cake covered with lit candles and another handed Larry a big knife. The crowd screamed and I put my arm around him as he cut the cake.

"What's your birthday wish?" I asked Larry while I held the microphone.

"My wish is that everyone lives out their dreams," he said, looking into the camera. "And to everyone who isn't here tonight you can read about this fabulous party in Kidd's column in the *South Beach Star* or watch him on *Star TV*." I was in shock at his kind words, and looked up to see Jeffrey giving me the look of death. If Jeffrey had been holding that knife it wouldn't be in the cake but in my heart. Remind me not to go to Jeffrey's birthday party.

After a few more quick interviews with guests, Jonathan thought we had enough coverage, so I helped him put the equipment in his car. Jonathan complimented me and said he couldn't believe that I didn't have any on-camera experience. That's when I told him about hosting the cable show in Virginia.

"Does Anthony know you hosted a cable show in Virginia?" he asked, a little surprised.

"Yes, he does," I said slowly, not sure if I should tell him the story or not. "Actually, it's a funny story. One night, I told Anthony all about hosting a cable show in Virginia, and how it cross-promoted the magazine that I edited. I told him that it had helped boost advertising on the magazine and was a great marketing tool. Anthony was drunk and I never thought he'd even remember. It was the very next morning that Anthony announced his idea about *Star TV*."

"Now I understand why he's been so hesitant to let you be a part of *Star TV*," said Jonathan. "He wants all the credit for coming up with the idea."

"Whatever," I said. "I'm going to try to get some sleep since I have to open the office in the morning, and in case anyone asks, I don't want any credit for the conception of *Star TV*."

The next morning I opened the office on time and wide awake. With a large café con leche in my hand and after several bumps of Tina, I was set to go. My head was spinning from the previous night's festivities, and I was still reeling from the words of praise from Larry Lucas. I had just turned on my computer so I could make notes on the party, when Anthony stormed through the door.

"Well, good morning, Kidd. I can't tell you how upset I am!" Anthony screamed.

"But Anthony," I began, thinking he was going to let me have it for doing the interviews for Larry Lucas' birthday party.

"I fell asleep on my couch. I missed Larry Lucas' birthday party. I can't believe I slept through it. Tasha will kill me. Larry will hate me." Anthony babbled on like a crazy man. "What'll I say? Was everybody there? Was it a great party? Did anybody ask about me?" he continued. "Did they get the party on video for *Star TV*?"

"Anthony you were there!" I stated loudly, trying to get him to calm down. "You were there." I couldn't believe he didn't remember being at Larry Lucas' party. He remembered, almost word for word, my conversation about my cable show in Virginia, but completely blanked out his attendance at this party. Go figure.

"What do you mean I was there?" he asked, looking at me like I was the crazy one.

"You were there," I said. "You obviously had been celebrating before you arrived. You kept walking around, yelling "surprise", and even did a bit on-camera for *Star*

TV. I was the on-camera host in case you didn't remember," I added. Anthony just looked at me like I was making it all up. "We have proof that you were there. I took your photo with Tasha and we have great footage for *Star TV* so yes, you were there." Anthony looked at me and shook his head and walked to the back office, but returned a moment later.

"Don't you dare tell anyone that I didn't remember being at Larry's party," Anthony demanded. I promised Anthony that I wouldn't tell a soul. Still I couldn't believe that Anthony had completely blanked out on the entire party. Hopefully, he would like my coverage of the party for *Star TV*. Now I had something on Anthony, and he owed me. But I could never collect, because I owed him so much more.

what's HAPPENING?
ramblings on South Beach nightlife
by KIDD

MEDIA FRENZY: The Miami premiere of the film *Curdled* held its opening night party at **The Forge**. The champagne flowed and the media swooped as the guests arrived to a mob of flashing cameras. **The Scull Sisters** (famed Miami artists) posed proudly for all the photographers while director **Quentin Tarantino** refused to be photographed. Camera crews from various networks (including *Star TV*) wandered throughout the party interviewing stars and local celebrities. The crowd enjoyed a taste of Hollywood as well as food samplings courtesy of The Forge. **SEEN *AT THE FORGE*:** Louis Canales, actress/singer **María Conchita Alonso, Eric Newill** (*Ocean Drive*), designer **Arthur Page, Glenn Albin** (*Ocean Drive*), socialites **Merle & Dan Weiss, Chris Paciello** (**Liquid**) & **Sofia Vergara** (**MTV**), **Jacquelynn D. Powers** (*Ocean Drive*), **Shareef Malnik** (owner of **The Forge**), **Michael Landau** (**Nicole Miller**), actress **Priscilla Barnes** (*Three's Company*), photographer **Jesse Garcia**, writer **Tasha Simon**, publicist **Susan Brustman** and columnist **Tara Solomon**.

SURPRISE FOR LARRY LUCAS: Queen of the Night **Tasha Simon** held an invitation-only surprise birthday celebration for South Beach Icon **Larry Lucas** at the **Astor Hotel**. DJ **Mark Leventhal** provided the music for the A-List crowd who packed the lobby, the bar area and the pool patio while waiting for the arrival of Larry Lucas. *South Beach Star* editor/publisher **Anthony Deerpark** wandered through the party yelling "surprise" while I strolled throughout the crowd with a microphone acting as on-camera host for *Star TV* getting birthday wishes for Larry from party-goers like **Merle and Danny Weiss, Crispy** (**821**), photographer **Jesse Garcia, Glenn Albin** (*Ocean Drive*), **Eric Newill** (*Ocean Drive*), **Debbie Ohanian**, designer **George Tamsitt, Gloria & Emilio Estefan, Jonathan Lucas** (*Star TV*), photographer **Iran Issa-Khan**, realtor **Renee Delaplaine, Gordon Chase** (*Spectrum*), **Jeffrey Scott** (*Star TV*), **Celia** (*Star TV*), **Brigitte Andrade** (*The Adventures of Bibi & Friends*), and writer **Brian Antoni**. Everyone cheered the giant birthday cake. (Watch my segment on *Star TV* (Thursday at 11 p.m. on Channel 3).

SEEN OUT: Jann Weiner (*Rolling Stone*) dining at **the Blue Door** in the **Delano**, **Madonna** at **Liquid**, singer **Ricky Martin** dining at **China Grill** and **Gloria & Emilio Estefan** dining at their own restaurant **Lario's**.

RESTAURANT OF THE WEEK: China Grill where Sunday Brunch has been added to its weekly fare. The food is delish and the cocktails divine. Now you can go directly from Saturday night after-hours to Sunday Brunch. Don't forget a change of clothes and to make reservations.

SHAMELESS PLUG OF THE WEEK: Watch me on *Star TV* (Thursday night at 11 p.m. on Channel 3) as the host for **Larry Lucas' Surprise Birthday Party.**

CLUBS OF THE WEEK: A TV Party for Generation X at **Tita's**, a new Friday night gay party called **HEAVEN** at **Rezurrection Hall**, an art opening at **BASH** on Thursday night, **KGB** (on Saturday night) and **Bar None** (whenever you can get in).

DRINK OF THE WEEK: Champagne!

TREND OF THE MOMENT: The Tango. It's a dance and it's a cocktail. You can enjoy them both on Thursday night at **Tango Martini**, a special night for dancing and martinis at **SWIRL**.

BARTENDER OF THE WEEK: Paul Sanchez, who you'll find behind the bar at **Escuelita**, the very same bar that those hot go-go boys dance on. Sometimes Paul takes off his shirt and gets more attention than the dancers and more tips.

QUOTE OF THE WEEK: "I'm also an escort when I'm not working here."

NEXT WEEK: Hot singer **Ricky Martin** is having an autograph party at **Spec's**. Until then, see you out.

TWENTY ONE

I Don't Have A Problem

My stint as an on-camera host on *Star TV* gave Jeffrey another reason to hate me and now he was even more determined to make my life miserable. The segment with me hosting at Larry Lucas' birthday party was a big hit, and was reviewed in the *Miami Herald,* giving it more attention than any previous segment. Who knew that the *Herald* would review that segment? Well, actually I did, because I was the one who made the call to the *Herald.* I figured it might be my last stint on the show, and I wanted it reviewed. So I called in a favor from a writer friend who happened to dislike Jeffrey. Imagine that?

The fact that Anthony had received phone calls requesting me to be the on-camera host for several special events also helped my cause. Even Anthony's aunt Rita raved about my performance on camera. She told him that she even liked me better than her friend Jonathan and had asked Anthony not to tell Jonathan but he did tell me.

Now Jeffrey completely ignored me when he entered the office and I, without saying a word, placed his messages on the desk for him to pick up. At first I enjoyed the newfound attention, but soon regretted doing the segment at all, since the tension in the office had become almost unbearable when Jeffrey was around. Everything finally came to a head during a staff meeting when Jeffrey started screaming that I was just a worthless nightlife reporter that could be replaced. Anthony shut him up by telling him that TV reporters could be replaced too and Jeffrey stormed out. It almost seemed like Anthony was on my side again but I had discovered that Anthony was on nobody's side but his own.

One morning Jonathan called to inform me that he had scheduled a facelift, and needed someone to fill in for him on *Star TV* while he recuperated. The Beach was filled with women who had been cosmetically enhanced, but this was the first man I had known who was going under the knife. Oh well, everyone needs to look young, especially if you're an on-camera host. Jonathan had worked out a trade deal with a plastic surgeon that he interviewed on *Star TV*. He would be getting the procedure for almost nothing, since all he had to pay for were the anesthesiologist's fees. Jonathan practically begged me to substitute for him, but I declined as I didn't want to cause any more tension and turmoil especially with Jeffrey. My life was already hell and I didn't need any more extra pressure or work.

Anthony called a special staff meeting and announced that he would have to hire a new on-camera host to fill in while Jonathan recovered since he would be out for at least a month and might not be camera-ready for six-weeks. Celia volunteered for the job, but Anthony told her that while she was the most beautiful on-camera reporter on the *Star TV* staff, the audience response to her segments had not been very favorable. Anthony told her that unless she was talking about herself, she came across as disinterested and a little boring. Imagine that. It was true but I can't believe Anthony said it to her face.

Jeffrey, who had been quietly brooding for most of the meeting, stood up and stated that since my stint as host at Larry Lucas' birthday party was such a success, I should fill in for Jonathan. Jeffrey knew that Jonathan and Anthony had asked me to substitute for him, and also that I had firmly declined. Jeffrey also knew that since our relationship had grown to just short of homicidal, I'd rather walk barefoot on broken glass while naked down Lincoln Road than work with him. So, when he made the suggestion that I should fill in for Jonathan, he was positive that I would decline. This action was just an opportunity for him to look good in Anthony's eyes. Jeffrey looked at me smiling, because he knew what I'm going to say.

"Jeffrey," I said, a bit surprised. "I don't think we'd be a good team. There seems to be a little tension between the two of us." I tried to control myself from saying another word. It could only have gotten worse.

"Nonsense," Jeffrey replied, saying his first words to me in weeks. "I think we would be a dynamite team. In fact, I'd love to work with you." He stood, looking down at me with a big smile, and then turned to look at Anthony. He was waiting for me to refuse so he would look like the noble one.

"Jeffrey," I said slowly. "Jonathan asked me to fill in for him but I refused and I even said no when Anthony suggested that I take over for Jonathan." I noticed that Jeffrey's smile widened. "But since you've asked me and you feel that we'd make a good team," I said, standing up slowly. "I accept." And I waited for his reaction.

"You what!" mumbled Jeffrey. "You accept?" Jeffrey sat down slowly, while the rest of the staff applauded. Clearly he had not expected me to agree, and now there was nothing he could do, since he had made the proposal himself. Jeffrey would be forced to work with me. Yes, it was my chance to get back at him. I announced that I would only fill in for Jonathan while he recuperated and would gladly relinquish the spot to him when he returned. Jeffrey sat in silence and it was the first time I had ever seen him at a loss for words.

The war was on between Jeffrey and me, but it was mostly one-sided. Jeffrey did everything he could to sabotage my shoots including giving me the wrong addresses, dates, and times. Once, he even claimed to have forgotten to let me know about a shoot, so he was forced, on purpose, to do all the on-camera interviews himself. While Jeffrey thought he was getting back at me, I always acted as if nothing was wrong, which drove him crazy. Jeffrey didn't realize it, but his actions were causing him more work and I still got paid. I didn't care if he wanted to do the whole show because I still got paid a weekly salary for working on *Star TV*, whether I did the segments or not.

When Jeffrey and I were on camera together, he always seemed tense because he kept trying to come up with situations that would throw me, however it never worked. I enjoyed working on camera. Most of his pranks made him look stupid. It wasn't hard to accomplish. Determined to get back at me, for landing the on-camera spot that she felt she deserved, Celia became Jeffrey's partner. Just when I thought that Celia and I might become good friends again, Jeffrey turned her against me. Since Celia wasn't being paid for her brief spots on *Star TV*, Jeffrey convinced Anthony to hire her as an ad rep for the *South Beach Star* so she could make some cash. That could have been a workable situation but Celia decided that, probably at Jeffrey's suggestion, the easiest accounts to get were mine. And so the war continued.

Suddenly my life was like a big Monopoly game and I had to pay dearly for every move I made. Jeffrey and Celia were dangerously competitive and both played to win. Every day the pressure swelled like a damn that was on the verge of bursting and I had to constantly watch my back. When Celia volunteered to watch the phones for me, I just assumed that she was being nice and was returning to my side. Later I discovered that she had rifled through my desk and copied all my advertising leads. She also had taken a message from one of my ad clients and told him that I wasn't handling advertising any more, so that account magically became hers.

Once again I felt like Tina was my only friend and luckily I could once again afford my habit and pay my bills. I never believed that I had a drug problem, I was able to work longer and stay alert as long as I did bumps of Tina. I would never let myself get out of control like some of the druggies that I had seen out in the South Beach clubs or the ones that hung out at my dealer's house. I had everything under control.

I remember the night that Sister, one of the tenants in my apartment building, was having an art exhibition at LINCOLN. The artist's name was actually Sam Murphy, but he had gone by the name Sister Sam for years. His friends just called him Sister. Sister Sam was the skinniest person that I knew. He resembled the Fagan character from *Oliver Twist*, but was much skinnier and very gay. Sister Sam was a notorious thief and drug addict, but he was also a very talented artist. Sister was the new featured monthly artist at LINCOLN. His art pieces were all large crosses made from found objects and some were quite beautiful. I had looked forward to the exhibition and had even included the event in the *Star's* calendar section.

While I could not kick my annoying habit of punctuality, the rest of South Beach did not follow suit and it was a rarity for anyone to arrive on time for any event. Everyone wanted to make an entrance so they all, especially the guest of honor, arrived fashionably late. I entered LINCOLN precisely on time, hoping to chat with Sister and take a few photos before the crowds filled the bar.

"Hey Kidd," shouted Billy, from behind the bar. "Have you seen Sister?" Billy knew I lived in the same building as Sister but I thought it strange that he asked.

"Isn't Sister supposed to be here for his opening?" I asked, taking the vodka cranberry that he offered.

"Yeah, but he hasn't shown up and he isn't answering his phone," stated Billy. "I know Sister likes to make a big entrance but the artists are supposed to be here on time. Nobody has heard from him since he hung his show earlier this afternoon."

"I'm sure Sister will get here any minute," I replied.

"I'm worried that Sister might be off on a drug binge or something," said Billy, looking a bit worried. "Today he sold one of his crosses while he was hanging the show. Someone offered Sister a couple hundred dollars for one of the pieces and instead of waiting until the show was over, he pulled it off the wall and took the cash. I've heard how Sister gets," he added. "I thought he might have bought drugs or something." Now that was a logical explanation considering Sister's history, but I hoped it wasn't the case.

"Don't worry," I said. "He'll show up. It's his opening after all." I had tried to reassure Billy but actually began to wonder myself. I knew how Sister got when he had cash. It all went to drugs and when he did drugs, he got a little crazed. Or so I'd heard.

"Greetings Kidd," shouted Lawrence. Even the owner of LINCOLN was on time for this opening. "Looks like quite an exhibition and a good crowd. I might even buy one myself," said Lawrence, who then turned and started chatting up the customers. The bartender motioned him over. They chatted a while, then Lawrence walked back over and sat next to me.

"Sister's crosses look great in here," I said.

"Yeah, but it seems that Sister is M.I.A.," Lawrence said, looking seriously at me. "Artists are pretty finicky and I'm not one to be praised for his punctuality but I am a little concerned about Sister. Three of the crosses have candles in them that Sister wanted to light for the exhibition. He didn't want anyone else to light them and swore he would be here early to light the candles himself. Could you do me a big favor and go check on him? I wouldn't ask you, but I know you're friends with Sister and he lives in your building so I know you can get in." Lawrence looked at me and I could tell he was worried.

"Sure," I said. "I'll run back and check on him. I'm sure he's okay."

I looked around at the crosses hung in the bar and suddenly got an eerie feeling that something might be wrong, so I rushed back to my apartment building. His apartment was just down the hall from mine. When I knocked on the door, no one answered. I listened with my ear against the door and could hear someone moving inside. I knocked again, but louder and started shouting.

"Sister, are you in there? It's Kidd," I screamed. "Sister, open up, you're late for your opening." Suddenly the door swung open and Sister was standing in the doorway with his eyes as big as saucers. He looked a little crazed and was not wearing a shirt.

"I can't find them," Sister said, a little frantically. I looked past him and could tell that he had torn up his entire apartment searching for something.

"Sister, what are you looking for?" I asked.

"My crosses are gone! I've got a show tonight and I need my crosses. I can't find them anywhere. How can I have a show without my crosses? They were here, but they've disappeared. What am I going to do? My crosses are gone." Sister was ranting like a crazy person and went back into his apartment and started walking circles in the middle of the floor. I walked in and looked around. I could see nails on the walls where his crosses had been hanging. I watched him look from one nail to the next, as if he were searching for the crosses.

"Sister, your crosses are hanging up at LINCOLN. You hung them there yourself, earlier today. Don't you remember?" I looked at Sister and saw that he was trying to remember. I also could tell that he was really high.

"My crosses are already at LINCOLN?" Sister asked. I could almost hear the gears of his mind working as he tried to remember. "You're right." It was as if a light went on in his mind. "What's wrong with me? I can't believe I forgot." He looked at me and smiled.

"You're having a show tonight and everyone is waiting? Let me help you get dressed so you can go to your opening." Sister was shirtless and needed to dress, so we could go back to LINCOLN. "What shirt are you going to wear?"

"I don't have anything to wear," Sister said, still standing in the same spot. "Kidd, I can't go. I look a mess, I'm not even dressed." Now he was standing in front of a full length mirror, looking at his own reflection, and giving himself a dirty look. It was the skinniest reflection I had ever seen.

"I have the perfect thing for you to wear," I said. "Remember that beautiful leopard shirt that Maria made for me? You've complimented me on it so many times. It will be just the thing for your opening."

"You'd let me wear that?" Sister asked sheepishly.

"Of course. In fact, if you like the way it looks, it's yours. You'll just have to make me a cross," I said, hoping that would put him in a good mood and we'd make it back to LINCOLN before the photographers left.

"I love that shirt," Sister said, smiling broadly. "Yes, that would be great."

"Okay, I'll run and get the shirt while you put on that great silver cross necklace of yours. Okay?" I left him standing in front of the mirror. I ran out the door and down the hall to my apartment. Luckily the shirt was hanging in my closet and not at the dry cleaners. I grabbed the shirt and threw it on the bed. Then I ran to the bathroom and took a quick look in the mirror. My reflection was also a bit thin. Because of the Tina, I was thinner than I had ever been in my life, except maybe when I was ten. I quickly splashed some cold water on my face and sprayed myself with a bit of cologne. I wanted to look presentable since I would be making an entrance with the artist. One quick bump and I rushed back to Sister's apartment. Sister was standing in the doorway wearing the silver cross that I had seen him wear so many times. He was also holding another smaller cross.

"Here, I have a cross for you, Kidd," he said. "It's the least I can do, since you've saved my life. I really thought someone stole all my crosses. I can't wait to see them at LINCOLN." He handed me the cross and I handed him the shirt. "This shirt is beautiful Kidd, and thanks for the cross," Sister said, looking at his reflection. I'm not sure why Sister had thanked me, he had just given me a cross. But thankfully, we were ready to go.

"Now, let's hurry before the photographers leave. That shirt looks great and you look fabulous. I've been photographed enough in that shirt. It's your turn to wear it and tonight is your night." Sister was smiling big time and I knew he was still very high. We walked into LINCOLN together and the crowd screamed. Sister immediately started posing for all the photographers and I took a quick photo then walked away to give him the spotlight. Sister was back in his element and no one realized that he was so high, he was practically flying. If they only knew the state I had found him in.

"Thanks Kidd," said Lawrence, who came over and handed me a glass of champagne.

"No problem," I said looking at him. I just hope someone would help me if I ever lost control like that. I was sure glad I had my life in check. I didn't have a drug problem. But I did.

what's HAPPENING?
ramblings on South Beach nightlife
by KIDD

SISTER'S OPENING AT LINCOLN: Artist/busybody **Sister Sam** (known as Sister) filled **LINCOLN** with art lovers for the opening of his art exhibition last Thursday night. Sister arrived fashionably late wearing a beautiful leopard shirt (**Zoo 14**) and one of his smaller handmade crosses around his neck. The walls were covered with beautiful large crosses made by Sister from found objects. Sister sold several pieces that evening and there was an empty spot on the wall where one piece had sold earlier in the day. SEEN AT LINCOLN: Writer **Tom Austin**, writer **Brian Antoni**, photographer **Jesse Garcia**, **Lawrence Freely** (owner of LINCOLN), **Eric Newill** (*Ocean Drive*), editor/publisher **Anthony Deerpark** (*South Beach Star/Star TV*), artist **Linda Faneuf**, promoter **Mary D.** and art collector **Craig Robins**.

ZOO 14 FASHIONS OPENS EQUUS: Last Thursday night the new restaurant/bar **Equus** opened with a packed house and a **Zoo 14** fashion show. Drag diva **Kitty Meow** and **Jeffrey Scott** (*Star TV*) emceed the event with South Beach celebrities like **Paulina DiSoto** and **Power** wearing the fashions. This was a wonderful showcase for **Maria Contessa**, owner/designer of Zoo 14. Maria has probably dressed every drag queen and go-go boy in town. SEEN AT EQUUS: Drag diva **Adora**, performers **Rubio & Kidd Madonny**, **Richard Trainor (TWIST)**, **Tony Miros (Mr. Nightlife)**, **Eric Newill** (*Ocean Drive*), **Arthur Page (24 Collection)**, and promoter **Jack Benggio (Liquid)**.

OUT AND ABOUT: After the Equus opening, I left with Jack Benggio and went to **Hombre** (conveniently located next door) but it was way too early for that late-night bar of sin. So it was on to **TWIST**, which was packed as usual, and owner **Richard Trainor** was in a very generous mood (passing out drink tickets). Next stop was **Groove Jet**, usually packed on Thursday, but even promoter **Doron** had left. No sign of owners **Nicole & Greg Brier** so we left and went to **Liquid** where he announced that he was drunk. I decided to call it a night but realized that I had left my bike locked up in front of **Hombre**. Back at Hombre, I had to go in for one more cocktail and the place was packed so I stayed. At the bar, I ran into the very straight club owner **David Landers**. The straight crowd fills Hombre after-hours when the other bars close. I tried to pretend that it was my first time at Hombre but one of the go-go dancers (on the bar behind me) leaned over and said "Hey, Kidd. It's good to see you again." That's the night I coined the phrase "I've never been here before, many times."

CLUBS OF THE WEEK: Every South Beach clubs is a club of the week because this week I've been in every one, often more than once.

ARTIST OF THE WEEK: Sister. Go see his exhibition at **LINCOLN**.

EVENT OF THE WEEK: Tuesday night at SWIRL. No special theme night but everyone, including the staff, was having too much fun. Speaking of too much, **Betty Too Much** made another appearance and took off all her clothes.

TREND OF THE MOMENT: Nipple Piercing. GW, The Gay Emporium on Lincoln Road has added a body piercing studio in the back of their shop. The studio, called **Pierced Hearts,** offers jewelry and all sorts of piercing (not just nipples).

COCKTAIL OF THE WEEK: The Recovery. This and other healthy cocktails (no alcohol) are available at **SoBe Smoothie.** If they were open at 5 a.m. when lots of us need to recover from a night of cocktails, they'd make a fortune.

RUMOR ON THE STREET: I hear that **Café Torino** is having some problems with their landlord and that the club next door, with the same landlord, wants to take over their space.

QUOTE OF THE WEEK: "Does anyone still go to **Liquid** on the weekends?"

TWENTY TWO

Who Was That Masked Man?

My nights were running into my days and I had lost count of how many times I had opened the *Star* office in the morning without having slept. I was so embarrassed that I not made even a feeble attempt at writing my novel and hoped, at least, I could use all this partying as research. Yeah, right. I had begun to hate the daily grind of answering phones and dealing with all the tension with Jeffrey and *Star TV*. I nearly jumped for joy when Jonathan returned to work after recouping from his facelift and resumed his position with *Star TV*. Jonathan asked me to continue to work with *Star TV* and do occasional segments but I refused. I couldn't stand the pressure of working with Jeffrey any longer. I didn't want to be a star, I wanted to be a serious writer but had become a mess. Jeffrey had completely wrapped Anthony around his little finger and was basically controlling Anthony's decisions. Jeffrey was happy that I wasn't working on *Star TV* but was still committed to totally annihilating me and wouldn't be completely satisfied until he had taken over my column. Wasn't he happy being the star of *Star TV?*

My nights had stopped being just research for my column, they had become a string of parties and I was an active participant. After a particularly long night out on the town I made it back to my apartment just in time to shower and change so I could go and open the *Star* office. Once again. I looked in the mirror and saw a thin blond-haired person that I really didn't know. If one thought that drugs and alcohol didn't affect your health, all they had to do was look at my reflection. Not a pretty picture in any light. I looked at my watch and noticed the time. I needed to hurry and frantically rushed around my apartment looking for something to wear. I stopped and realized that I was acting like a crazy person and it reminded me of the day I discovered my artist friend Sister in his apartment looking for his crosses. My life was falling apart and I had no one to help me pull it together. My crosses hadn't disappeared, it was my life that I had lost track of.

Unlocking the door of the *Star* office, I walked in to find that someone had left the lights on. Obviously someone had been working in the office in the middle of the night and forgot to turn them off when they left. In the back office I found that Jeffrey's computer was still on and a letter was up on the screen. It was a letter addressed to one of my biggest advertising accounts. Jeffrey was trying to take over my account by convincing the client that I had slandered them in my column. Of course it wasn't true, but he made it sound like I was blackballing this client. In the letter Jeffrey claimed that Anthony was going to fire me for writing such negative comments about a client. Anthony ridiculed clients weekly in his editorial so I knew it wasn't true. But of course, that was Anthony and not me. Was Jeffrey controlling Anthony to the point that he would fire me?

My mind was reeling and anger consumed my body. I started pacing around the office, trying to figure out what to do. If I stopped walking, I knew that I'd smash Jeffrey's computer. Finally I stopped and printed out the letter and put it on Anthony's desk. I wrote in big letters on top of the paper "I CAN'T WORK WITH THIS" and signed my name.

My time at the *South Beach Star* was over. Anthony had hired me as his assistant and I had miraculously become the *Star's* star columnist. Without realizing it, I had acted like a diva and mocked the whole scene. I had been invited everywhere but had eventually relinquished it all for drug parties. I had lost control of my life and I had no one to blame but myself. I was sick of Jeffrey's games and this was the last straw. I had to escape this madness and couldn't work at the *Star* one more day.

I needed to get out of the *Star* office and fast, but before I left I went to my computer and deleted all my files which included all my contacts, my columns and advertising lists. I gathered everything that I cared about and locked the door. I dropped the key to the office into the mail slot and walked back to my apartment.

Not wanting to stay at home, I called Denny, my dealer friend. Denny's apartment was always filled with his tweaker friends and clients. I rarely stayed and partied but visited just long enough to get my supply of Tina since I always had somewhere to go. Now things had changed, I had no job and no where to go. But I wanted my friend Tina.

Denny lived in a security building on West Avenue where all visitors had to be announced before they were allowed past the front desk. When I arrived at Denny's apartment he greeted me at the door and led me back into his bedroom where he did business. Along the way we passed another room where his friend Mitch was working on an art project. Mitch was there most of the time, as a companion and watchdog, in case anything went wrong during one of Denny's drug transactions. Mitch and Denny were good friends and always seemed to be up working on some task or another. I sat on Denny's bed and poured my heart out, telling him what I had just done. I felt better for a moment but then I realized my situation and felt dead.

"I have no life now," I said. "I have no idea what I'm going to do."

"Here take this," Denny said, as he threw a bag of Tina at me. Just as I was about to open it, the doorbell rang.

"Must be my neighbor," Denny said, since no one had called up from downstairs. As Denny went to answer the door, I sat in a daze with the bag of Tina in my hand. Suddenly I heard shouting and running. I turned around and someone wearing a ski mask was pointing a gun at me.

"You're kidding," I laughed. I thought it all a joke but quickly saw that it wasn't.

"Shut up and get on the floor," the masked-man shouted. My first thought was that this was a bust so I quickly hid the bag of Tina in the bed before I hit the floor. Maybe if I wasn't caught with drugs on me I could say that I was just visiting and had no contact with drugs. Who was I kidding? Not even a nun caught in this situation could get away with it. I was in a drug dealer's apartment and there were drugs everywhere.

"On the floor," he screamed, with the gun in my face. "Get down on the floor now, asshole," said the man in the ski mask. He then grabbed me and threw me to the floor. Before I knew what was happening he dragged me down the hall to the living room. I was pushed face first to the floor. "Keep down asshole or you'll be sorry," he shouted.

Someone was taping my hands together behind my back and then taping my feet as the masked gunman held me down. Next someone grabbed my head and lifted it while someone else wearing a mask taped my mouth. Every time I tried to sneak a peek I was hit on the head with the gun.

"Stay down if you want to live," said a voice into my ear.

Everything happened so quickly and it was very clear that it wasn't a bust. It was a robbery. I was shaking on the floor not knowing whether I was going to live or die. Someone walked over me and then pulled my wallet out of my pocket. My last bit of cash and my identification. What a day to get robbed. There was loud shouting and noise in the bedroom and suddenly a gun fired. Then there was running and someone jumped over me and I heard a door slam. Then there was silence. For a moment, time stood still. It was like a scene from a movie and I was waiting for the director to yell cut.

The apartment was dead quiet and I listened for some sort of sound hoping that I'd hear someone say that everything was okay. Nothing. Had my friend been shot? I tried to twist my arms and wrestle out of the tape but couldn't. I heard someone walking and I froze.

"Are you okay?" came Mitch's voice, as he pulled the tape off my mouth.

"I think so," I said. He undid my hands and feet. I saw that he had been roughed up and there was still tape hanging from one of his ankles. Somehow he had been able to wrestle free.

"I'm going to check on Denny," Mitch said, then ran into the bedroom. I laid there on the carpet in shock. What had just happened? How did masked robbers with guns get into the building? There was security and Denny's apartment was on the eighth floor. This whole scene had been like something out of a Quentin Tarantino movie and I was terribly miscast. Maybe I wasn't but I didn't want this role.

"Is everyone okay?" I yelled, as I pulled myself up to a standing position. My body ached like I had been beaten and I felt dizzy. I walked slowly back to Denny's bedroom afraid of what I'd find. Denny and Mitch were sitting on the bed talking. There was no blood, so no one had been shot.

"Are you alright?" I asked, as I walked into the room.

"Yeah," said Denny. "They took everything. My drug box and all my money. I'm wiped out. I can't believe it."

"I heard the gun shot," I said. "I thought they shot you." I had pictured my friend lying dead on the bedroom floor.

"It was just a scare tactic," Denny said softly. It was obvious he was in shock and wasn't the perky funny Denny that we all knew. Guns tend to scare the perkiness out of people. I went over and sat on the bed with Mitch and Denny. We all just looked at each other, not knowing what to say.

"When the guy came in the bedroom, I laughed at him," I said. "I thought it was a joke."

"Yeah, some joke," said Denny.

The three of us sat there in silence. Silence had never sounded so quiet before. Denny had been robbed of all his money and his drug supplies. This was not one of those situations where you could just call the police. Denny was a drug dealer and couldn't even report the incident. While we were sitting there my mind raced and then made a quick stop. Reality hit me right in the face. I had no job, no money, no life, and no Tina. That's when I saw the bag of Tina that I had hidden in the bed. It was still lying under the sheet where I had stashed it. I casually slipped over like I was making myself comfortable on the bed and grabbed the little bag of crystal. Now I had no job, no money, no life, but I had Tina.

"What are you going to do?" I asked Denny. Maybe his answer would give me some insight as to what I should do with my life. He had just lost all his money and job, so to speak, so maybe he could give me some advice on what to do with my life.

"I have no idea," Denny said, calmly. "I need to try to figure out who these guys were and how they got in. They must have come up the fire stairs which are just across the hall from my door. They probably have been planning this for a while. These guys knew I had drugs and I had cash. I'm screwed now. I don't have anything." Denny looked at me as if I might have an answer but of course I had none.

"Wow," I said. "I'm in shock. I've never been involved in anything like this before," I added, not knowing how to make a graceful exit. I knew it was strange to just get up and leave. "Denny, I'd better get going. I've got to figure out what I'm going to do. Call me if you need anything, okay?" I wanted to get out of there fast in case the guys decided to come back. But since all the drugs and money were gone, they had no reason to return. Someone in the building must have heard the gunshot and called the police. I didn't want to be around for that scene either. The real truth was that I wanted to go home so I could do a bump of Tina. Crystal always made me feel better and I didn't want to share. How selfish was that? Now I knew that I had a drug problem but that certainly wasn't my real crisis. I was jobless and broke.

I rode down the elevator in a daze. What was I going to do with my life? When I arrived home I pulled out the Tina and crushed it so I could do a bump. I reached in my back pocket for my wallet and it was gone. That's when it really hit me what had happened. I could have been killed. I started shaking so badly that I could barely scrape the Tina into a line, but at the time it was the most important thing I had to do. I did a big line and took a deep breath waiting for it to hit me. I wanted to feel better so I did some more.

I stripped my clothes off so I could take a shower. Looking in the mirror I could see marks around my mouth where the tape had been. My eyes were big and empty and my white hair stood up in clumps and the dark roots were showing. I didn't like what I saw in the mirror. I had exchanged one persona for another and now I didn't know who I was. I didn't want to be Kidd any more. I reached under the cabinet for the package of hair-dye that I had bought a couple of weeks ago. I had grown tired of my bleached white hair and felt now was the perfect time to get rid of it.

After my shower I looked in the mirror again and saw a new reflection look back at me. No longer the blond-haired Kidd who was once mistaken for Jean Paul Gaultier, this was more like the old Jamie Kidd, however, a little skinnier and worn at the edges. Without a job, I had no life. I had no one to call. My former best friend Celia had turned into a competitive enemy. I couldn't call anyone at the *South Beach Star* since I had quit. I really didn't feel like talking to anyone. All I could think to do was to go out and lose myself in the crowds of one of South Beach's nightclubs. For the past couple of years I had prowled the nightlife scene as Kidd the nightlife columnist from the *South Beach Star*. Now that I wasn't a nightlife columnist I didn't know what else to do. I was Jamie Kidd again and I felt I didn't belong. Anywhere.

TWENTY THREE

Alone in A Crowd

As a South Beach nightlife columnist I had been given the red carpet treatment and welcomed with open arms to every club and event in town. Velvet ropes were never a problem and the very doormen who controlled the crowds and snubbed the uninitiated or those not on the list treated me like their best friend. My signature white hair always stood out in a crowd and I was always ushered in ahead of the lines. Even though no one in town could possibly know that I had left my job at the *South Beach Star,* my confidence had disappeared and I felt like a fraud. South Beach was one of the shallowest towns I had ever encountered and I was afraid that I had become one of the superficial locals. The South Beach crowd was fickle and they followed anything or anyone that was hot. Everyone wanted to be photographed or included in my weekly nightlife column but now that I had no column, how many would still pretend to be my friend? Now I would find out who my real friends were. How frightening was that?

Liquid, a club frequented by the likes of Madonna, Gianni Versace, Rupert Everett, Kate Moss and any other celebrity that happened to be in town, always had an eager crowd waiting at the door. Normally crowds parted for me when given the nod from the doorman but tonight the doorman acted as if I wasn't even there. Easing my way through the mob to the front I shouted the doorman's name. Gilbert was one of the doormen that I had befriended and he and I had bonded in a casual sort of way. Gilbert, a handsome black man with bleached white hair, was a legend on the beach and was always hired to man the door at the hot club of the moment. Looking toward me he looked away, then did a double-take and turned back smiling.

"Kidd, I didn't recognize you," yelled Gilbert, coming over to the rope. "I like the new look but not the serious expression. What's up?" he asked, genuinely concerned.

"I thought it was time for a change," I said, trying to smile. "How are things with you?"

"Same shit, different night," said Gilbert. "I'm beginning to hate this door scene. Let's go inside for a drink. I'm buying."

"Boy, could I use a drink right now," I said. Gilbert walked me into club leaving the screaming crowd outside. The lingering crowd was spread out on the sidewalk on both sides of the door and spilled out into the street, but Gilbert had left them all outside to wait while we went inside for a drink. I still had one friend.

Gilbert and I found a place at the end of the bar in the lower lounge of Liquid, right by the door. The bartender was Jeff, who always snapped to attention whenever I entered and then brought me a vodka cranberry without my asking. Tonight he ignored me but saw Gilbert waving his hand. Greeting Gilbert with a nod, Jeff was all smiles when he came over but acted like I was invisible.

"Cocktails please, Jeff. An Absolut martini for me and an Absolut cranberry for Kidd," Gilbert ordered. Jeff did a take when he heard my name and looked my way.

"Kidd, I didn't recognize you," apologized Jeff. "How are you tonight? You look different with dark hair. Are you incognito?"

"Apparently I'm in hiding without trying," I said. "Maybe tonight I won't be bothered by millions of requests to take photos of strangers and star-wannabes." It was also the first time I had been out in almost two years without my camera. What a load off my shoulder that was, literally and figuratively.

"Gilbert, who's manning the door?" asked Jeff.

"The security guys are restraining that obnoxious mob while I take a much deserved break with my friend here," said Gilbert, who was truly one of the nicest people that I had met on the Beach. From the first night I met Gilbert he had always treated me like a friend. Gilbert even remembered my birthday and I remembered his. Gilbert was real and didn't put on any airs. He either liked you or didn't, and you knew it.

The night that I met Gilbert would always be etched into my mind. Holly had taken it upon herself to escort me around town and wanted to take me to the spots she considered hot. Holly always boasted that every man in town was after her. After spending a few nights out with her I realized that Holly was living in a fantasy world. I'm not stupid but I was giving her the benefit of a doubt, but while no one was ever rude to her, I noticed several guys laughing at her behind her back. Typical of South Beach, many pretended to be Holly's friend. She always carried her camera with her and everyone wanted to be photographed for her OUT WITH HOLLY photo section in the *Star*. It was a simple case of smile for the camera but not always for the photographer.

That night Holly was taking me to a Monday night party called Back Door Bamby at a club called Lua. While I was skeptical about the popularity of a Monday night party, Holly raved about the party, the promoter, the club, and the crowd as well as the legendary doorman, Gilbert. When we walked up to the door Holly introduced me to Gilbert. He smiled and grabbed me for a hug and a kiss on each cheek which I discovered was the typical greeting on South Beach. It was a little dramatic but I sensed that it was sincere from Gilbert. Gilbert either kissed you or ignored you.

"So you're Kidd," bellowed Gilbert, whose rich baritone voice sounded theatrical and I could immediately imagine him on stage playing the role of

King Lear. I would later discover that he treated each door as his stage. "I'm a great fan of your column," he added. "It's so refreshing to read a nightlife column by someone who actually goes out and covers the scene. You tell it like it is without taking yourself so seriously. Your column is witty and it's fun to read. I knew I'd like you."

"Thank you very much," I replied, quite taken aback. "I'm glad to meet you too."

"No, the pleasure is all mine and you will be treated as royalty whenever I'm at the door," announced Gilbert. My column, which had been running about a month then, had received great feedback, but this was the first time I had received such a gushing compliment in person. Holly grabbed me and pulled me inside the club. She was used to being the star.

"Holly darling," yelled a handsome man with long hair who rushed over and hugged her. "I'm glad you made it. Did you bring your camera?"

"Yes, Mykel," said Holly, a little put off. "You know I always bring my camera. I also brought someone I'd like you to meet," she said, turning to me.

"I'm Kidd," I said, putting my hand out in greeting. "I write the nightlife column in the *South Beach Star*," I added, thinking this Mykel might not know about my column.

"Holly, you should have told me you were bringing Kidd, I would have reserved a table," bellowed Mykel. "Welcome to Back Door Bamby," said Mykel, as he moved in to shake my hand. I wasn't prepared for such a welcome.

"Thank you, Mykel," I replied. "Is this your club?"

"No, it's just my party. Back Door Bamby is the hottest party on the Beach. Let me introduce you around." Mykel grabbed my arm and led me toward the bar, leaving Holly standing alone. Holly wasn't used to being overshadowed and found the attention I was getting from the promoters and club owners a little disconcerting. Promoters really kissed up to nightlife columnists as they understood the power of the press and knew they were essential to making a party successful. While I always thanked Holly for the tours and introductions, eventually she stopped asking me out. I'm pretty sure it was because I was getting too much attention. Holly was used to being the celebrity because of her photo column in the *Star*. Everyone wanted to be her friend because they wanted their photo in the *Star* but Holly never really got it. I found started hitting the scene on my own until I hooked up with Celia.

On this occasion I could certainly have used Holly by my side since no one recognized me and for the most part I was treated like a regular customer. Listen to me. This was what South Beach had done to me. I wasn't used to being treated like everyone else. I knew that everyone gave me special treatment and I had become jaded. Gilbert left me alone at the bar since he had to return to his post at the door. Liquid was one of my favorite clubs and I always had a great time but now I felt like a stranger in a strange land. I wandered upstairs where the majority of the crowd partied until five a.m. and searched for a friendly face.

Pushing my way through the crowd, not one person gave me a second glance, even the club kid Marty Campbell who I had dubbed as Marty "take my picture" Campbell. The first time I met him he asked who I worked for and when he discovered I had a column in the *Star* he grabbed his friend and posed, saying, "Take my picture, I'm a friend of Madonna's." Whenever Marty saw me he would wave and often yell "take my picture" and then pose. I usually took his photo. It was a lot easier than having him follow me around the club all night. I learned to never take his photo with any of his boyfriends since he would always have a new one by the time the photo ran. I usually photographed Marty with his best friend, who was always by his side. They were so camera-ready, they must have practiced at home because they were always prepared with a series of poses. This was the first time that Marty had ever walked by me without demanding a photo. He didn't even recognize me. Being a brunette might not be so bad after all.

Liquid's upstairs had four different bars but I always went to the small bar in the VIP section. Standing at the ropes that separated the VIP section from the main room was Stephen, a cute feminine gay guy who was one of Jeffrey's party companions and was only friendly to me when Jeffrey wasn't around. Luckily Jeffrey was no where in sight.

"Hey Stephen, it's Kidd," I said, knowing that he might not recognize me with my new hair color. "How's your night been?" I asked, hoping he'd be cordial and open the ropes without any drama.

"Oh, it's Kidd," Stephen said, so smugly and cold, I knew something was up. "Jeffrey told me you left the *Star* but he didn't tell me you'd changed your hair color. Sorry, this section is for VIPs," he announced, then turned his back to me while he opened the rope for some other people who he considered to be actual VIPs. So Jeffrey had told Stephen that I had left the *Star*. That meant that Stephen had told half the regulars in the club.

"Is Jeffrey here?" I asked Stephen.

"Please step aside," Stephen snapped. "I need to keep this area clear for VIP entrance." Stephen then smiled and stood erect as if he were guarding the Buckingham Palace. My world had changed and I was being pushed to the curb. Stephen was definitely one of those fair weather acquaintances.

Wandering back through the crowd I remembered that I had another friend who worked at the back bar. When I was finally able to push my way into a spot at the end of the bar I waved to Cliff, another bartender who always brought me my cocktail without me having to order. In fact, Cliff usually stayed to chat, about celebrities and which parties were hot, whatever. On this night, Cliff was busy and obviously had no idea who I was. Then it hit me, I had no idea who I was either. I wasn't Kidd the nightlife columnist anymore so what was I doing here? The loud music buzzed in my head and I glanced around at all the beautiful people dressed in designer duds smiling and parading under the flashing lights. I didn't fit in and since I didn't write for the *Star*, I had no reason to be there. In fact I wasn't really sure why I had landed at Liquid except that I was high on crystal and didn't know what else to do.

"Cliff, it's Kidd," I yelled, half heartedly hoping to be heard over the roar of the music. Looking down the bar I saw Jeffrey standing with Celia. My heart sank. Both looked my way but didn't recognize me. When Cliff made no effort to come my way I turned to leave and bumped into Debbie, one of the club kids who frequented any party where there was an open bar or the possibility of finding drugs.

"Watch where you're going asshole," said Debbie, as she pushed by me and took my spot at the bar. I could understand Cliff not recognizing me but I was baffled and hurt by Debbie's snub since we had spent so many nights together drinking and doing bumps of Tina. We were friends or so I thought. I looked back and I heard her say "what an asshole" to Cliff, who looked up and gave me a dirty look. It was clear that I wasn't welcome. I was certain that Jeffrey was spreading the news of my demise, so I decided to exit as quickly as I could.

What hurt me the most was seeing Celia with Jeffrey. Celia and I had been best friends and always went out together. Celia had been the one person that I could always count on and I could tell her anything. Even though Celia's world had always been about Celia, she was always there for me. Not always on time, but she'd be there if I needed her. I know she loved me and I loved her, but now she had joined forces with Jeffrey and had become my enemy.

The crowded club and the loud music made me want to scream. I never felt so alone in my life. I pushed my way through the crowd and passed several familiar faces that had claimed to be my friend but not one of them gave me a nod. For the first time since I had been in South Beach I really felt unwelcome and out of place. I couldn't get out of there fast enough. But where would I go?

"Kidd, you're not leaving so soon?" said Gilbert, as I stepped outside the door.

"I think I am, my friend. I'm not having a very good night," I replied, not wanting to explain myself.

"When has Kidd ever had a bad night?" asked Gilbert, grabbing me for a one armed hug.

"Jamie, is that you?" came a voice from the crowd that waited on the other side of the rope. I immediately looked to see who was calling my name. It had been such a long time since anyone had called me Jamie.

"Jamie, over here! It's Greg." I looked over to see my former lover and ex-partner from Virginia, the very one who had left me heartbroken, causing me to take flight to South Beach. Of all people in the world, I actually never thought I'd see him again and here he was. My first impulse was to punch him in the face but oddly enough, I was happy to see him.

"Greg," I shouted, not knowing what else to say. I walked over to where he stood. "What are you doing here in South Beach?"

"I'm so glad to have found you. I knew you were here somewhere and I need to talk to you. I called the *South Beach Star* where you worked and they said that you didn't work there any more and wouldn't give me your number. So much has happened since I left Virginia. I'm working at a magazine in New York and wanted to offer you a job."

"What!" I was more than dumbfounded, I was speechless.

"Let's go somewhere and talk. I need to explain everything and apologize." This had been some night and seeing Greg again was a little too much. Not to mention that he was offering me a job.

"How about we go inside for a drink?" I asked, knowing that I needed to calm down a bit before we did any talking. "Gilbert, I think I've changed my mind. Can I get my friend in so we can go in for another drink?"

"Of course, any friend of yours is a friend of mine," said Gilbert, while he opened the rope letting in Greg.

"Let's go in for a cocktail so you can explain everything. An apology would be a good start." After all I'd been through, I was happy to see Greg. It was like the prodigal son had returned home. I had punched him, kicked him, and even killed him in my mind over and over but had finally released it all. I knew that I probably would have done the same thing in Greg's situation. I finally came to the conclusion that it was really my fault, for allowing myself to get involved in a secret relationship. And if that wasn't enough, I did it again with Jeffrey and that ended even worse. I was anxious to talk to Greg and hear about this magazine job. "Gilbert, this is my friend Greg, who is also in the publishing business. We used to work together in Virginia. How about joining us inside for a cocktail?" Gilbert, a closet-writer who claimed to be writing the next great novel, always enjoyed networking, but more importantly Gilbert would get us cocktails immediately and gratis.

"South Beach is crazy," screamed Greg, as we were ushered in after Gilbert had ordered the security guys to hold the door. "I don't know how you can deal with all the craziness," yelled Greg, trying to be heard over the music as we made our way to the bar. I could see the concern in Greg's eyes but he smiled every time he looked at me.

Greg chatted up his job in New York and raved about the publication. Gilbert was impressed and took a card before he returned to the screaming mob outside. With Gilbert gone, I bared my soul to Greg and told him that I had fled Virginia almost immediately after he had left. I had landed in South Beach but was now fed up with the whole scene and had quit my job that very day.

"Looks like I arrived at just the right time," added Greg. "One of my jobs is hiring writers and we have a position to fill. I actually came looking for you. You're a hard man to find. Consider yourself hired. How long will it take you to pack your things?" he asked. "You're moving to New York." He just looked at me with a steady smile. Was this really happening?

"What?" I stammered. "Are you serious?"

"Sorry," Greg injected. "I didn't even give you a chance to say yes, but you better not turn me down. I owe you and I'm going to make it up to you for leaving like I did. I was just going through so much and I'm really hoping you'll forgive me. Anyway, considering your situation, you can't say no. You'll fit in perfectly. I was hoping to run into you but I never thought you'd be looking for a job. This is perfect." Greg looked at me smiling and waited for a response.

"Wow, I can't believe this," I replied, with a big smile. My first real smile in a long while, I'm sure. "I guess I could leave as soon as tomorrow," I said. Shocked and elated at the job offer, I was more than dazed at all that had happened. I've heard of knights in shining armor who come to save the day. Talk about arriving just in the nick of time. My emotions were flooding over and my head was spinning. Today had been quite a day. I had abruptly left my job at the *Star*, I had been threatened and robbed at gun point, and tonight I had been snubbed by my friends as if I didn't exist. I had gone from blond to brunette, from a fabulous nightlife columnist to unemployed and alone, all in one day. Now I had just been offered a job in New York City. What timing. Boy, did I need to leave town.

"Greg, you have no idea how you've just saved my life, literally," I said. I had never felt so low or worthless. I actually thought that I would have been better off if those masked gunmen had shot and killed me. Thankfully that didn't happen. Now I had a job and an identity again. I could leave all this South Beach craziness behind. All I wanted to do was to grab Greg and hug him as hard as I could.

"Kidd, let's go back to your place and talk. I'll help you pack. I'll call my office tomorrow morning and let them know that I've hired you and arrange for your airline ticket. I want you to stay with me in New York until you get settled. I have a great apartment on First Avenue and I've plenty of --."

"Wait a minute," I said, stopping him mid-sentence. "Greg, I'm speechless," I said, trying to hold back tears. Suddenly the impact of the day hit me. I felt an emotional meltdown coming on but didn't want to share it with the crowd at Liquid. Wait till I tell Greg about the drug robbery and being threatened and tied up by masked gunmen. And my drug problem. Maybe I better not tell him about that. I still couldn't believe that Greg was there. It was like one of those amazing moments that you see in movies that just didn't happen in real life, but it did.

"Don't say a thing," said Greg, then he grabbed me by the shoulder. "It's my way of repaying you for what I did to you but more importantly, it's my way of thanking you. I'm so glad I found you and you must know how I really feel about you. And besides all that, you're a talented writer and the magazine will be lucky to have you. Have you started that novel that you talked about?"

"No, I haven't. I've lived it but I haven't written a word. Let's get out of here," I said. "I have a lot of packing to do if we're flying out tomorrow." We walked out of the club to find a crowd of people still waiting behind the velvet ropes. I could never understand how anyone could stand so long just to get into a club. Apparently Gilbert was on another break since he wasn't at his post by the ropes. Greg and I pushed our way through the crowd and walked arm in arm down Lincoln Road back to my apartment. It was a beautiful South Beach night and the sky was filled with stars and the moon was as full as I've ever seen it. It was one of those magical Miami nights that you read about. Suddenly a shooting star fell from the sky, the first I'd ever seen. Maybe that was my star falling from the sky. It was time to find a new place in the sky.

TWENTY FOUR

Another Suitcase, Another Job

The ringing phone woke me up, and I slowly rolled over in my sea of blankets and reached for the phone like a drowning man grabbing for the hand of his rescuer. The reality of Greg's voice on the phone rekindled the memory of the previous night when my ex-partner and secret lover had not only magically appeared but had offered me a job in New York City. Yesterday I discovered the reality of how shallow South Beach was and it didn't take me long to sink to the bottom.

My time in South Beach had been wonderful and sometimes I felt like I had followed Peter Pan to a world called Neverland filled with a colorful assortment of characters that included drag queens, fairies (some like Tinkerbell, others more like pirates), celebrities, fashionistas, models, designers and lots of lost boys. Unfortunately I had fallen in with the lost boys and gotten hooked on fairy dust. But now it was all over.

The South Beach that I experienced was a very special place unlike any other place in the world. It seemed like such a long time ago when I first landed in Miami after my escape from Virginia. On the map this little sandbar was just a tiny spot on the southeastern tip of the United States however South Beach didn't really feel like a part of America at all. The South Beach that I knew was a fairyland (in more ways than one) where everyone was my friend and the party never ended. Maybe it had all been a dream.

"Jamie, it's Greg," came the voice from the phone.

"Hello," I said, trying to wake up. I looked at the clock on my nightstand and noticed it was nearly noon. Normally I would have been at the *South Beach Star* office for three hours manning the phones and dealing with the daily drama of the competing staffs of the *South Beach Star* and *Star TV*. Luckily that was all behind me and I was poised to start a new life.

The universe has a funny way of taking care of us and once again I found myself starting yet another new life. Only a couple of years ago I had escaped from my trauma in Virginia by coming to South Beach where I got a fresh start as a nightlife columnist for the *South Beach Star*. Now the very man that had caused me to flee Virginia had magically appeared to save the day. Now that's something no one would believe if they read it. I was still in shock from seeing Greg again and didn't quite know how our lives would fit together now.

It seemed like such a long ago when Anthony had rescued me from drowning in despair and self pity when he offered me a job as his assistant at the *South Beach Star*. Possibly he was my Peter Pan, but it was my nightlife column that gave me flight. South Beach opened its arms to me and I flew from club to club, landing at openings, fund-raisers, special events, and exclusive private parties.

My life as a nightlife reporter was truly blessed as every day was an adventure that often lasted late into the next morning. In South Beach everyone was a star; just ask them, so my nightlife column made me everyone's friend. Every busboy, waiter, promoter, club owner, model, and doorman wanted to be included in my column with their names in bold print. Some were featured in the photos that accompanied my weekly column and those people became my closest friends or at least told everyone that they were. Although my weekly paycheck was meager, my job afforded me many perks including free dinners, complimentary cocktails at every club, free theatre tickets, designer clothes, massages, and invitations to the best parties.

My life was a dream existence that most people envied, thinking how wonderful it must be to have a job covering nightlife. In the beginning it was an amazing lifestyle but things went haywire and I left reality behind. In order to keep up with my overbooked schedule I had to have an endless supply of that magical fairy dust called Tina (why it's called that I still don't know). Tina kept me flying but coming down often produced a crash landing.

"Are you packed?" asked Greg, bringing me back to the moment. "You're booked on United flight 2720 and it leaves at four thirty-five this afternoon."

"I'm ready to go," I said. The previous night, Greg had helped me pack and we talked until the time he finally left at 4 a.m. He invited me to spend the night with him in his hotel room but my emotional state wouldn't allow it. As much as I wanted to throw myself into his arms, I remembered how things ended in Virginia and we were going to be working together in New York. I told him that I wanted to spend my last night in South Beach in my apartment. I had a lot of memories there and needed the time alone to say goodbye.

"Good. I'm glad you're all set. It's almost noon so I've gotta get to the airport. My flight is at one. I wish I could have gotten you on the same plane but it was all booked. I was lucky to get you this flight; it was the last seat available. You should get to the airport at least a half hour early," Gregg said. "The crowds going back to New York are going to be crazy. We're going to have fun in New York. I'm glad we reconnected. I missed you." Now those were words that were wonderful to hear. 'I missed you.' I could tell that Greg had changed and was more secure about himself. I had missed him too.

"I can't wait to get to New York," I said, looking at my packed suitcases sitting by the door. My Tina buzz was still going when we arrived at my apartment. I packed and talked while Greg sat on my bed and watched. I knew that I'd be totally useless the following day without crystal so I made sure I finished packing for the trip before passing out. Saying goodbye to South Beach meant I had to say farewell to Tina and learn to fly solo. It was time. It was also time to say goodbye to Neverland and grow up.

"Great! I don't know how you do it," said Greg. "I'm a mess today and when I got back to my hotel last night I fell right into bed." As much as he pretended, I knew that Greg could tell that I was on drugs.

"I'm pretty beat today myself but I'm ready to go," I said, as I walked around looking at my apartment. If he only knew what had given me the energy to pack. "I have to tell you that I really had convinced myself that I hated you but I was so glad to see you last night. Thanks again Greg, you're really a life-saver."

"Stop it," Greg quickly replied. "I'm the one that owes you. I promise to make it up to you in New York and I'm looking forward to working together again. Just swear to me that you won't go after my job," he said laughing.

"Now would I do that?" I said, smiling. Yes, I was smiling and had a good reason to be happy. I could barely remember the feeling of being happy without the assistance of drugs or alcohol. Hey, I couldn't remember being happy even with the assistance of drugs and alcohol.

"Oh, one more thing," Gregg added. "When you get to New York there will be a driver waiting for you and he's going to take you to my apartment. The doorman knows you're coming and will let you in. Just make yourself at home and I'll be back after I get home from work. I need to go in for a few hours."

"What about me?" I said. "When will I start work?" I was eager to start a new job but a little scared about a whole new beginning in New York City.

"Just relax," said Greg. "I'm sure you could use a break. It sounded like you've been working non-stop without a vacation at all. You won't have to start working right away."

"A little time off would be nice."

"You'll get a little time to reacquaint yourself with New York," said Greg. "Once you start working, the city will become a blur anyway and the only thing you'll see will be deadlines. I called my boss and he's extremely pleased that I hired you and we'll both go into the office together on Monday."

"Thanks, that sounds great." I was standing in front of the mirror in my bathroom and couldn't believe that the smiling face staring back at me was mine. Still not used to being a brunette again, I was amazed to see the reflection that looked back at me. I was glad to see Jamie Kidd instead of the blond Kidd. I was happy to be me again. Wow, I was happy.

"Now, I'd better run or I'm going to miss my flight. I'm glad I found you and I'll see you in New York."

"I can't wait. See you later and you have a great flight too," I said. I stood looking at my reflection thinking about my time in the crazy world of South Beach.

Sadly enough I could see that the party world of South Beach probably wouldn't last much longer. The realtors and developers were already buying up all the prime South Beach property and stuffing cash in the pockets of the local politicians. Already scheduled for a major revitalization, I had a feeling that the bohemian South Beach that I knew would soon disappear. I hoped the developers wouldn't ruin South Beach and turn it into one big mall and start building tall condos everywhere.

Stripping off my clothes I let them fall to the bathroom floor and stepped into the shower. The cold water felt great and my blood seemed to speed up with a renewed energy. My life was finally back on track and my mind flashed back over my time in South Beach. It was like trying to remember three years worth of watching movies. Every night was a different film, the characters, the actors, the plots, the endings, all blended together into one giant cinematic epic that had finally come to an end. While my memories included many wonderful times like going to Madonna's party, meeting Versace before he died, and hanging out in the backroom of the Living Room with beautiful models like Helena Christenson, I couldn't erase the image of that masked robber with a gun pointed right at my head and walking through Liquid as if I were an invisible ghost.

Stepping out of the shower, I grabbed a towel and walked through my apartment as I dried off. My closet was still filled with the flashy designer fashions that I wore to parties. Those were Kidd's clothes and Jamie Kidd, the serious journalist, wouldn't need them anymore. I dressed in my uniform of black jeans, black t-shirt and a black jacket. I thumbed through the pages of my phone book and couldn't believe how many unlisted numbers of celebrities and models I had accumulated. I'd probably never call any of them again but I thought I'd keep it anyway. Who knows, one day I might want to reconnect. I might even come back one day.

My walls were plastered with posters of events and theme nights at various parties including one that featured my photo along with Courtney Love. Our images were side by side on the poster, but I didn't meet her until years later. Another club paid her to host a party and she arrived with an entourage. The tabloids had printed photos of the drunken Courtney, before and after rehab, and her current publicist was picky about who photographed her. I met her when she entered the club but the club's promoter escorted her and her entourage to the club's office where they hung out for a while. I wasn't allowed in and realized why when the group finally emerged, all looking stoned and wild eyed. Every poster and flyer that hung on my wall invoked a memory and I closed my eyes to block it all out. There were too many recollections of the past coming at me at once.

I flashed on the classic film *The Wizard of Oz* and know exactly how Dorothy felt when she woke up in her bed after returning from Oz. My time in South Beach had been like a colorful dream and every night I strolled down that yellow brick road where I ran into so many interesting characters. Never did I run into a scarecrow, a tin man or a cowardly lion, but everyone I met seemed to be in need of a heart, a brain or courage. (Real courage, not the temporary type afforded by illegal substances).

With a couple of hours before my flight I thought about who I should call before I left. There was not one person that I had any desire to talk to. I hated goodbyes and mentally I had already left. How different this day would have been if Greg had not come along. With no job, no money and no prospects, the tropical paradise known as South Beach was not a very pretty place.

The phone rang, breaking my stroll down memory lane. Who could be calling me? I let the phone ring until it stopped, then picked it up and called a cab. I had already called the apartment super and left a message that I was leaving so I just left my keys on the dresser. I grabbed my suitcases and camera case and walked out into the hallway. I closed the door behind me and walked down the steps for one last time. Downstairs I was surprised to find a waiting cab. I could not remember how many times I had stood looking at my watch cursing at the cab company.

"Hey buddy," yelled the cabbie. "Are you going to the airport?"

"Yes I am," I said smirking. The suitcases must have given it away.

"Let me help you," said the driver, a pudgy Latin man wearing a baseball cap. He quickly grabbed my bags and headed back to the cab. The cabbie threw my bags into the trunk as I got in the back of the cab.

"Were you here on vacation?" asked the cab driver. How unusual to find a helpful and courteous cab driver, most were grumpy and barely spoke.

"No, I lived here for several years. Now I'm moving to New York," I answered. The streets of South Beach flashed quickly by as the cab headed towards the airport like he actually knew where he was going and driving at a normal speed. There was a running joke about cabs in South Beach that went "How do you get a cab to slow down?" Answer: "Get in it." Cabs were known for their erratic driving and speed except when you needed to get somewhere fast. This driver was not only considerate and efficient but was driving swiftly towards the airport.

"Good for you," he said. "South Beach is a party town filled with liars and crooks. I always say, Come and play but don't stay," he said, laughing.

"I wish I had gotten in your cab when I first arrived here," I said. But did I really? While my South Beach adventure had ended badly, for the most part I had really had a wonderful time, but like *Alice in Wonderland*, I had fallen down some long hole. Although I felt like I was flying, I was actually falling the entire time. Luckily I landed on my feet while many others had not. The South Beach lifestyle had produced many casualties and my address book was filled with many names of those who had died from AIDS, suicide or overdosed on drugs. I thanked God that I had survived and was now moving on to a new life. Who knows, I might even write that novel.

"Which airline are you flying?" asked the driver.

"I'm flying United," I replied. I looked back at South Beach as we crossed the MacArthur Causeway. The view was magnificent. On my right I saw the beautiful home of Gloria and Emilio Estefan on Star Island and on my left was Government Cut, the strip of water that linked the Port of Miami to the Atlantic Ocean used primarily by cruise ships. I laid my head back against the seat of the cab and closed my eyes. For the first time in months my mind was racing without the benefit of drugs. My exodus from South Beach came just in the nick of time and I was afraid to look back. I was amazed that I had survived but I'd never forget the *South Beach Star*.

December 3, 2007

TWENTY FIVE

There's No Place Like Home

Walking through the Miami airport I looked anxiously at the faces I passed, thinking that I would run into someone from my past. Once there was a time that I could barely go anywhere in Miami without running into someone I knew or at least someone who recognized me because of my column in the *South Beach Star*. I had not stepped foot in Miami in years and it had changed considerably since I had left. I was excited to see how Miami had progressed but was also afraid to run into my past.

I'm sure no one would recognize me now that so many years had passed and I had become the respectable Jamie Kidd. My friends in New York could not accept the fact that I once called myself Kidd and sported bleached white hair. Or that I was a fixture on South Beach's nightlife scene and covered the waterfront as they say. I couldn't believe that one local magazine had gone as far as to say that "it's not a party unless Kidd is in attendance." Now my work schedule is so overloaded with appointments, interviews, book promotions, and deadlines I have no time for parties. The truth is that I've not seen the inside of a nightclub in years. Not that I'm complaining but my life is worlds apart from the life I led in South Beach.

When I left South Beach nearly ten years ago I left behind a lifestyle that practically killed me. Arriving in

New York I still had the habit but not the desire but I didn't realize what hell I would have to go through because of my crystal addiction. Innocently I thought I could just say goodbye to the drug and that would be it but the need for Tina did not leave. At first I tried to hide my situation from Greg but I couldn't hide my symptoms. Unknown to me, Greg had also kicked a drug addiction and realized almost immediately that I was in withdrawal. Greg became my savior and sponsor in a drug treatment program and helped me through the horrendous ordeal of kicking a nasty drug habit. Now years later, we are both drug-free but we still go to meetings.

You're probably thinking that we reconnected as lovers and everything worked out just like the ending to some sappy movie. That didn't happen even though Greg did come to grips with his sexuality. We did however become the best of friends and that was much more important to me. I was currently in a relationship with an artist that I had met four years ago when I interviewed him for a feature in one of magazines that I write for. This was not a secret relationship. I had learned my lesson.

The crowd of people rushing from their planes to the luggage checkout reminded me of the excited mobs who pushed and shoved past the velvet ropes in front of the South Beach clubs when I used to live here. I always hated crowds but loved to be near the masses of people packed into the clubs because of the incredible energy. There's nothing like the power from an overcrowded dance floor filled with writhing bodies all dancing together to some throbbing base beat controlled by a world renowned DJ. Now I was uneasy just making my way through the jammed terminal even though I encountered the same sort of crowds daily on the streets of New York City. I was out of my element and frankly I was a little scared even though I had no reason to be.

Up ahead a line of limousine drivers holding signs waited for their clients and I looked for one holding my name. A handsome Latin man with a shaved head in a black suit held a cardboard sign bearing my name.

"I'm Jamie Kidd," I said, giving him a little wave.

"Welcome to Miami, Mr. Kidd," he said. "I'm Juan Carlos, your driver. Let me take your bag."

"Thank you. I'll carry my camera bag but I have two more bags that are checked," I added, showing him the luggage tickets. I was lucky that the magazine had booked a car service for my entire stay in Miami.

"I'll take care of that for you Mr. Kidd," he said, taking the tickets. "Let me take you to the car and then I'll get your bags."

Outside the terminal the warm air that hit my face brought back memories of my time in Miami. I had become accustomed to New York winters and had forgotten that the temperature in Miami, even in December, rarely dropped below sixty degrees. The temperature this morning back in New York City was a chilly forty-one degrees and I welcomed the warmth of the Miami sun. I took off my jacket and carried it on my arm. The driver quickly led me to a black town car and opened the back door for me. The cold air from the car's air conditioner did little to cool me down as adrenaline pumped through my body. Normally cool and collected in the tensest of situations I was sweating bullets and my hands were shaking. One would have thought I was on my way to the gas chamber or electric chair instead of headed for a week of parties and art events in South Beach.

Why was I returning to South Beach? Last week I passed a girl on Madison Avenue that was the spitting image of my old friend Celia. It had been more than ten years since I had thought about Celia. We had been close friends when I had lived in South Beach but frankly my hectic life in New York afforded me little time to keep in touch with my current friends and I had lost touch with most of my friends who lived here. I often wondered where life had taken Celia. Blessed with beauty, charm and a gorgeous body, Celia treated life as if it was just a gigantic cocktail party and she was always on the guest list.

That same afternoon, I was thumbing through a portfolio of an artist I was considering for an art feature and came upon an image that bore an uncanny resemblance to Celia. Suddenly I couldn't stop thinking about her. Was this one of those strange signs from the universe? Still staring at the image, I picked up the phone and called the artist so I could arrange a meeting. Maybe the painting actually was of my long lost friend. Oddly enough, the artist's voicemail said that he was in South Beach and would be there through the middle of December.

That was all I needed to hear. Like a master detective putting all the clues together, I had "proof" that the painting was of Celia. I sat looking at the photo and memories of South Beach hit me in the face like a video on fast-forward. For some reason, I had the urge to see if I could find Celia.

A call to my agent revealed that Pedro Cruz, the artist, was in South Beach for Art Basel Miami Beach, the international art fair. I had attended Art Basel in Switzerland, but had never attended the newer Art Basel in Miami. My agent must have been reading my mind when he offered to send me to Miami for a week to cover the event. So here I was back in Miami, after a very long absence.

Juan Carlos put my luggage safely in the trunk, then took his place at the wheel and nodded to me in the rear view mirror.

"Everything okay, Mr. Kidd?" asked Juan Carlos, with a twinkle in his eye. Miami was filled with Latinos, particularly Cubans, in fact when I lived in South Beach I had the numbers of three Juan Carlos' in my phone book and was always calling the wrong one.

"Yes, thank you," I replied. "I'm just not used to the heat."

"South Beach is very hot. You should know that Kidd," Juan Carlos said. He smiled at me in the mirror.

"Excuse me," I said, a bit shocked to be called Kidd. No one had called me that in years.

"Kidd, it's me," he said, with a chuckle. "Your old friend Juan Carlos, I used to dance at Liquid and Hombre. We used to have some great times back then. Don't you remember?"

"My god, Juan Carlos," I said. "Of course I remember. You look great. I didn't recognize you wearing clothes," I joked, but in reality it was true. I couldn't remember him wearing more than a g-string and he looked like a different person dressed in a chauffeur's uniform. Dancers like Juan Carlos made their living from their bodies and the less they wore the more cash they generated. My friends would never believe it if I told them that I hung out with male go-go dancers. Actually, I could hardly believe it myself.

"I don't dance anymore," Juan Carlos said. "Those times were great but I'm married now and have a three year old son. I'm the owner of this limo company but I'm glad to be driving for you. I will be your personal driver for your entire stay in Miami," he said smiling. "And please tell all your friends coming down to Miami about my company. I'll give them a good deal."

"Great," I said quickly. "I'm glad you'll be my driver. I have a very busy schedule and I haven't been back here in nearly ten years." Juan Carlos had changed so much. I remembered the wild dancer who worked the clubs and danced for tips. Now he owns his own limousine company and is married with a son. Wow. Both our lives have transformed us into different people. I'm sure he doesn't announce the fact that he used to be an exotic dancer as I don't make it known that I was a wild blond party boy with a nightlife column.

"The Beach isn't the same as it used to be, Kidd," Juan Carlos announced. "But you have me as your guide. Most of the old clubs have closed but I can show you the new clubs and the scene in downtown Miami."

I looked out the window as we crossed the MacArthur Causeway. The last time I had crossed the causeway, I was heading towards the airport excited about my new job in New York City. I had no idea if I would ever return. Now I was psyched to see the new South Beach.

Surely Juan Carlos meant those words to reassure and calm me but somehow they had the opposite effect. I was here to cover Art Basel Miami Beach which was the most important art fair in the United States with a week of art exhibitions, art related events and private collectors' parties. I was already overwhelmed by my schedule and didn't have much time for extracurricular activities. Looking out the window to my right I saw a fleet of cruise ships docked at the Port of Miami. Yes, I was definitely back in Miami and South Beach was just minutes away. The car drove quickly towards the Beach and soon we were driving up Collins Avenue towards the Delano Hotel where I was staying.

"Kidd, have you kept in touch with anyone from the old crowd?" asked Juan Carlos.

"No, I haven't Juan Carlos," I replied. I was wondering just who he might be thinking about. "My schedule in New York gives me little time to connect with my friends there." Part of the reason that I was nervous about returning to Miami was that I would run into some of the old crowd. I had left town abruptly and there might be a few questions about my exit. I had thumbed through my phone book so many times looking at the names of my friends in Miami but I didn't contact anyone. Not even Celia, who I could never stop thinking about. I wanted to call her so many times but I always remembered the last time I saw her with Jeffrey and I just couldn't do it.

"We're here Kidd," Juan Carlos announced, as we pulled into the curved driveway in front of the Delano. During my time living in South Beach I had been to many parties at the Delano Hotel, the all white Philippe Starck designed hotel known for its trendy owner and clientele like Madonna, who was once an investor in the restaurant. This was my first time arriving as a guest. The truth was that I could never have afforded to stay at the Delano or even eat there unless I was getting a press comp.

Juan Carlos took care of my bags and gave me his card while I walked up the white steps through the white curtains to the entrance. As I strolled through the lobby I recalled the many late-nights that I had wandered through this lobby and for a while I even had a membership at the David Barton Gym located in the basement. Oh, the memories. One of the best parties of my life was a New Year's Eve party held here that was hosted by New York party goddess Suzanne Bartsch, wife of fitness guru David Barton, which featured drag queens performing throughout the courtyard and dressed as mermaids swimming in the pool. Stepping up to the front desk a voice quickly brought me back to the present.

"Welcome to the Delano Mr. Kidd," said a familiar voice. I looked up and was shocked to see the beautiful face of my old friend Celia staring at me with a big smile. "It's really you. When I saw your name on the printout for check-ins I couldn't believe my eyes. It's been a long time." Celia looked as beautiful as ever and the years had been good to her. Celia's pleasant greeting wiped away all the bad things that had happened and I forgave her for everything. I was so happy to see her, I could barely contain myself. I knew that it more than fate that had brought us together again. Celia had once been my closest friend and we were inseparable but unfortunately circumstances turned things around. I had thought about her so many times and wondered what she was doing. Celia's smile made this trip worthwhile. Now she was a concierge at the Delano Hotel.

"Yes, it has been a long time," I said, not knowing how to react. This wasn't the Celia that had turned on me and had partnered with Jeffrey, my nemesis at the *South Beach Star*. This was the happy and gorgeous Celia that I remembered as my dear friend and I wanted to give her a big hug.

"I'm so glad to see you," Celia said sincerely. "I do hope you've forgiven me. I was so mean to you. Jeffrey turned me against you. When you disappeared I cried so hard. I was so ashamed how I treated you and I really missed you. You were my best friend you know?" Celia looked at me and I could tell she was truly sorry.

"The past is the past," I said. "I don't blame you and I regretted leaving without saying goodbye but you know I just had to get out of here." I really didn't want to relive the past, especially any part where Jeffrey was involved, but I was so happy to see Celia.

"You've done quite well for yourself," said Celia. "I'm proud of you. You're the only one from our group that really succeeded. Did you hear about Jeffrey?"

"No, I didn't Celia," I said, smiling at her. "Now why would I have kept tabs on someone like Jeffrey who stole my best friend from me?" I really did blame Jeffrey for turning Celia against me. Unfortunately I had heard that Jeffrey had died of AIDS a couple of years ago. While Jeffrey was the one responsible for me leaving my position at the *South Beach Star* and had instigated a one-man hate campaign against me, I was still sad when I heard the news of his death. "I have reconnected with Anthony," I added. Anthony Deerpark had been my savior and was a wonderful and talented man. Anthony had contacted me several times through one of the New York publications that published my work. Anthony had even called me once when he was in New York and I chatted with him briefly but couldn't see him because of my busy schedule. I had put in a call to him and told him I was coming to South Beach for Art Basel and hoped to have an opportunity to meet with him over lunch or dinner.

"I understand," said Celia, handing me my room key. "I saw your byline in *Vanity Fair* a couple of years ago and was quite impressed." Celia smiled at me like she used to. She was still a strikingly beautiful woman but I could see a change in her eyes. She had grown up as I had.

"Thanks Celia," I said and looked into her eyes. "Now what night can we have dinner? I'm only here for a week and we have about ten years of catching up to do." I looked at her and waited for her reply.

"Are you busy tonight? I can book us a table at the hotel's restaurant." Celia was smiling but her eyes filled with tears. I could tell they were real tears and they were tears of joy.

"Great. Book the table and we'll plan the week. How can I go out on the town in South Beach without my girl on my arm?" My regrets about returning to South Beach had all disappeared. I was so happy to be reunited with my dear friend Celia. We had been apart for such a long time but our bond was there.

"I'm so happy to see you Kidd. I'll call you as soon as I reserve a table." I couldn't believe that this was my Celia, the same Celia that kept me waiting for hours and had me go from bar to bar while she was getting dressed for the opening of her friend's club.

"Until later then," I said. I turned and walked to the elevator and rode to the sixth floor. My room was stylishly chic and decorated in all white. On the desk was a stack of local publications including the *South Beach Star*. The publication looked nothing like the weekly tabloid that I once wrote for and I didn't recognize one name on the masthead. Anthony had told me he had sold the publication and the current reincarnation of the *Star* was filled with pages of event photos but had very little content. Every local publication I looked at was stocked with similar pages of party photos of beautiful people, not one person did I recognize. Maybe South Beach hadn't changed that much after all.

From the balcony in my room I had an incredible view of the ocean and looked down at the pool. South Beach was a tropical paradise and was still a favorite playground of the rich and famous. When I lived here I partied with the A-list crowd as if I was one of them and my life seemed like a fairy tale. Every night was an adventure and I was either attending some great event or writing about it. When I try to remember all the wild nights I'm still amazed when I think of all the people that I partied with, the places that I went, the things I saw, and the long nights. It was a magical time where life was a constant party and everyone was my friend. Celebrities like Madonna, Naomi Campbell, Kate Moss, Ricky Martin, Mickey Rourke, Sylvester Stallone and designer Gianni Versace were regular faces in the clubs who all hung out with the local celebrities including the drag queens, male strippers and drug dealers. The paparazzi had yet to invade South Beach and no one hid from the cameras. South Beach was a fantasy world like Neverland and every club was filled with Peter Pans and Tinkerbells and there was lots of fairy dust.

Once again I had landed in South Beach but had outgrown Neverland. I had returned this time to work and there was little time to play. I had once fantasized about a world where no one had to work and everyone played all night. But I grew up.

Whenever I think of my time in South Beach it all seems like a dream. Sometimes I wonder if it all really happened. My South Beach was a swirl of wild parties, drugs, crazy situations, endless cocktails, drugs, long nights, drugs, and a cast of wonderful friends. My last day here was pretty unbelievable in itself. I know that I'll never be able to return to that time in my life but I'm so happy to be able to come back for a visit and reconnect with friends like Celia.

I knew what I had to do. I walked to my shoulder-bag and took out my lap-top. I sat down and decided to write the story about my adventures in South Beach. Certainly no one would ever believe that it all really happened. It was the novel that I had been meaning to write for years. I looked across the room and saw my reflection. It looked nothing like that blond nightlife writer named Kidd who rode the nights like a wild stallion.

"White hair a la Jean Paul Gaultier was just the touch I needed to strut among the fabulous shallow South

Beach royalty and even pass as one myself." It was my time in Neverland and I had to write about it.

Made in the USA
Columbia, SC
08 January 2023